"Just one thing," Gavin said, his features set angrily. "Why did you marry a bastard like Brooks?"

"It's none of your business," Melanie lied. She grappled with the truth, wishing she could tell him about the baby they'd never shared.

"Was it because of his money?" he said, his voice low. "Was that what you found so attractive?"

There was nothing she could say to change the past, and with a sinking sensation, she realized that telling Gavin the truth would only increase the tension between them. "I don't think your question merits an answer."

"You walked out on me—"

"Correction, Gavin. You did the walking—or, to be more precise, the skiing," she accused, unable to keep the bitterness out of her tone. "You just skied your way out of my life, and I fell in love with someone else."

Gavin's eyes narrowed. "Save that for someone who'll believe it."

Dear Reader,

Welcome to the Silhouette **Special Edition** experience! With your search for consistently satisfying reading in mind, every month the authors and editors of Silhouette **Special Edition** aim to offer you a stimulating blend of deep emotions and high romance.

The name Silhouette **Special Edition** and the distinctive arch on the cover represent a commitment—a commitment to bring you six sensitive, substantial novels each month. In the pages of a Silhouette **Special Edition**, compelling true-to-life characters face riveting emotional issues—and come out winners. All the authors in the series strive for depth, vividness and warmth in writing these stories of living and loving in today's world.

The result, we hope, is romance you can believe in. Deeply emotional, richly romantic, infinitely rewarding—that's the Silhouette **Special Edition** experience. Come share it with us—six times a month!

From all the authors and editors of Silhouette **Special Edition**,

Best wishes,

Leslie Kazanjian,
Senior Editor

LISA JACKSON

Double Exposure

Published by Silhouette Books New York
America's Publisher of Contemporary Romance

SILHOUETTE BOOKS
300 East 42nd St., New York, N.Y. 10017

ISBN: 0-373-09636-4

First Silhouette Books printing November 1990

Printed in the U.S.A.

Books by Lisa Jackson

Silhouette Intimate Moments

Dark Side of the Moon #39
Gypsy Wind #79
Mystic #158

Silhouette Special Edition

A Twist of Fate #118
The Shadow of Time #180
Tears of Pride #194
Pirate's Gold #215
A Dangerous Precedent #233
Innocent by Association #244
Midnight Sun #264
Devil's Gambit #282
Zachary's Law #296
Yesterday's Lies #315
One Man's Love #358
Renegade Son #376
Snowbound #394
Summer Rain #419
Hurricane Force #467
In Honor's Shadow #495
Aftermath #525
Tender Trap #569
With No Regrets #611
Double Exposure #636

Silhouette Romance

His Bride to Be #717

LISA JACKSON

was raised in Molalla, Oregon, and now lives with her husband, Mark, and her two sons in a suburb of Portland, Oregon. Lisa and her sister, Natalie Bishop, who is also a Silhouette author, live within earshot of each other and do all their work in Natalie's basement.

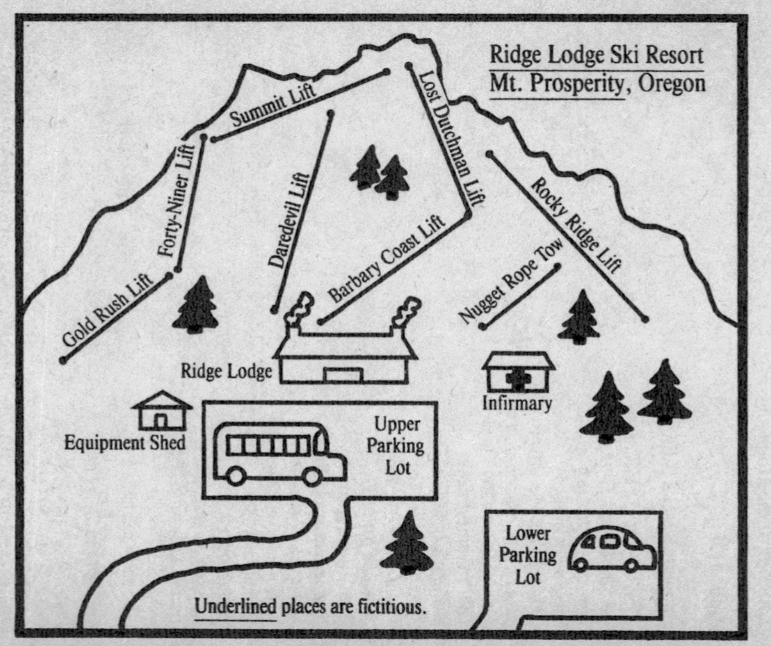
Ridge Lodge Ski Resort
Mt. Prosperity, Oregon
Summit Lift
Lost Dutchman Lift
Forty-Niner Lift
Daredevil Lift
Rocky Ridge Lift
Barbary Coast Lift
Nugget Rope Tow
Gold Rush Lift
Ridge Lodge
Infirmary
Equipment Shed
Upper Parking Lot
Lower Parking Lot
Underlined places are fictitious.

Prologue

Taylor's Crossing, Oregon

The wipers slapped the snow away and the windshield fogged with the cold, but Melanie Walker barely noticed. She drove by rote, unseeing as the miles from the clinic downtown slipped beneath the old truck's tires.

One of her favorite songs was playing on the radio, fighting a losing war with static, but she didn't concentrate on the melody. She couldn't. Her mind wouldn't focus on anything but Gavin and the last time she'd seen him, three weeks before.

His naked body had been the only heat in the hayloft, and his legs and arms had been entwined with hers. The smell of musty hay and animals had filled the air.

"Wait for me, Melanie," he'd whispered against the curve of her neck. His breath had been as warm as a summer wind, his tawny eyes seductive in the half light of the barn. "Say you'll wait for me."

"You know I will," she had foolishly vowed, unaware that fate was against her. At the time she'd known only that she loved him with all of her young heart. And that was all that mattered.

Until today.

She swallowed a hard lump in her throat and shoved the gearshift into third. Her rendezvous with Gavin had taken place three weeks ago and she hadn't seen him since. And now, all their plans and her entire future had changed.

As she drove through the snow-packed roads, she forced her wobbling chin up and clamped hard on her teeth. She wasn't going to cry, no matter what.

Gavin was over a thousand miles away, chasing a dream, and she was alone in a small Oregon town—and two months pregnant.

Her hands clenched over the wheel as she struggled with the right words to explain to her father that she was carrying Gavin Doel's child.

Snowflakes drifted from a gray sky and melted against the windshield as the pickup rumbled along the slippery highway. To the west, the town of Taylor's Crossing nearly bordered Walker land. To the east, fields and pine forest covered the foothills of the Cascades.

Melanie snapped off the radio and glanced into the rearview mirror. Worried hazel eyes stared back at her.

Pregnant. And unmarried. And seventeen. Even in the cold, her hands began to sweat.

The fact that her father had let Melanie see Gavin had been a miracle. He despised Gavin's father, and heaven only knew why he'd allowed Melanie to go out with "that kid from the wrong side of town," the boy who had the misfortune of being Jim Doel's son.

"Help me," she whispered, feeling entirely alone and knowing she had no option but to tell her father the truth.

If only Gavin were still here, she thought selfishly, then whispered to herself, "You can handle this, Melanie. You have to!"

She shifted down and turned into the short lane near the house. The truck slid to a halt.

All Melanie's newfound convictions died on her tongue when she saw her father, axe propped over one shoulder, trudging through the snow toward the barn. The pup, Sassafras, bounded at his heels.

Hearing the rumble of the pickup's engine, Adam Walker turned and grinned. He yanked his baseball cap from his head and tipped it her way, exposing his receding hairline to the elements.

Melanie's mouth went dry. She cut the engine, pocketed the keys and sent up a silent prayer for strength. As she opened the truck's door, a blast of chill winter wind swirled inside. "It's now or never," she told herself, and wished she could choose never.

Stuffing her hands into the pockets of her fleece-lined jacket, she plowed through a blanket of snow. Four inches of powder covered the frozen ground of the small ranch—the ranch that had been her home for as long as she could remember. Though the town of Taylor's Crossing was steadily encroaching, her father had refused to sell—even after his wife's death.

Melanie shivered from the vague memory of losing her mother—and the sorry reasons behind Brenda Walker's death. Her father still held Jim Doel responsible.

Oh, Lord, why did it seem that her entire life had been tangled up with the Doels?

"I'd about given up on you." Her father squared his favorite old Dodgers' cap back onto his head, then brushed the snow from the shoulders of his jean jacket.

Melanie wanted to die.

"Go into the house and warm up some coffee. I'll be back as soon as I feed the stock and split a little kindling." Whistling, he turned and started for the barn.

"Dad?" Her voice sounded tiny.

"Yeah?"

"I'm going to have a baby."

Time seemed to stand still. The wind, raw with the breath of winter, soughed through the pines and cut through her suede jacket. Her father stopped dead in his tracks and turned to face her again. His jaw dropped, and denial crept over his strong features.

"You're pregnant?" he whispered.

Nodding, Melanie wrapped her arms around her middle.

"No!"

She shifted from one foot to the other and tried to ignore the sudden bow in her father's shoulders. All expression left his face, and he looked older than his forty-seven years. His throat worked and his brown gaze drilled into hers. "Doel?" he asked in a voice barely audible over the wind.

She nodded, listening to the painful drum of her heart.

His face turned white. "Oh—Mellie."

"Dad—"

"That black-hearted son of a bitch!" he suddenly growled, wincing as if physically wounded. The small lines around his mouth turned white.

Melanie didn't have to be reminded of the hatred that still simmered between the two families. And she hadn't meant to fall in love with Jim Doel's son; she really hadn't. But Gavin, with his warm eyes, enigmatic smile, lean, athletic body and razor-sharp wit, had been irresistible. She'd fallen head-over-heels in love with him. And she'd thought, foolishly perhaps, that the love they shared would bridge the painful gap between their families—the gap that had been created by that horrible accident.

"You're sure about this?" her father whispered, his gloved fingers opening and closing over the smooth wood of the axe handle.

"I saw the doctor this afternoon."

"Damn!" Adam's teeth clenched. He took up the axe and swung it hard into the gnarly bark of a huge ponderosa pine. "He's just like his old man!" An angry flush crept up his neck, and he muttered an oath under his breath. Kicking the toe of his boot into the base of the tree, he grappled with his rage. "I should never have let you see him—never have listened to that stupid brother of mine!" he raged. "But your damned uncle convinced me that if I'd forbidden it, you'd have started sneaking behind my back!"

"Dad, I love Gavin—"

"Love? *Love!* You're only seventeen!" he bellowed, placing both hands on the fence. He breathed deeply, as he always did when he tried to regain his composure. His breath fogged in the air. "I don't have to tell you about the pain Jim Doel has caused this family." His face twisted in agony, and he leaned heavily against the tree.

"I—I know."

"He's a bastard, Mellie, a drunken, useless—" His voice cracked.

"Gavin's not like his father!"

"Cut from the same cloth."

"No—I mean, Dad, I *love* him. I—I want to marry him."

"Oh, God." Setting his jaw, he said more quietly, "And Gavin—how does he feel?"

"He loves me, too."

Snorting, Adam Walker ran a shaky hand over his lip. "He only loves one thing, Melanie, and that's skiing. Downhill racing was his ticket out of Taylor's Crossing and believe me, he's going to use it to stay away."

Melanie's heart wrenched. Some of what her father was saying was true—she'd told herself that the death-defying runs down the face of a rugged mountain were and always would be Gavin's first love, his mistress—but she didn't want to believe it.

Her father glanced through the trees to the snow-laden mountains in the distance. Absently he rubbed his chest. "I don't say as I can blame him."

"But, when he gets back from Colorado..." she protested as the wind tossed her hair in front of her face.

"He won't be coming back. He's gonna make the Olympic team." Her father's gaze returned to hers. The sadness in his eyes was so profound it cut to her soul. "Sweet Mary, you're just a child."

"I'm—"

"Seventeen, for God's sake!" His breath whistled through his teeth.

"It doesn't matter."

"Life hasn't begun at seventeen." He reached into the pocket of his work shirt for his cigarettes, then swore when he discovered the pack was missing. He'd quit smoking nearly three years before.

Walking on numb legs, Melanie crossed the yard and propped her elbows on the top rail of the fence. Through the pines she could see the spiny ridge of the Cascade Mountains. The highest peak, Mount Prosperity, loomed over the valley.

Her father's throat worked as he followed her. He touched her gently on the shoulder. "Doc Thompson at the clinic, he can—"

"No!" she cried, pounding her fist against the weathered top rail. "I'm having this baby!" She turned, appalled that he would suggest anything so vile. "This is *my* child," she said, tossing her black hair from her eyes. "My child and Gavin's, and I'm going to keep him and raise him and love him!"

"And where does Gavin figure into all this? Does he know?"

She shook her head. "Not yet. I just found out this afternoon."

Adam Walker looked suddenly tired. He said softly, "He may not want it, you know."

"He does!" Her fists clenched so hard that her hands ached.

"He might consider a wife and baby extra baggage."

She'd thought of that, of course. And it worried her. Gavin, if his dream were realized and he made the Olympic team, might not be back for months. Unless he felt duty bound to give up everything he'd worked for and return to support a teenage wife and child. Nervously, she chewed on the inside of her lip.

"What do you think he'll do when he finds out?"

"Come back here," she said weakly.

"And give up skiing?"

Though she felt like crying, she nodded.

He sighed loudly. "And that's what you want?"

"No. Yes! Oh, Dad, yes!" She threw up her hands. How could anything so wonderful as Gavin's child make life so complicated? She loved Gavin, he loved her, and they would have a baby. It was simple, wasn't it? Deep in her heart, she knew she was wrong, but she didn't want to face the truth.

She felt her father's hand on her shoulder. "I'll see you through this, Melanie. You just tell me what you want."

Melanie smiled, though her eyes burned with tears. "I want Gavin," she said.

Her father's hand stiffened, and when she glanced up at him, she saw that his face had turned ashen. He measured his words carefully. "You didn't plan this, did you?"

"Plan what?" she asked before she realized the turn of his thoughts. She felt the color drain from her face. "No!"

"Some women work out these things ahead of time—"

"No!" She shook her head. "The baby was an accident." *A glorious, wonderful accident!*

"Good." He pressed his lips together. "'Cause no man wants to feel trapped."

"I—I know," she whispered.

He touched her chin with a gloved finger, and his expression became tender. "You've got a lot going for you, girl. Finish high school and go to college. Become a photographer like you wanted—or anything else. You can do it. With or without Gavin."

"Can I?" she asked.

"'Course you can. And Gavin's not the only fish in the sea, you know. Neil Brooks is still interested."

Melanie was horrified. "Dad, I'm pregnant! This is for real!"

"Some men don't mind raising another man's child and some men don't even know they've done it."

"What's that supposed to mean?" she demanded, but a sick feeling grew inside her as she grasped his meaning.

"Only that you're not out of options."

She thought about Neil Brooks, a boy her father approved of. At twenty-two, he was already through college and working full-time in his father's lumber brokerage. Neil Brooks came from the right side of the tracks. Gavin Doel didn't.

"I'm not going to lie to Neil," she said.

"Of course you're not," her father agreed, but his eyes narrowed just a fraction. "Go on now, you go into the house and change. I'll take you into town and we'll celebrate."

"Celebrate what?" she asked.

He rolled his eyes to the cloud-covered heavens. "I suppose the fact that I'm going to be a grandfather, though I'll have you know I'm *much* too young." He was trying to cheer her up—she knew that—but she still saw pain flicker in his eyes. She'd wounded him more than he'd ever admit.

Gritting his teeth and flexing his muscles, he walked back to the ancient pine and wiggled the axe blade from the bole, leaving a fresh, ugly gash in the rough bark.

He headed for the barn with Sassafras on his heels again. But he was no longer whistling.

Melanie shoved her hands into her pockets and trudged into the old log house that had been in her family for three generations. Inside, the kitchen was warm and cheery, a fire burning in the wood stove. She rubbed her hands near the stove top, but deep inside she was cold—as cold as the winter wind that ripped through the valley.

She knew what she had to do, of course. Her father was right. And, in her heart, she'd come to the same agonizing conclusion. She couldn't burden Gavin with a wife and child—not now. *Not ever,* a voice inside her head nagged.

Climbing the stairs to her room, she decided that she would never stand between Gavin and his dream. He'd found a way to unshackle himself from a life of poverty and the ridicule of being the town drunk's son. And she wouldn't stop him. She couldn't. She loved him too much.

On his way to Olympic stardom as a downhill skier, Gavin couldn't be tied down to a wife and child. Though he might gladly give up skiing to support her and the baby, one day he would resent them both. Unconsciously, Melanie rubbed her flat abdomen with her free hand. She smiled sadly. If nothing else, she'd have a special part of Gavin forever.

Her pine-paneled room was filled with pictures of Gavin—wonderful snapshots she'd taken whenever they were together. Slowly, looking lovingly at each photograph of his laughing gold-colored eyes, strong jaw and wind-tossed blond hair, she removed every memento that reminded her of Gavin.

She closed her eyes and, once again, remembered the last time she'd seen him. His tanned skin had been smooth and supple beneath her fingers. His pervasive male scent had mingled with the fragrance of hay in the loft.

"Wait for me," he'd whispered. He had cupped her face in his hands, pressed warm kisses to her eyelids, touched a part of her no other man would ever find.

She remembered, too, how he had traced the slope of her jaw with one long finger, then pressed hard, urgent lips to hers. "Say you'll wait for me."

"You know I will," she'd vowed, her fingers tangling in his thick blond hair, her cheeks, wet from tears, pressed to his.

His smile had slashed white in the darkened hayloft. "I'll always love you, Melanie," he'd sworn as he'd kissed her and settled his hard, sensual body over hers.

And I'll love you, she thought now, as she found a pen and paper and began the letter that would set him free.

Chapter One

Taylor's Crossing, Oregon
Eight Years Later

Flags snapped in the breeze. Barkers chanted from their booths. An old merry-go-round resplendent with glistening painted stallions pumped blue diesel smoke and music into the clear mountain air. Children laughed and scampered through the trampled dry grass of Broadacres Fairgrounds.

Long hair flying behind her, Melanie hurried between the hastily assembled tents to the rodeo grounds of the annual fair. She ducked between paddocks until she spied her Uncle Bart, who was holding tight to a lead rope. On the other end was the apple of his eye and the pride of this year's fair—a feisty Appaloosa colt appropriately named Big Money.

Whip thin and pushing sixty, Bart strained to keep the lead rope taut. His skin had become leathery with age, his hair snow-white, but Melanie remembered him as a younger man, before her father's death, when Bart had been Adam Walker's best friend as well as his older brother.

"Thought you might have forgotten us," Bart muttered out of the corner of his mouth. His eyes were trained on the obstinate colt.

Melanie slid through the gate. "Me?" She looked up and offered him a smile. "Forget you? Nah!" Opening her camera bag, she pulled out her favorite .35-millimeter and removed the lens cap. "I just got caught up taking pictures of the fortune teller and weight lifter." Her eyes twinkling, she glanced up at Bart and wrinkled her nose. "If you ask me, Mr. Muscle hasn't got a thing on you."

"That's what all the ladies say," he teased back.

"I bet. So this is your star?" She motioned to the fidgeting Appaloosa.

"In the flesh."

Melanie concentrated as she gazed through the lens of her camera. *Okay,* she thought, focusing on the horse, *don't move.* But the prizewinning colt, a mean-spirited creature who knew he was the crowning glory of this fair, tossed his head and snorted menacingly.

Melanie smothered a grin. She snapped off three quick shots as the horse reared suddenly, tearing the lead rope from Bart's grip.

"You blasted hellion," Bart muttered.

Melanie clicked off several more pictures of the colt prancing, nostrils flared, gray coat catching the late afternoon sunlight.

"Come here, you devil," Bart muttered, advancing on the wild-eyed Big Money, who, snorting, wheeled and bolted to the far side of the paddock. "You know you're something', don't ya?"

The horse pawed the dry ground, and his white-speckled rump shifted as Bart advanced. "Now, calm down. Melanie here just wants to take a few pictures for the *Tribune*."

"It's all right," Melanie called. "I've got all I need."

"You sure?" He grabbed the lead rope and pulled hard. The colt, eyes blazing mischievously, followed reluctantly behind.

"Mmm-hmm. In next week's edition. This is the twenty-second annual fair. It's big news at the *Trib*," Melanie teased.

"And here I thought all the news was the reopening of Ridge Lodge," Bart observed. "And Gavin Doel's broken leg."

Melanie stiffened. "Not *all* the news," she replied quickly. She didn't want to think about Gavin, nor the fact that a skiing accident may have ended his career prematurely, bringing about his return to Taylor's Crossing.

Uncle Bart wound the rope around the top rail of the fence and slipped through the gate after Melanie. "You been up to the lodge lately?"

Melanie slid him a glance and hid the fact that her lips tightened a little. "It's still closed."

"But not for long." Bart reached into his breast pocket for his pack of cigarettes. "I figured since you were with the paper and all, you'd have some inside information."

"Nothing official," she said, somehow managing to keep her composure. "But the rumors are flying."

"They always are," Bart agreed, shaking out a cigarette. Big Money pulled on the rope. "And, from what I hear, Doel thinks he can pull it off—turn the ski resort into a profit-making operation."

Melanie's heart skipped a beat. "That's the latest," she agreed.

"Gavin tell you that himself?" he asked, lighting up and blowing out a thin stream of smoke.

"I haven't seen Gavin in years."

"Maybe it's time you did."

"I don't think so," Melanie replied, replacing the lens cap and fitting her camera back into its case.

Bart reached forward and touched her arm. "You know, Mellie, when your dad died, all the bad blood between Gavin's family and ours dried up. Maybe it's time you buried the past."

Oh, I've done that, she thought sadly, but said, "Meaning?"

"Look up Gavin," he suggested.

"Why?"

"You and he were close once. I remember seeing you up at the lodge together." He slanted her a sly glance. "Some fires are tough to put out."

Amen! "I'm a grown woman, Bart. I'm twenty-five and have a B.A., work for the *Trib* and even moonlight on the side. What would be the point?"

He studied her through the curling smoke of his cigarette. "You could square things up with Jim Doel. Whether your dad ever believed it or not, Jim paid his dues."

Melanie didn't want to think about Jim Doel or the fact that the man had suffered, just as she had, for that horrid night so long ago. Though she'd been only seven at the time, she remembered that night as vividly as any in her life—the night Jim Doel had lost control of his car, the night she'd lost her mother forever.

"As for Gavin," Uncle Bart went on, "he's back and unmarried. Seeing him again might do you a world of good."

Melanie shot him a suspicious glance. "A world of good?" she repeated. "I didn't know I was hurting so bad."

Bart chuckled.

"Believe it or not, I've got everything I want."

"Do you?"

"Yes."

"What about a husband and a house full of kids?"

She felt the color drain from her face. Somehow, she managed a thin smile. She still couldn't think about children without an incredible pain. "I had a husband."

"Not the right one."

"Could be that they're all the same."

"Don't tell your Aunt Lila that."

"Okay, so you're different."

Bart scratched his head. "Everyone is, and you're too smart not to know it. Comparing Neil Brooks to Gavin Doel is like matching up a mule to a thoroughbred."

Despite the constriction in her throat Melanie had to laugh. "Don't tell Neil," she warned.

"I don't even talk to the man—not even when he shows up here. Thank God, it's not too often. But it's a shame you didn't have a passel of kids."

Her insides were shaking by now. "It didn't work out," she said, refusing to admit that she and Neil could never have children, though they'd tried—at least at first. She and Neil had remained childless, and maybe, considering how things had turned out, it had been for the best. But still she grieved for the one child she'd conceived and lost.

Clearing her throat, she caught her uncle staring at her. "I—I guess it's a good thing we never had any children. Especially since the marriage didn't work." The lie still hurt. She would have loved children—especially Gavin's child.

Uncle Bart scowled. "Brooks is and always was an A-number-one bastard."

Melanie didn't want to dwell on her ex-husband, nor the reasons she'd married him. They came too close to touching Gavin again. With a sigh, she said, "Look, Bart, I really can make my own decisions."

"If you say so." He didn't seem the least bit convinced.

She said, "Not many people in town know or remember that Gavin and I had ever dated. I'd like to keep it that way."

"Don't see why—"

She touched his arm. "Please."

Deep furrows lined his brow as he dropped his cigarette and ground it out under the heel of his scruffy boot. "You know I can keep a secret when I have to."

"Good," she said, deciding to change the subject as quickly as possible. "Now, if you want to see Big Money's picture in the *Tribune* next week, I've got to run. Give Lila my love." With a wave she was off, trudging back through the dry grass, ignoring the noise and excitement of the carnival as she headed toward her battered old Volkswagen, determined not to think about Gavin Doel again for the rest of the day.

Unfortunately, Gavin was the hottest gossip the town of Taylor's Crossing had experienced in years.

Back at the newspaper office, Melanie ran the prints in the darkroom and was just returning to her desk with a fresh cup of coffee when Jan Freemont, a reporter for the paper, slammed the receiver of her phone down and announced, "I got it, folks—the interview of the year!"

Melanie cocked a brow in her direction. "Of the year?"

"Maybe of the decade! Barbara Walters, move over!"

Constance Rava, the society page editor, whose desk was near Melanie's work area, looked up from her word processor. A small woman with short, curly black hair and brown eyes hidden by thick reading glasses, she studied Jan dubiously. "What've you got?"

"An interview with Gavin Doel!"

Melanie nearly choked on her coffee. She leaned her hips against her cluttered desk and hoped she didn't look as apoplectic as she felt.

"No!" Constance exclaimed.

"That's right!" Jan said, tossing her strawberry blond hair away from her face and grinning ear to ear. "He hasn't granted an interview in years—and it's going to happen tomorrow morning!"

Every face in the small room turned toward Jan's desk.

"So he's really here—in Oregon?" asked Guy Reardon, a curly-haired stringer and part-time movie critic for the paper.

"Yes, indeedy." Jan leaned back in her chair, basking in her yet-to-be-fulfilled glory.

"Why didn't we know about it until now?"

"You know Doel," Constance put in. She rolled her eyes expressively. "He's become one of those Hollywood types who demand their privacy."

Melanie had to bite her tongue to keep from saying something she'd probably regret. Her hands trembled as she set down her cup. Gavin had always created a sensation, probably always would. She'd have to get used to it. And she'd have to forget that there had ever been anything between them.

But the fact that he was back—*here*—caused her heart to thump crazily. Not that it mattered, she told herself. What Gavin did with his life was his business. Period. Except, of course, when it came to news. And though she was loath to admit it, Gavin Doel was news—big news—in Taylor's Crossing. The epitome of local boy does good.

Sidestepping the tightly packed desks in the newsroom, Jan threaded her way to Melanie's work area. "Can you believe it?"

"Hard to, isn't it?" she murmured, wishing the subject of Gavin Doel would just go away.

"Oh, come on. This is a coup, Mel. A real coup!"

"I know. But we've heard this all before. Someone's always going to reopen the resort."

"This is a done deal."

Melanie's heart sank. She'd hoped that, once again, the rumors surrounding Ridge Lodge were nothing more than idle speculation—at least as far as Gavin was concerned. Melanie welcomed the thought of the lodge opening, but why did Gavin have to be involved?

Jan wrinkled her nose thoughtfully. "I just got off the phone with Doel's partner, what's his name—" she glanced at her notes "—Rich Johanson. He said Doel would meet me tomorrow at nine at the main lodge!" Opening her hands in front of her, she added dramatically, "I can see it now, a full-page spread on the lodge, interviews with Gavin Doel and maybe a series of articles about the man, his personal and professional life—"

"Don't you think you're pushing things a bit?" Melanie cut in a little desperately. Few people had been with the paper long enough to know about her romance with Gavin, and she intended to keep it that way. "Constance just told us how private he is—"

"But he'll need the publicity if the ski lodge is to reopen for the season. And we all know how Brian feels about this story—he can't wait!"

Brian Michaels was the editor-in-chief of the paper.

"He'll want to run with this one. Now," Jan said, chewing on her lower lip, "we'll need background information and photos. Then, tomorrow, when we're at the lodge—"

"We're?" Melanie repeated, reaching for her Garfield coffee cup again. She took a sip of lukewarm coffee as her heart kicked into double time.

"Yes—us," Jan replied as if Melanie had developed some sort of hearing problem. "You and me. I need you for the shoot."

This was too much. Despite her professionalism, Melanie wasn't ready to come face-to-face with Gavin. Not after the way they'd parted. He'd asked her to wait for him and she'd vowed that she would. But she hadn't. In fact, within the month she'd married Neil Brooks. "Can't Geri do the shoot?" she asked.

"She starts vacation tomorrow, remember?" Jan shoved a stack of photographs out of the way and plopped onto the corner of Melanie's desk. Crossing her legs, she leaned over Melanie's In basket. "Don't you want a chance to photograph one of the most gorgeous men in skiing history?"

"No."

"Why not?"

Melanie dodged that one. There wasn't any reason to tell Jan all about her past—a past she'd rather forget. At least not yet. "I've heard he's not too friendly with photographers."

"Too many paparazzi," Jan surmised, waving off the statement as if it were a bothersome mosquito. "But that's what he gets for going out with all those famous models. It comes with the territory." She leaned closer. "Confidentially, this paper needs the kind of shot in the arm that Gavin Doel's fame and notoriety could give it. I don't have to tell you that the *Trib*'s in a world of hurt."

Guy, who had wandered over from the copy machine, glanced over his shoulder. "Do you think he brought any of his girlfriends back with him? I'd love to meet Gillian Sentra or Aimee LaRoux."

"You and the rest of the male population," Jan replied dryly.

Melanie's heart wrenched, but she ignored the familiar pain.

"I don't think there will be any women with him," Constance said from her desk. "He hasn't been seen with anyone since he broke his leg in that fall last spring. The way I understand it, he's become a recluse."

"But not a monk, I'll bet," Guy joked. "Doel's always surrounded by gorgeous women. Anyway, Melanie's right—the guy's just not all that friendly with the press. I can't believe he's going along with the interview."

"Well," Jan said, "I didn't actually talk to Doel himself. But Johanson says he'll be there." Jan checked her watch and glowered at the digital display. "Look, I've got to run. I want to tell Brian about the interview."

"He'll be ecstatic," Melanie predicted sarcastically. Since the rumors had sprung up that Ridge Lodge was reopening, the editor-in-chief had been busy coming up with articles about the lodge—its economic impact on the community, the environmental issues, the fact that one of the most famous skiers in America had returned to his small home town. Yes, Gavin was big news, and the *Tribune* needed all the big news it could get.

Jan's brown eyes slitted suspiciously. "You know, Melanie, everyone in Taylor's Crossing is thrilled about this—except for you, maybe."

"I'm all in favor of Ridge reopening," Melanie said, taking another gulp of her coffee and frowning at the bitter taste. She shoved her cup aside, sloshing coffee on some negatives. Sopping the mess with a tissue, she muttered, "Idiot," under her breath and avoided Jan's curious gaze.

"So what's the problem?" Jan persisted.

"No problem," Melanie lied, tossing the soppy tissue into her wastebasket. "I just hope that it all works out. It would be a shame if Ridge Lodge reopened only to close again in a year or two."

"No way—not if Doel's behind it! I swear, that man has the Midas touch." Jan slung the strap of her bag over her shoulder just as Brian Michaels shoved open the door to his glassed-in editor's office and made a beeline for her desk. A short, lean man with prematurely gray hair and contacts that tinted his eyes a darker shade of blue, he dodged desks, glowing computer terminals and overflowing wastebaskets on his way toward the photography section.

"You got the Doel interview?" he asked Jan.

"Yep." Jan explained about her conversation with Gavin's partner, and Brian was so pleased he managed a nervous smile.

"Good. Good. We'll do a story in next week's issue, then follow up with articles between now and ski season." Tugging thoughtfully at his tie, he glanced at Melanie. "Dig out any old pictures we have of Doel. Go back ten years or so—when he was on the ski team for the high school, then the Olympic team. And find everything you can on his professional career and personal life. And I mean everything." He swung his gaze back to Jan. "And you talk to the sports page editor, see what he's got on file and double-check with Constance, see if he's up to anything interesting personally. It doesn't really matter if it's now or in the past. Don't forget to rehash the accident where he broke his leg—poor son of a bitch probably lost his career on that run."

For a split second, Melanie thought she saw a glimmer of satisfaction in Brian's tinted eyes. But it quickly disappeared as he continued. "And check into his love life before he left town, that sort of thing."

Melanie's heart turned stone-cold.

"Will do," Jan said, then frowned at Melanie, who was standing stock-still. Jan pursed her lips as she glanced at her watch again. "I've really got to get moving—the park dedication's in less than an hour. I'll meet you up at the lodge tomorrow morning."

Unless I chicken out, Melanie thought grimly as Brian and Jan went their separate ways. So she had to face Gavin again. She felt a premonition of disaster but squared her shoulders. The past was ancient history. There wasn't any reason Gavin would drag it up.

Even so, her stomach tightened at the thought. How could she ever explain why she'd left him so suddenly? Why she'd married Neil? Even if she could say all the right words, it was better that he never knew.

She wasn't looking forward to tomorrow in the least, she thought grimly. The last person she wanted to see was Gavin Doel.

"I want it off, and I want if off today!" Gavin thundered, glaring darkly at the cast surrounding the lower half of his left leg.

"Just another couple of days." Dr. Hodges, who looked barely out of his teens, tented his hands under his chin and shook his head. He sat behind a bleached oak desk in his Portland sports clinic, trying to look fatherly while gently rebuffing Gavin as if he were a recalcitrant child. "If you want to race professionally again—"

"I do."

"Then let's not push it, shall we?"

Gavin clamped his mouth shut. He wanted to scream—to rant and rave—but knew there was no reason. The young sandy-haired doctor knew his business. "I've got work to do."

"The lodge?"

"The lodge," Gavin agreed.

"Even when you get the cast off, you'll have to be careful."

"I'm tired of being careful."

"I know."

Gavin rubbed an impatient hand around his neck. He hated being idle, hated worse the fact that he'd been sidelined from the sport he loved, but at least he had the resort to keep him busy. Though his feelings about returning to Taylor's Crossing were ambivalent, he was committed to making Ridge Resort the premier ski resort in the Pacific Northwest.

"Come back in on Friday. I'll check the X rays again and then, if the fracture has healed, you can go from a walking cast to only crutches. With physical therapy, you should be back on the slopes by December."

"This is September. It's already been over six months."

"That's because you rushed it before," Hodges said with measured patience. "That hairline fracture above your ankle happened during the spring season and you reinjured it early this summer when you wouldn't slow down. So now you have to pay the price."

Gavin didn't need to be reminded. He shoved his hands through his hair in frustration. "Okay, okay, you've made your point."

"Friday, then?"

"Right. Friday." Helping himself up with his crutches, he started for the door. He made his way through the white labyrinthine corridors to the reception area. He passed by posters of the skeletal system, the neurological system, the human eye and heart, but he barely noticed. He was too wrapped up with the fragility of the human ankle—his damned ankle.

And now he had to drive nearly three hundred miles back to Taylor's Crossing, a town he despised. He would have picked any other location in the Cascades for his resort, but Taylor's Crossing, his partner had assured him, was perfect. The price was right, the location ideal. If only Gavin could get over his past and everything that the town represented.

Meaning Melanie.

Uttering an oath at himself, he shouldered open the door and hobbled across the parking lot to his truck. He shoved his crutches inside and climbed behind the wheel. As he flicked on the ignition, he told himself yet again to forget her. She was out of his life—had been for eight or nine years.

She was married to wealth and probably had a couple of kids by now. Scowling, he threw the truck into reverse, then peeled out of the lot. He didn't want to drive back to Taylor's Crossing tonight, would rather stay in Portland until Friday, when the cast had better come off.

Portland held no bittersweet memories for him. Taylor's Crossing was packed with them. Nonetheless, he headed east, back to Mount Prosperity, where so many memories of Melanie still lingered in the shadowy corners of Ridge Lodge.

At five-thirty, Melanie ignored the headache pounding behind her eyes, stuffed her camera into her bag, snagged her jacket from the closet and headed out of the newsroom. The afternoon had flown by and she hadn't had a chance to dig through the files on back issues and dredge up pictures and information on Gavin. She was glad. She'd heard enough about him for one day, been reminded of him more times than she wanted to count. An invisible, bittersweet cloud of nostalgia had been her companion all afternoon. Seeing pictures of him would only intensify those feelings.

She would save the thrilling task of wading through Gavin's award-strewn past for tomorrow.

Tomorrow. She hardly dared think about it. What would she say to Gavin again? What would she do? How could she possibly focus a camera on his handsome features and not feel a pang of regret for a past they hadn't shared, a future they would never face together, a baby who had never been born?

"Stop it," she chastised herself angrily, shoving open the door.

A wall of late summer heat met her as she walked out onto the dusty streets. A few dry leaves skittered between the parking meters lining the sidewalk. Melanie climbed into the sun-baked interior of her old Volkswagen, rolled down the window and headed east, through the heart of town, past a hodgepodge of shops toward the outskirts, where she lived in the log cabin her great-grandfather had built nearly a hundred years before, the home she'd left eight years ago.

She might not have returned except that her father's illness had coincided with her divorce. She'd come back then and hadn't bothered to move. There was no reason to—until now. If she could part with the home that was part of her heritage.

The log house had originally been the center of a ranch, but Taylor's Crossing, barely a fork in the road in her great-grandfather's time, had steadily encroached and now street lamps and concrete sidewalks covered what had once been acres of sagebrush and barbed wire. In the past few years there had been big changes in the place. Acre by acre the ranch had been sold, and now the property surrounding the house was little more than two fields and a weathered old barn. The log cabin itself, upgraded over the years, now boasted electricity, central heating, plumbing and a new addition that housed her small photography studio.

She parked her car near the garage, stopped off at the mailbox and winced at the stack of bills tucked inside. "Great," she muttered as Sassafras, her father's collie whom she'd inherited along with the house, barked excitedly. Wiggling, he bounded ahead to the door. "Miss me?" she asked, and the dog swept the back porch with his tail. She petted his head. "Yeah, me, too."

Inside, she tossed the mail and camera on the kitchen table, refilled Sassafras's water bowl and poured herself a tall glass of iced tea. Her headache subsided a little, and she glanced out the window to the Cascade Mountains. The craggy peak of Mount Prosperity, whereon Ridge Resort had been built years before, jutted jaggedly against the blue sky. She wondered if Gavin was there now. Did he live in the resort? Was he planning to stay after it was opened? Or would he, once his ankle had healed, resume his downhill racing career?

"What does it matter?" she asked herself, her headache returning to pound full force.

Tomorrow she'd have all her answers and more. Tomorrow she'd meet Gavin again. And then what—oh, God, what—could she possibly say to him?

The next morning, as shafts of early sunlight pierced through thick stands of pine, Melanie drove up the series of switchbacks to the ski resort.

A few clouds drifted around the craggy upper slopes of Mount Prosperity, but otherwise the sky was clear, the air crisp with the fading of summer.

Located just below the timberline, Ridge Lodge, a rambling cedar and stone resort that had been built a few years before the Great Depression, rose four stories in some places, with steep gables and dormers. The building had been remodeled several times but still held an early-twentieth-century charm that blended into the cathedral-like mountains of the central Oregon Cascades.

Melanie had always loved the lodge. Its sloped roofs, massive fireplaces and weathered exterior appealed to her as much today as it had when she was a child growing up in nearby Taylor's Crossing. She'd lived in the small town most of her life, except for the six years she'd been married to Neil and resided in Seattle. Ridge Lodge had been an important part of her youth—a special part that had included Gavin.

As she parked her battered old Volkswagen in the empty lot, her pulse fairly leaped, her skin covered in goose bumps. The thought of seeing Gavin again brought sweat to her palms.

"Don't be a fool," she berated herself, climbing out of the car and grabbing her heavy camera bag. *He's long forgotten you.* Shading her eyes, she looked over the pockmarked parking lot and noted that Jan's sports car wasn't in sight. "Terrific."

She started up the path, noticing the bulldozers and snowplows standing like silent sentinels near huge sheds. Behind the lodge, ski lifts—black poles strung together with cable—marched up the bare mountainside.

"It's now or never," she told herself. Keyed up inside, her senses all too aware, Melanie swallowed back any lingering fear of coming face-to-face with Gavin.

She pounded on the front doors, and they creaked open against her fist. "Hello?" she called into the darkened interior.

No one answered.

Hiking her bag higher, she squared her shoulders and strode inside. The main desk was empty, the lodge still, almost creepy. "Hello?" she yelled again, and her voice echoed to the rafters high overhead. Summoning all her courage, she said, "Gavin?"

The sound of his name, from her own voice, seemed strange. Her nerves, already strung tight, stretched to the breaking point. Where was Jan?

Maybe Gavin had changed his mind. Or, more likely, maybe Rich Johanson had spoken out of turn. Probably Gavin wasn't even here. Disgusted, she turned, thinking she'd wait for Jan outside, then stopped, her breath catching in her throat.

Blocking the doorway, crutches wedged under his arms, eyes hidden behind mirrored aviator glasses, Gavin Doel glared at her.

Melanie's heart nearly dropped through the floor. She tried to step forward but couldn't move.

He was more handsome than before, all boyishness long driven from the bladed angles and planes of his face. His expression was frozen, his thin lips tight. The nostrils of his twice-broken nose flared contemptuously at the sight of her.

In those few heart-stopping seconds Melanie felt the urge to run, get away from him as fast as she could. The once-dead atmosphere in the lodge came to life, charged and dangerous.

Gavin shifted on his crutches, his jaw sliding to the side. "Well, *Mrs.* Brooks," he drawled in a cold voice that disintegrated the remnants of her foolish dreams—dreams she hadn't even realized she'd kept until now. "Just what the hell are *you* doing here?"

Chapter Two

Gavin ripped off his sunglasses and impaled her with his icy gaze. "Well?" he demanded, his eyes slitting dangerously. His jaw thrust forward impatiently. Undercurrents of long-dead emotions charged the air.

"I was waiting for you."

"For me?" His mouth tightened. "Well, now, isn't that a switch?"

The words bit.

"You know, Melanie, you were the last person I expected to run into up here." He dug in his crutches and hobbled past her to the bar.

"I was waiting for you because—"

"I don't want to hear it. In fact," he said, glancing over his shoulder, "I don't think we have anything to say to each other."

Melanie was stunned. This cold, bitter man was Gavin—the boy she'd loved so passionately. Where was the tenderness, the kindness, the laughter she remembered so vividly? "Let's just get through this, okay?"

"What? Get through what? Oh, hell, it doesn't matter." He turned his attention to the dusty mirrored bar.

"Of course it matters! I've got a job to do—"

He frowned, his eyes narrowing on her camera case. "A job?"

"Yes—"

"Just get out."

"Pardon me?"

"I said 'Get out,' Melanie. Leave. I don't want to talk to you."

"But you agreed—"

"Agreed?" he roared, his fist banging the bar. "Unless memory fails me, the last time we agreed to anything, I was going to Colorado and you *agreed* to wait for me."

"Oh, God." This was worse than she imagined. "I couldn't—"

"And guess what? The minute I'm out of town, you left me high and dry."

"That's not exactly how it was," she snapped back.

"Oh, no? Then you tell me, how was it?"

"You were in Colorado—"

"Oh, right, I left you. Look, it doesn't matter. It's over. Period. I shouldn't have brought it up. So just go." Swearing under his breath, he propped himself up with his crutches and scrounged around behind the oak and brass bar, searching the lower cupboards.

From her vantage point, Melanie saw his reflection in the dusty full-length mirror. He was wearing cutoff jeans, and the muscles of his thighs, covered with downy gold hair, strained as he leaned over.

"You did leave me," she pointed out, refusing to back down.

"And you said you'd wait. Stupid me, I believed you."

"I meant it."

"Oh, I get it," he said, glaring at her again. "I just didn't put a time limit on the waiting, is that it? I assumed you meant you'd wait more than a few weeks before you eloped with someone else."

The hackles on the back of her neck rose as he turned his attention back to the cupboard. "You don't understand—"

"No, damn it, I don't. *I*—" he hooked a thumb at his chest "—wasn't there, was I? I didn't have the advantage of seeing you moving in on Brooks."

"I didn't move in on—"

"Okay, so he moved in on you. Doesn't matter."

"Then what're we arguing about?" she demanded, the heat rushing to her cheeks.

He let out his breath slowly, as if trying to control a temper that was rapidly climbing out of control. "What're you doing here, Melanie? I thought you lived in Seattle and probably owned a Mercedes and had a couple of kids by now."

"Sometimes things don't turn out the way you want them to," she said.

He glanced over the top of the bar, his brows pulled together. "Philosophy? Or real life?"

"Both," she replied, holding up her chin. "I'm here with the *Tribune*."

"The what?" he asked without much interest.

"The *Tribune*. You know, the local newspaper."

"Oh, right." He snorted, returning his attention to the contents of the bar. "So you're a reporter these days? What's that got to do with me?"

"I'm a photographer," she replied quickly. "Not a reporter, but I'm supposed to take pictures of you for the interview."

"I don't give interviews."

Melanie's temper began to simmer. "But yesterday your partner said you'd talk to us—"

His head snapped up, and the look he sent her over the bar was positively furious. "Rich said *what*?"

"That you'd grant an interview to the *Trib*—"

"No way!"

"But—"

"Hey, don't argue with me," he bit out. "You, of all people, should understand why I don't talk to the press. It has to do with privacy and the fact that there are some details of my life I'd rather keep to myself."

"Why me 'of all people?'" she flung back at him.

His lips thinned. "As I remember it, there's still some bad blood between our families and a whole closet full of skeletons that are better left locked away."

She couldn't argue with that, but she wanted to. Damn the man, he still had a way of getting under her skin—even if it was only to irritate her. But he did have a point, she thought grudgingly. She didn't want anyone dredging up their affair or the scandal concerning her mother and his father.

"I'll make sure this is strictly professional."

"You can guarantee that?"

"I can try."

"Not good enough. The *Tribune* doesn't have the greatest reputation around."

"I know, but—"

"Then no interview. Period," he growled, rattling glasses until he found a bottle, yanked it out and blew the dust from its label.

"Let's start over."

He didn't move, but his gaze drilled into hers. "Start over," he repeated. "I wish I could. I would've done a whole lotta things differently."

A lump jammed her throat. Her voice, when she found it, was soft. "I—uh, that's not what I meant. I think we should start the interview over."

"Like hell!" Wincing as he straightened his leg, he rained a drop-dead glance her direction.

Her temper flared. "Look, Gavin, I don't want to be here any more than you want me here!"

"Then leave." He cleaned the bottom of a short glass with the tail of his shirt, then uncapped the bottle.

"I have a job to do."

"Oh, yeah. Pictures for the *Trib.* I forgot." He poured three fingers of whiskey into the glass and tossed back the entire drink, grimacing as the liquor hit the back of his throat.

"Isn't it a little early—?"

"I don't need any advice," he cut in. "Especially from you!" A sardonic smile twisted his lips, and he leaned across the bar, holding the bottle in one hand. "Excuse my manners," he bit out, obviously intending to bait her. "Would you like to join me?"

Melanie narrowed her eyes, rising to the challenge. Why not? She'd taken all the flak she intended to, so she'd beat him at his own game! "Sure. And make it a double."

A spark of humor flashed in his tawny eyes. "The lady wants a double." He twisted off the cap. "You never did anything halfway, did you, Melanie? All or nothing."

"That's me," she mocked, but her pulse jumped as he looked her way again, and she remembered him as he had been—younger, more boyish, his hard edges not yet formed. He'd always been striking and arrogant and fiercely competitive, but there had been a gentle side to him, as well—a loving side that she'd never quite forgotten. Now it seemed that tenderness was well hidden under layers of cynicism.

She felt a stab of guilt. How could their wonderful love have turned so bitter?

Forcing a smile, she fought the urge to whisper that she was sorry. Instead she took the glass he offered and sipped the fiery liquor. "Ah..." she said, remembering the words her grandfather had used when tasting expensive Scotch, "smooth!"

"Right...smooth," he challenged, his eyes glinting again. "Good ol' rotgut whiskey. I'll give you a clue, Melanie, it's not smooth. In fact it burns like a son of a bitch."

He was right. The whiskey seared a trail down her throat. She pushed her glass aside and met his gaze squarely. "If you say so."

"I do."

"Then that must be the way it is," she replied smartly, wishing he wasn't so damned handsome. If only she didn't notice the way his dark lashes ringed his eyes, the cut of his cheekbones, the down hair of his forearms. "Now that we've gotten past going for each other's jugular—maybe we can quit sniping at each other long enough to get down to business."

"Which is?"

"The interview. And pictures for it."

His mouth tightened, and he shoved a wayward lock of blond hair from his eyes before taking another long, slow sip from his glass.

Several seconds ticked by, and he didn't move a muscle. The subject of the interview was obviously closed.

"Right. Well, I tried." With the tips of her fingers Melanie nudged her business card across the bar. "In case you change your mind. And when Jan gets here, would you tell her I went back to the office?"

"Who's Jan?"

"The reporter. The one from the *Tribune* who planned to write a stunning article about your lodge. As I pointed out earlier, I'm just the photographer and I don't care whether you want to be photographed or not. But Jan might see things differently. She's under the false impression that you agreed to an interview."

"She's wrong."

"You can tell her." She started for the door and said sarcastically over her shoulder, "Thanks for the drink."

Shoving his crutches forward, Gavin hobbled around the bar and placed himself squarely in her path to the door. "What is it you're really doing here, Melanie?" he asked.

A surge of anger swept through her. "You think I'm lying?"

"I don't know." His lips twisted cynically. "But then, you've had a lot of practice, haven't you?"

That did it! She slung her bag over her shoulder. "For your information, I don't want to be here. In fact, if I could, I'd be anywhere on God's green earth rather than here with you!" She spun, but quick as a striking snake his hand shot out, steely fingers curled over her wrist and he whirled her back to face him.

"Before you leave," he said so quietly she could barely hear him, "just answer one question."

Melanie's heart thumped, and her wrist, where his fingers wrapped possessively over her pulse, throbbed. Her throat was suddenly dry. "Shoot."

"Where is your husband?"

"I don't have a husband anymore."

His eyes narrowed as if he expected everything she said to be a lie. She turned back to the door, but he wouldn't release her. "So what happened to good ol' Neil?"

She swallowed hard. "We, uh, we're divorced."

Something flashed in his eyes. Regret? "I guess I should say I'm sorry."

"No need to lie."

His face softened slightly. "Believe it or not, Melanie, I only wanted the best for you," he said suddenly. "I just didn't think Neil Brooks could make you happy."

"I guess it's a moot point now."

"Is it?" Again the pressure on her arm, the spark in his eyes.

Nervously she licked her lips, and his attention was drawn for a second to her mouth.

His jaw worked, and he said softly, "You know, Melanie, I think it would be best if you didn't come back."

"I only came here because of my job."

"Oh?" he said, eyebrows lifting, the fingers on the inside of her wrist pressing slightly against her bare skin. "So you weren't curious about me?"

"Not in the least."

"And you didn't think because you shed yourself of your husband that we could pick up where we left off?" His voice had grown husky, his pupils dilating in the darkened lodge.

"That would be crazy," But her heart was pumping madly, slamming against her ribs, and she could barely concentrate on the conversation as his fingers moved on her inner wrist.

"Probably—"

The huge double doors were flung open, and Jan, her briefcase swinging at her side, strode into the lobby. "So here you are! God, I've had a terrible time getting here—" She took one look at Gavin and Melanie, and her train of thought seemed to evaporate.

Self-consciously, Melanie yanked her arm away from Gavin.

"Well," Jan said, as if walking in on an intimate scene between one of her co-workers and an internationally famous skier were an everyday occurrence, "I see you've already started."

"Not quite," Melanie replied, but Jan plunged on, walking up to Gavin and flashing her businesslike smile.

"I'm Jan Freemont. With the Taylor's Crossing *Tribune*." She flicked a confused glance at Melanie, "But I suppose you already guessed."

"I assumed."

Jan dug into her heavy canvas bag. She withdrew a card and handed it to him. "So, you've already met Melanie."

Gavin's mouth quirked. "Years ago."

"Oh?" Jan's brows lifted in interest, and Melanie could have throttled Gavin right then and there.

Instead, she managed a cool smile. "Gavin and I both grew up around here," she explained, hoping that would end this turn in the conversation. She was probably wrong. Jan wasn't one to let the subject drop. Her reporter instincts were probably going crazy already.

"Sorry I'm late," Jan apologized. "I had trouble with my car again."

"I don't think it matters," Melanie said.

Jan was busy extracting her pocket recorder and steno pad.

Melanie threw Gavin a look that dared him to disagree as she said, "Mr. Doel and I were just discussing the interview."

"Mmm?" Jan asked, searching through her large black shoulder bag.

"There isn't going to be one," Gavin said.

Melanie lifted a shoulder. "Apparently he didn't know about it."

"I didn't," Gavin clarified.

Melanie charged on. "And he's not interested in going through with it."

"You're kidding, right?" Jan asked.

"'Fraid not," Gavin drawled.

"But I spoke with your partner, Mr.—" she flipped open a note pad "—Johanson. He said you'd be glad to talk to us."

"Oh, he did, did he?" Gavin seemed faintly amused. "Well, he was wrong."

Oh, this is just wonderful, Melanie thought, wishing she could disappear. She'd known this session would be a disaster, but neither Brian Michaels, the *Trib*'s editor-in-chief, nor Jan, the paper's crack reporter, had listened to her. Jan saw herself as a new Barbara Walters and Brian was hoping he could turn the *Tribune* into the *Washington Post*. Never mind that the *Tribune* was a small newspaper in central Oregon with a steadily declining readership.

Jan wasn't about to be thwarted. She explained about her phone call to Gavin's partner. She also went into an animated dissertation about how she wanted to write a "local boy does good then returns home" type of story.

Gavin wasn't buying it. He listened to all her arguments, but his hard expression didn't alter and his gaze drilled into her. "If you want information on the lodge, you'll have to get it from Rich," he finally said.

"But our readers will want to know all about you and your injury—"

"My personal life is off limits," Gavin muttered, and Melanie felt a tremor of relief.

"But you're a celebrity," Jan cooed, trying desperately to win him over. "You have fans who are interested—"

"Then they can read all about it in some cheap rag at the checkout counter of their local market. It might not be true, but it's guaranteed to be sensational."

"Now, wait a minute." Jan wasn't about to take this lying down. "Reopening Ridge Lodge is a big story around here! People will be interested and it's great publicity for you—"

"I don't want publicity," he said, glancing icily at Melanie. "I think I've had enough." He hobbled to the door. "If you want to do an article on the lodge reopening, that's fine with me. But I want my name kept out of it as much as possible."

Jan's smile was frozen. "But doesn't that defeat the point? It's your name that's going to bring people here, Mr. Doel. Your face in the paper that will make people interested. You're an international skier. You've endorsed everything from skis to lip balm. Your face will guarantee public interest, and that's what you need to reopen the lodge successfully." She gestured expansively to the inside of the resort. "I know I can convince my editor to do a series of articles about the lodge that will keep public interest up. I'll also free-lance stories to ski magazines that are distributed everywhere in the country, so by the time the snow hits and the season is here, you're guaranteed cars in the parking lot, skiers on the runs and people in the bar."

Melanie expected Gavin to say "Bully for you" or something along those lines, but he kept silent.

Jan pressed her point home. "My guess is you need all the publicity you can get."

"I've given you my answer. Rich'll be back here this afternoon. Since he's the one who agreed to this damned interview in the first place, you can talk to him."

He shoved his crutches in front of him and moved awkwardly through the front door.

"That man is something else!" Jan whispered, letting out her breath. "You know, he almost acts like he's got something to hide."

"Constance said he doesn't talk to the press," Melanie reminded her.

"Yeah, but she didn't say why." Jan's lips thinned as she turned to Melanie. "And what was going on between you two when I first got here? You looked like you were deciding whether to kill each other or make love."

Melanie's stomach tightened. "You're exaggerating."

"Nope. And you didn't tell me that you knew him."

Lifting a shoulder, Melanie replied, "It didn't seem important."

Jan's expression clouded with suspicion. "Oh, sure. That's like saying storm warnings aren't important when you're heading out to sea in a small boat."

Slinging the strap of her camera bag over her shoulder, Melanie said, "Look, I've got another shoot in twenty minutes, so I'm not going to waste my time here."

"But you'll fill me in later?"

"Sure," Melanie replied, wondering just how much she could tell Jan about Gavin as she shoved open the door and stepped into the warm mountain air.

Across the parking lot, near the equipment shed, she spied Gavin leaning hard on his crutches, talking to a man in an orange pickup. A sign on the pickup's door read Gamble Construction.

The two men were engrossed in conversation. Gavin's reflective aviator glasses were back in place, and the late morning sunlight glinted in his hair. His cast-covered leg looked awkward.

Melanie wondered if the rumors were true that his career was over.

He didn't glance her way as she unlocked her car, and she didn't bother trying to get his attention. The less she had to do with him, the better.

Gavin watched the little car speed out of the lot and felt the tension between his shoulder blades relax. He hadn't counted on seeing Melanie again. What was she doing back in Taylor's Crossing, working at that rag of a paper? And why had she and Neil split? Maybe Brooks wasn't making enough money for her now.

But would she give up the good life of luxury to work on a small-time newspaper? Nope, it didn't make sense.

"...so the crew will be here at the beginning of the week, and I think we can make up for some of the time lost by the strike," Seth Gamble, owner of Gamble Construction, was saying as he leaned out the window of his pickup. Gavin forced his attention back to the conversation.

"Good. I'll see you then." Gavin thumped the dusty hood of the truck with his hand, and Seth, grinning, rammed the pickup into gear and took off.

Shoving the damned crutches under his arms, Gavin started back for the lodge and found Jan whatever-her-name-was, the blond reporter, sweeping toward him. Her expression had turned hard, and he was reminded why he didn't trust reporters. They didn't give a damn about the subject—just that they got the story.

"Mr. Doel!" she said, striding up to him and trying her best to appear hard-edged and tough. "My editor expects a story on the lodge—the story we were promised."

"As I said, you can talk to my partner."

"Is he here?"

"No," Gavin admitted.

"When do you expect him?"

"I don't know. He had business out of town."

"Then it looks like we're left with you if we want to make next week's edition. Right?" When Gavin didn't reply, she said, "I'm sorry if we inconvenienced you, Mr. Doel, but what's going on here—" she made a sweeping gesture to the lodge "—is news. Big news. And so, unfortunately, are you. You can't expect the *Tribune* to ignore it, nor, I would think, would you want it ignored."

She stood waiting, cool green eyes staring up at him, firm jaw set, and he couldn't fault her logic. Besides, he wanted to get rid of her. "All right," he finally agreed. "When Rich gets back. Tomorrow. He and I will tell you all about our plans for the resort, but I want my private life kept out of it."

"But not your professional life," Jan said quickly. "People will need to know why you're involved. Some people, believe it or not, might not be familiar with your name."

"My professional life is a matter of record."

"Good. Then we understand each other." She offered her hand, shook his and marched to a red sports car, which coughed and sputtered before sparking to life and tearing through the dusty lot.

"Now you've done it, Doel," he muttered. Inviting the reporter back was probably a mistake. No doubt Melanie would accompany her. His fingers tightened over the handholds on his crutches. Seeing Melanie again wasn't in his plans.

The sight of Melanie brought back memories he'd rather forget forever, and touching her—good God, why had he done such a fool thing? Just the feel of her skin made his blood race.

Leveling an oath at himself, he plunged the tips of his crutches into the pavement and headed back for the lodge, intending to throttle Rich Johanson when he showed up. They'd had an agreement: Rich would handle all the publicity, the legal work and financial information; Gavin would supervise the reconstruction of the lodge and the runs. Gavin had made it clear from the onset that he wasn't going to have a passel of nosy reporters poking around, digging into his personal life.

He hadn't lied to Melanie when he'd mentioned skeletons in the closet. There were just too damned many. Unfortunately, Melanie knew about a lot of them. Her family and his could provide enough scandal to keep the gossip mill in Taylor's Crossing busy for years.

Gavin opened the door to the lodge. There on the bar was the bottle of whiskey. And two glasses—his and Melanie's.

Just what in the hell was she doing back in town?

By the time Melanie shoved open the doors of the newspaper office, Jan had caught up with her. "Let me handle Brian," Jan insisted as she followed Melanie inside.

"He's not going to be thrilled about losing the interview," Melanie predicted.

Jan flashed her a grin and winked. "All is not yet lost."

Melanie stopped short. "What?"

"I think I've convinced the arrogant Mr. Doel to see things our way."

Melanie couldn't believe her ears. Gavin had been adamant. "How'd you do that?"

"Well, I did have to make a few concessions."

"I bet."

Constance, a worried expression crowding her features, was scanning the society and gossip columns of other papers. Looking up, she waved two fingers at Melanie, beckoning her over.

Jan made a beeline for the editor's office, but Melanie paused at Constance's desk.

"How'd it go?" Constance asked, once Melanie was in earshot.

"Not so good. You were right. Doel refused."

"Privacy is that man's middle name. So you got nothing?"

"Not so much as one shot," Melanie said, tapping her camera bag, "but Jan's convinced that he's changed his mind."

"I hope so." Constance's wide mouth pinched at the corners. "Brian's on a real tear. Geri called in and said she wanted to extend her vacation by a couple of days—and he told her not to bother coming back."

Geri was Melanie's backup—the only other photographer for the *Tribune*. Suddenly Melanie felt cold inside. "You mean—"

"I mean she's gone, kaput, outta here!" Constance sliced a finger theatrically across her throat.

"But why?"

"I don't know, but my guess is he's getting pressure from the owners of the paper." Her voice lowered. "We all know that sales haven't been so hot lately. In fact, Brian's counting on the interest in Ridge Resort to drum up business."

"Oh, great," Melanie said with a sigh. "In that case I'd better go help bail Jan out when she drops the bomb that we came up empty today."

She left her camera at her desk, then marched to Brian's office and knocked softly on the door.

"It's open!" Brian barked angrily.

Melanie slipped into the room as Jan coughed nervously. She was seated in a chair near the desk, notebook open, a pencil ready. "I was just explaining that getting an interview with Gavin Doel was tantamount to gaining an audience with God himself."

Melanie took a chair and nodded, swallowing a smile. "She's right."

"But somehow," Brian said, "she's managed to change his mind."

"Not somehow—I used my exceptional powers of persuasion," Jan remarked. "We're going back up there tomorrow. You know what they say about the mountain and Muhammad."

"He really agreed?" Melanie asked, dumfounded.

"Of course he did," Brian said with a sneer. He rubbed his chin with his hand. "No matter what else he is, Doel's no fool. And he can't snake his way out of this one. I've already devoted half the front page for the story."

Melanie couldn't believe it. What had made Gavin change his mind? And why was Brian so edgy?

"There is a catch," Jan explained.

Brian's lips turned down at the corners.

"Doel only wants his name used professionally. He doesn't want any part of his private life included."

Brian snorted. "That's impossible."

"But that's the deal," Jan insisted.

"Can't we hedge a little?"

Melanie shook her head. "I don't think that would be a good idea."

"Why not? As long as everything we print is true, he can't sue us," Brian argued. "And the way I see it, publicity will only help Ridge Lodge, of which he owns a large percentage."

Melanie squirmed. She wasn't afraid to speak her mind—she and Brian had locked horns more often than not, but when it came to Gavin, her emotions were still tangled in the past. "Gavin Doel won't take kindly to us digging through his private life. And I think we should keep good relations with him—at least as long as he owns and runs the resort."

Jan scribbled a note to herself. "Don't worry about it, Melanie, I'll handle the interview. Just get me some shots of the lodge, a few of the ski runs and the mountain and some closeups of Doel."

Brian tugged at his tie. "I'm counting on this article, men," he said, and Melanie laughed a little. Ever since she and the rest of the female staff had objected to being called girls, Brian had responded by referring to all reporters, photographers, secretaries and receptionists as men, female or male.

Melanie noticed the lines of worry etching Brian's forehead and the pinch of his lips. His complexion was pale, and she wondered, not for the first time, if he were ill. A bottle of antacids sat on the corner of his desk, next to his coffee cup and a half-full ashtray.

Brian's phone jangled, and he reached for it. "Okay, that's everything. Let's get on it," he said, lifting the receiver as he dismissed them.

"I want to talk to you," Jan whispered to Melanie as they walked back to the newsroom.

Here it comes, Melanie thought, but fortunately Constance waved Jan to her desk and Melanie escaped an inquisition on Gavin, at least for the time being.

She spent the rest of the afternoon sorting through the prints she'd taken of the fair the day before, picking out the shots of children riding the roller coaster and eating cotton candy. She worked on the shots of Uncle Bart's colt, as well, choosing a photograph of Big Money standing calmly by Bart for the next edition. She sorted through the shots again, found one she thought Bart would like and placed it in an envelope. She'd enlarge it later.

When she could no longer put off digging up pictures of Gavin, she set about looking through the files, sorting through old pictures and microfiche, rereading all about Gavin Doel. The photographs brought back memories of Gavin as a young man so full of life and expectation.

His skiing had been remarkable, gaining him a berth on the Olympic team and taking him on a road to fame and fortune. He'd been tough, fearless, and had attacked the most severe runs with a vengeance. His natural grace and balance had been God-given, but his fierce determination and pride had pushed him, driven him, to become the best.

Melanie stared wistfully at the photographs, noting the hard angle of his jaw and the blaze of competitive fire in his eyes before each race—and his smile of satisfaction after a win.

The most recent photographs were of Gavin losing that blissful God-given balance, tumbling on an icy mountainside and finally being carried off in a stretcher, his skin taut over nose and cheekbones, his mouth pulled in a grimace of pain.

"Oh, Gavin," she whispered, overcome by old feelings of love. "What happened to us?"

Hearing herself, she slammed the drawer shut and closed her mind to any of the long-dead emotions that had torn her apart ever since she'd heard he'd returned to Ridge Lodge. "Don't be a fool."

Stuffing the pictures she thought would be most useful into an envelope, she opened the drawer again. She slid Gavin's file into its proper slot and noticed the other slim file marked Doel, James.

Melanie's mouth went dry as she pulled Jim Doel's file from its slot and looked inside. She cringed at the first photograph of Gavin's father. Jim's eyes seemed vacant and haunted. His hands were shackled by handcuffs, and he was escorted by two policemen. In the background a frightened boy of twelve, his blond hair mussed, his pale eyes wide with fear, watched in horror. Restrained by a matronly social worker, Gavin was reaching around her, trying to get to his father as Jim was led to the waiting police car.

"Oh, God," she whispered. Her throat grew hot, and she pitied Gavin—an emotion he would abhor.

Chewing on her lower lip, she slipped the photograph from the file and tucked it quickly into her purse. No, that wasn't good enough. Jan or Brian would just dig deeper. Stomach knotted, she pulled the entire file from the drawer then took anything damaging from Gavin's file as well. There was no reason for Brian or anyone else from the *Tribune* to lay open Jim Doel's life and persecute him again. Nor, she thought, did she want to be reminded of her mother's death. She'd just take the file home and keep it locked away until all the interest in Gavin Doel faded.

She slammed the drawer quickly, and for the first time since returning to Taylor's Crossing two years before, Melanie wondered if coming home had been a mistake.

Gavin rammed his crutches into a corner of his office and glared at his partner. "A reporter and photographer from the *Tribune* were here today," he said. "Seems you gave them the okay for an interview."

Rich shoved a beefy hand through his graying hair and sighed loudly. Tall and heavyset, he looked more like a retired guard for a professional football team than an attorney. "Don't tell me, you threw them out."

"You could have had the decency to let me know about it."

"You were gone," Rich pointed out. "Besides, I thought we agreed that we should start publicity as soon as possible."

"But not with personal interviews!"

Rich was irritated. "For God's sake, what've you got to hide?"

Gavin's jaw began to ache, and only then did he realize he'd clenched it. "I just don't want this to turn into a three-ring circus."

"Four rings would be better," Rich said, dropping into a chair. "The more interest and excitement we can generate, the better for everyone."

Gavin snorted. Ever since seeing Melanie again, he'd felt restless and caged and he'd been out of sorts. "Look, I'm all for publicity about the resort. But that's as far as it goes. I like my privacy."

"Then you chose the wrong profession." Rich stuffed his hands in his pockets and jangled his keys nervously. "I know you don't want to hear this, but I think public interest in you is healthy."

"Meaning?" Gavin asked suspiciously.

"Meaning that people aren't really all that interested in your professional life. Hell, the Olympics were eons ago. And only a few dyed-in-the-wool fans will care about ski clinics you developed." His pale blue eyes lighted, and he wagged a finger at Gavin. "But the fact that you jetted all over the continent, skiing with famous celebrities, dating gorgeous women, partying with glamorous Hollywood types—now *that* will get their attention!"

"The wrong kind."

"Any kind will help."

Gavin scowled. "The tabloids made more of it than there was," he said slowly.

"Doesn't matter. The public sees you as an athletic playboy—a guy who hobnobs with the rich and beds the beautiful."

Gavin grimaced. "Then the public would be disappointed if it knew the truth."

"Let's not allow that to happen," Rich suggested slyly. "What does it hurt to keep the myth alive?"

"Just my reputation."

Rich chuckled as he crossed the room and poured himself a cup of coffee. "Don't you know most men would kill for a reputation like yours?"

"Then they're fools," Gavin grumbled, hobbling over to the window and staring at the windswept slopes of the mountain rising high behind the lodge. Without snow, the ragged slopes of Mount Prosperity seemed empty and barren.

He thought of Melanie, and his frown deepened. No doubt she'd be back tomorrow, along with the pushy reporter. It didn't matter that he didn't want to see her again.

"Just one more session," he muttered to himself.

"What?" Rich asked.

"Nothing," Gavin replied. "I was just thinking about the interview tomorrow."

"What about it?" Rich blew across his coffee cup.

"I can't wait for it to be over!" he declared vehemently. Maybe then he could close his mind to Melanie. Even now, eight years later, her betrayal burned painfully in his gut.

Maybe he'd get lucky and they'd send someone else. But more likely he'd have to face her again and find some way of being civil. He doubted he was up to it.

Chapter Three

The morning sun gilded the steep slopes of Mount Prosperity as Melanie again met Jan at Ridge Lodge Resort. She turned from the view of the mountain to the old rambling cedar and shake lodge. She wished she could be anywhere other than here.

"It'll be over soon," she muttered under her breath.

"What will?" Jan asked, approaching her car.

"This interview."

"You want it over? But why? This has to be the most interesting story we've done all year!"

"Is it?" Melanie asked, leaning inside her warm Volkswagen and snatching her camera case and tripod.

"What is it with you?"

"I don't like Doel's attitude," she replied, starting across the path leading to the front door of the lodge.

"Give him a chance. My bet is he'll grow on you."

"You'll lose your money," Melanie predicted.

They started to the building, but Jan suddenly stopped short. "Okay, Melanie, are you going to hold out on me forever or are you going to tell me what's going on between you and—" she cocked her head toward the lodge "—our infamous new neighbor?"

"There's nothing going on."

"Didn't look that way yesterday."

"We got into an argument, that's all."

"And it looked like a doozy," Jan exclaimed. "You know you're going to have to tell me the truth about all this. You grew up with the man."

"It wasn't all that interesting," Melanie lied, but Jan simply smiled as they headed up the path leading to the main doors.

Gavin was waiting for them.

Lounging at one of the tables near the bar, his leg and cast propped on the seat of another chair, he looked up as they entered but didn't bother trying to stand.

"So you didn't change your mind," he said, his tawny eyes moving from Jan to Melanie.

"Nope," Melanie replied.

"News in Taylor's Crossing must be slow." The weight of his gaze landed full force on Melanie, but she tossed her bag onto the table and unzipped the padded canvas, pretending she didn't care one way or the other that he was staring at her.

Jan slid into a chair opposite him. "Ready?" she asked.

"As I'll ever be." He glanced down at his stiff leg and the plaster cast surrounding his ankle. Grimacing, his jaw rock hard, he added irritably, "Rich isn't here right now."

"But he'll be back?" Jan asked.

"He'd better be," Gavin growled.

Jan looked smug. "We can manage without him."

Melanie set up her tripod near the bar and adjusted its height, then double-checked the film in her camera.

Frowning, Gavin muttered, "Let's get the damned thing over with."

"That's a healthy attitude," Melanie shot back, and Jan stared at her as if she'd lost her mind.

Scowling, Gavin reached behind him, grabbed his crutches, stood and made his way to the other side of the bar. Rock-solid muscles supported him, though he slouched to fit the tops of the crutches under his arms. "What do you want to know?"

"Everything," Jan replied brightly, reaching into her oversized bag for her pocket recorder, steno pad and pen. "The reopening of Ridge Lodge is big news. But then, everything you do is news."

"If that's true, then the world's in worse shape than I thought," Gavin remarked, setting out two glasses and his favorite bottle on the top of the bar. "Join Melanie and me for a drink?" he asked.

"A drink?" Jan's brows rose. "At eleven in the morning?"

"Right. Kind of a celebration, eh, Melanie?"

"Don't ask," Melanie advised Jan as she set her camera onto the tripod.

Gavin was already searching for another glass, but Jan held up her hand. "It's too early for me," she said, curiosity filling her gaze.

"Melanie?" he asked, motioning to the two glasses already placed on the bar. "Another *smooth* one?"

Jan shot her a look that said more clearly than words, *what's he talking about?*

Shrugging, Melanie found the lens she wanted and screwed it onto the camera. Then she checked the light with a meter. "Not today," she replied.

"Too early?" he mocked, pouring himself a hefty shot.

"I'm working." She moved to the windows with her light meter.

"All work and no play?"

"Oh, you know me, nose to the grindstone all the time," she flung back, unable to help herself. Why was he baiting her?

Jan eyed them both. "You two *do* know each other," she said speculatively while casting Melanie a look that could cut through steel.

"You could say that," Gavin answered evasively.

"How well?" Jan's eyes were full of questions when she turned them on Melanie.

"Gavin and I went to school together—grade school," Melanie replied quickly, silently cursing Gavin. What was he doing firing up Jan's reporter instincts? He was the one who wanted his damned privacy.

Gavin's jaw grew tight. "Small world, isn't it?"

Jan reached for her pen and paper. "Then you're family friends?"

Melanie's heart began to thud, and she felt sweat gather along her spine.

Gavin didn't answer, and the silence stretched long. "Not exactly," he finally said.

"Then 'exactly' what?"

"Acquaintances," he clipped. "Nothing more."

Melanie, wounded, nodded. "That's right. Acquaintances. Mr. Doel is—"

"Gavin, please," Gavin drawled. "No reason to be so formal."

Melanie bristled. "*Gavin*'s a few years older than I am."

Jan lifted a brow as Melanie suggested, "Maybe we should just get started."

Gavin forced a cold smile. "I can't wait."

"So you went to school at Taylor High?" Jan began, but Gavin cut her off.

"Nothing personal, remember?"

You started it, Melanie thought.

"Okay, okay," Jan said amiably. "We can begin with the lodge. When is it going to reopen? Is it going to be changed in any way? And tell me why you think you and your partner can make it work when the last operation went bankrupt?"

Jan's questions were fair, Melanie decided. Her ear tuned to the conversation, she busied herself with her equipment. Now that Gavin had steered Jan to safe territory, she was sticking to questions Gavin could answer without much thought. Leaning on the bar for support, he ignored his drink and answered each question carefully. No more spontaneous remarks—just the facts.

Melanie lifted the camera and focused on Gavin. He didn't seem to notice, and the lens only magnified his innate sexuality, the hard slope of his jaw, the bladed features of his face, the glint of his straight white teeth and the depth of his eyes, cautious now and sober.

She clicked off a few shots, and he glanced her way. Her heartbeat accelerated as he smiled—that irreverent slash of white against his tanned skin that had always caused her heart to trip.

"You want a tour?" he asked, flicking his gaze back to Jan.

"That would be great!"

Melanie watched him maneuver to the main lobby. Beneath his shirt his shoulders flexed, straining the seams of the white cotton while his hips shifted beneath his shorts and his tanned thighs and one exposed calf strained.

Even though Gavin was on crutches, Jan had to hurry to keep pace with him. Melanie grabbed another camera, double-checked that she had film and switched on the flash as she followed.

Gavin moved quickly across the main lobby, gesturing to the three-storied rock fireplace, scuffed wooden floors and soaring ceiling. Around three sides of the cavernous room, two tiers of balconies opened to private guest rooms. The other wall was solid glass, with a breathtaking view of Mount Prosperity. Now the ski runs were bare, the lifts still, the pine trees towering out of sheer rock. Dry grass and wildflowers covered the slopes.

Showing off the office, kitchen, exercise room and pool room, Gavin explained how the lodge was set up, when it was built and how he planned to restore it. Eventually they returned to the main lobby, and Gavin stopped at a group of tables with chairs overturned on their polished oak surfaces. Balancing on his good leg, he yanked three chairs down and shoved them around a battered table.

Jan plopped down immediately. Gavin kicked a chair Melanie's way, but rather than sit so close to him, she said, "I think I'll look around."

"Not interested in hearing about the lodge?" Gavin baited.

"I can read about it," she tossed back. "Fascinating as it is, I've got work to do."

Jan, sensing the changed atmosphere, said, "Melanie's the best photographer on the paper."

Melanie shot Jan a warning glance. "Right now I think I'm the *only* photographer." *Just let me get through this,* she prayed silently, wishing she could be aloof and uncaring when it came to Gavin Doel. She unzipped her bag and sorted through the lenses, cameras, light meters and rolls of film.

Jan leaned across the table to Gavin and turned the questions in a different direction. Writing swiftly in her own fashion of shorthand, she asked about his career as an international skier, his bronze medal from the Olympics nearly eight years before, his interest in the lodge itself. Gavin answered quickly and succinctly, never offering more than a simple, straightforward answer.

He's used to this, Melanie realized, wondering how many reporters had tried to pin him down, how many other newspapers had tried to dig into his personal life. Even though the *Tribune* had been known to downplay scandal in the past, especially about a local hero, there were other newspapers that wouldn't have been so kind.

Seeing this as her chance to escape, Melanie wandered through the old rooms, and memories washed over her. She'd been here often, of course, before the last owners had filed for bankruptcy and closed the runs and the lodge for good. She'd even skied here with Gavin, but that had been ages ago. She'd been seventeen, sure of her love of him, happy beyond her wildest dreams. And he'd been on his way to fame and fortune. She sighed. How foolish it all seemed now.

Measuring the light through the large glass windows, she caught sight of her own pale reflection and wondered what Gavin thought about her. Gone was her straight black hair, replaced by crumpled curls that fell past her shoulders. Her eyes were still hazel, her cheekbones more exposed and gaunt following her divorce from Neil. She'd lost weight since Gavin had known her. But it didn't matter. What had happened between Gavin and her was long over—dead. She'd killed whatever feelings he'd had for her, and she'd destroyed those emotions intentionally when she'd eloped with Neil Brooks.

She glanced back to the table. Gavin was leaning back in his chair, answering Jan's questions, but his eyes followed her as she moved from one bank of windows to the next.

She snapped off a few shots of the interior of the lodge, then, as much to get away from the weight of Gavin's gaze as anything else, wandered down the hallways to the spaces where the shops and restaurant had been housed in years past.

In the tiny shops the shelves and racks were empty. Dust collected on display windows, and the carpet was worn and faded where ski boots had once trod throughout the winter. Bleached-out Clearance signs were stacked haphazardly against the walls.

The interior seemed gloomy—too dark for the kind of pictures Brian wanted for the layout. Maybe exterior shots would be better. Even though there wasn't a flake of snow on the mountain, shots of the lodge, the craggy ridge looming behind its gabled roofline, would give the article the right atmosphere.

Outside, she snapped several quick shots of the lodge, a few more of the empty lifts and others of the grassy ski runs.

The mountain air was clear and warm, and a late September breeze cooled her skin and tangled her hair. The scents of pine and dust, fresh lumber and wildflowers mingled, lingering in the autumn afternoon.

"Get what you wanted?" Gavin's voice boomed, startling her.

"What?" Whipping around, she squinted up and found him seated on the rail of a deck, his cast propped on a chair, his eyes shaded by reflective glasses. The deck, because of the lack of snow, was some five feet in the air and he stared down at her.

"What I wanted?" she repeated, shading her eyes with one hand and attempting to hide the fact that at that height he was incredibly intimidating.

"The pictures."

"Oh." Of course that's what he'd meant. For a moment she thought he'd been asking about her life. *You're too sensitive, Melanie. He doesn't give a damn.* "Enough to start with." She noticed his mouth turn down at the edges. "But you never can tell. If these—" she patted her camera fondly "—aren't what Brian had in mind, then I'll be back."

Gavin's jaw clenched even tighter. "So when did you take up photography?"

"I've always been interested in it." *You know that.*

"But as a career?"

"It started out as a hobby. I just kept working at it," she replied, not wanting to go into the fact that after she'd married Neil, she'd taken photography courses. She'd had time on her hands and empty hours to fill without the baby.... Neil's money had provided her with the best equipment and classes with some of the Northwest's most highly regarded instructors, and she'd spent hour upon hour learning, focusing on her craft. When she'd landed her first job, Neil had been livid. It was ironic, she supposed, that her hours of idleness and Neil's money had provided her with her escape from a marriage that had been doomed from the start.

Clearing her throat, she looked up and found Gavin staring at her, looking intently, as if he could read her thoughts. "So you took your 'hobby' and started working for the *Tribune.*"

"That's a shortened version of it, but yes." Why explain further? "Where's Jan?" she asked, changing the subject as she packed her camera back in its case.

"She took off."

Melanie was surprised. "Already?"

Gavin's lips twitched as she started to climb onto the deck. "She asked one too many personal questions, and when I objected, I guess she thought I was being rude."

Melanie skewered him with a knowing look as she crossed the deck. "Were you?"

"Undoubtedly. She asked for it." Wincing, Gavin swung his leg back to the decking and balanced on his good foot while he scrabbled for his crutches. "Damn things," he growled when one crutch clattered to the cedar planks. He twisted, and his face grew white.

"I'll get it."

Melanie started to pick up the offending crutch, but Gavin bent over and, swearing, yanked it out of her hands. "Leave it!"

Melanie's temper flared. "I was only trying to help."

"I don't need any *help*." He didn't say it, but from the flare of his nostrils she expected him to add, "Especially from you." A few beads of sweat collected on his upper lip, but his skin darkened to its normal shade.

"You know, Gavin, you could relax a little. It wouldn't kill you to let someone lend you a hand once in a while."

His lips thinned. "I learned a long time ago not to depend on anyone but myself. That way I'm never disappointed."

Her throat went dry and she felt as if he'd slapped her, but he wasn't finished.

"As for these," he said, shaking a crutch, "I can handle them myself. And I don't need your advice, or your help, or your damned pity!" By this time he was standing, leaning on his crutches and breathing hard as he glared at her through his mirrored glasses.

"Then I'm out of here," she said, forcing an icy smile. "If you don't want my help or my advice or my pity, then there's no reason for me to stay."

"No reason at all."

"And I'm sure the shots I've taken will be good enough for the paper. You won't have to worry about me intruding again."

"Good."

"Goodbye, Gavin," she said, swinging her camera case over her shoulder, "and good luck with the lodge."

"Luck has nothing to do with it."

"I'll remember that if we don't get any snow until next February," she said sweetly, turning on her heel and marching through the lodge to the main doors. Her footsteps rang loudly on the weathered flooring, and her fists were clenched so tightly her fingers began to ache. How could she have loved him? *How?* The man was rude, arrogant, and carried around a chip on his shoulder the size of a California sequoia! Muttering under her breath, she shoved open the doors and escaped into the hot parking lot. Heat rose form the dusty asphalt in shimmering waves, only adding to the fire burning in her cheeks.

How could he have changed so drastically? Gavin was positively insufferable! She unlocked her car door and climbed into the suffocatingly hot interior. Rolling down the windows, she wondered if somehow she were to blame for this new cynical, horrible beast named Gavin Doel. Had she wounded him so badly by marrying Neil—or had he, at last, shown his true colors?

Her father had always warned her that Gavin was cut from the same cloth as Jim Doel, but she'd never believed him. Now she wasn't so sure, and it worried her. Twice in two days Gavin had poured himself healthy doses of Scotch before noon.

But she hadn't seen him drink any this morning. It had just been a game. He'd been baiting her again.

"Well, he can drown in his liquor for all I care!" she grumbled as she rammed a pair of sunglasses onto the bridge of her nose and glanced in the side-view mirror. In the reflection she saw Gavin standing in the doorway of the lodge, leaning hard on his crutches and frowning darkly.

She ground the gears of her battered old car and sped out of the lot. Maybe, if she was lucky, she'd never have to deal with him again!

Gavin swore roundly and stared after the car. "You're a fool, Doel," he growled, furious with himself for noting that Melanie was more beautiful than he remembered. Her black hair shimmered blue in the sunlight, and her eyes were round and wide, a fascinating shade hovering between gray and green.

So what? Her beauty meant nothing. He'd loved her more than any other woman and she'd betrayed him as callously as if his feelings hadn't existed. So why should he care?

"Damn it, why now?" he muttered. He didn't want to deal with any latent feelings he might still harbor for her. And he wouldn't. Just because she was in the same neck of the proverbial woods didn't mean he had to fall all over himself chasing after her.

No, he decided, his lips compressing thoughtfully as the dust from her car settled back onto the asphalt, this time he'd be in control. This time Melanie Walker Brooks wouldn't get close to him. No matter what.

"...he might be the rudest man I've ever met!" Jan charged. Her eyes were bright, her cheeks flushed at the memory of her interview with Gavin. "And, unfortunately, maybe the best looking."

Melanie couldn't agree more. She'd heard the tail end of the conversation between Jan and Guy as she returned to the office. "I take it you're talking about the new owner of Ridge Resort?"

"You got it," Jan said. "And I'm not kidding. I've met some jerks in my time—good God, I've dated more than my share—but this guy takes the cake!"

"What exactly did he say?"

Jan puffed up like a peacock. "I just mentioned that he'd been linked to several famous models and I brought up Aimee LaRoux's name."

"And?" Guy prodded.

"And he asked me who I'd been linked to. I, uh, said, it was none of his business and he said 'Precisely.' "

"That doesn't sound so bad to me."

"It gets worse," Jan assured them. "I kept bringing it up and he finally asked me why, if I was so interested in Aimee LaRoux's love life, I just didn't call her and ask her out! Then he had the audacity to scribble a phone number on a book of matches and toss it to me."

Despite her foul mood, Melanie laughed. "You're right," she said. "Doel's obnoxious."

Jan glared at her. "He's got one dismal sense of humor!"

"You think it's really Aimee's number?" Guy asked, his eyes bright.

"No, I don't!" Jan snapped. "And you can quit drooling."

Guy pulled a face. "Is it that obvious?"

"Very."

Melanie said, "Just be glad the interview's over. We won't have to deal with Doel again."

"Oh, I wouldn't be so sure of that," Guy disagreed. "Brian seems to think that stories about Gavin Doel and Ridge Lodge can only increase circulation. I think he's planning a series of articles about Mount Prosperity and the lodge and guess who?"

"Gavin Doel," Jan said, grimacing.

"You got it."

Melanie sighed inwardly. She didn't think she could face Gavin again. And the thought of Gavin's personal life being ripped open put her on edge. "I think Brian's putting too much emphasis on Doel."

"Yeah, it's almost as if he has an axe to grind with him," Guy agreed.

"An axe? What're you talking about?"

Guy shook his head. "Just a feeling I have. I don't think there's any love lost between Brian and Doel."

"Do they know each other?" Melanie asked.

"Beats me."

Jan's purse landed on her desk with a thump. "Well, Brian had better get himself another reporter," she declared flatly. "I'm not going to put myself through that ringer again. Doel won't open up at all. Guards his privacy as if there's something dark and dangerous in his past."

"Maybe there is," Guy said, throwing a leg over Jan's desk and tapping the side of his face with the eraser end of his pencil. "After all, what do we know of the guy—really?"

Jan turned thoughtful eyes on Melanie. "We know more than most," she said, her mouth curving thoughtfully upward.

Melanie steeled herself. Obviously Jan thought she could get information on Gavin through her. Well, she could guess again. For now Melanie's lips were sealed.

"He grew up around here," Jan told Guy. "Melanie went to school with him."

"Did you?" Guy was impressed.

"Well, not really. He's five years older than I am," Melanie countered. "He was out of high school before I entered."

"But you said you knew him," Jan persisted, "and he concurred. In fact, I'd be willing to bet you two knew each other better than you're letting on."

"What's this?" Guy asked, interested.

Melanie decided it was time for evasive tactics, at least until she knew just how far Jan was willing to dig. "Jan's exaggerating. I knew *of* him," she corrected, her palms beginning to sweat. "Everyone in town did."

She should probably just tell Jan part of the truth right now and get it over with, but she couldn't. Where would she stop? How would she explain that she married Neil to protect Gavin from the burden of a wife and child? Gavin didn't even know that she'd been pregnant. She certainly wasn't going to tell Jan or Guy or anyone else.

And beyond that, she didn't want the scandal of her mother's death raked up all over again.

"What was Gavin like as a kid? Doesn't he have a no-good for a father?" Jan asked, the wheels turning in her mind.

"I thought you weren't interested in interviewing him again," Melanie said.

Jan shook her head. "You know me. I was just mad. I let the guy get to me. It was my problem, not his. But it won't happen again. Besides, Barbara Walters wouldn't have let Doel intimidate her, would she? Nope, I've just got to fight fire with fire. So, what was Gavin Doel like before he became famous?"

Melanie thought for a moment, remembering Gavin as he had been. "He was . . . determined and ambitious and dedicated to being the best skier in the world."

Jan sighed and blew her bangs out of her eyes. "I know all that. But what about the man behind the image? Did you know him?"

Better than anyone. Melanie lifted a shoulder. "Not well enough to be quoted. Besides, the way he is about his private life, I think the *Trib* would be better off if we asked him. That way there's a chance we won't get sued!"

"He won't sue us," Jan said.

"Why not?"

"Bad publicity. He can't afford it. But right now he won't tell me anything." She smiled slyly. "This is going to call for some research. What's in the files?"

"I checked yesterday," Melanie said, walking briskly to her desk and knowing there was nothing the least bit damaging in the envelope she snatched from her cluttered In basket. She tossed the packet on Jan's desk and waited while Jan quickly flipped through the stack of photos as if it were a deck of cards. "Nothing else?" she asked, looking disappointed.

"Nothing interesting."

"You checked the copy that went along with these?"

"Yep."

"Damn!" She pursed her lips and eyed the photographs again. "Well, these are good. . . ." She picked up a glossy black and white of Gavin poised at the top of a ski run. His face was set, his body tight, his gloved hands wrapped around his poles, every muscle ready to spring forward at the drop of a flag. "But I think it would give some dimension to our story if we knew a little more about him." Tapping a long fingernail on the photograph, she said, "Privacy or no privacy, I think we should dig up *everything* we can find on one Mr. Gavin Doel. We can check with the high school, find out who he dated, if he was ever employed around town."

"I think most of his relatives moved away a long time ago. And as for his employment, he worked at the lodge before it closed down," Melanie offered, hoping to steer Jan away from Gavin's love life.

"Well that doesn't do us a lot of good. Unless he bought the damned thing for sentimental reasons. But we'll find out. The next time I interview him, I'll be ready with a little personal ammunition to get him to talk."

"It's your funeral," Guy said, straightening from the desk.

And just possibly mine, Melanie thought inwardly. "I'll do the research," she offered, hoping that she could circumvent any old news story that might prove uncomfortable for Gavin or herself.

"Good." Jan checked her watch. "Look, I've got to run over to the school and talk to the principal about the new gym. Melanie—are you coming with me?"

"No, I've already got the pictures. They'll be on your desk tomorrow."

"Good. Thanks." Jan grabbed her bag and headed out of the office.

Melanie was left with the sinking sensation that Gavin's personal life—as well as her own—was about to be splashed all over the front page of the Taylor's Crossing *Tribune*!

Chapter Four

Brian Michaels did indeed want to do a series of articles on Ridge Lodge and he wasn't the least bit concerned with Gavin's desire for privacy. In fact, he had his own reasons for wanting to see Gavin's life plastered all over the newspaper. But he kept those to himself.

"He's a public figure, for crying out loud," Brian said the next afternoon as he shook a cigarette from his pack. Jan and Melanie were seated on two worn plastic chairs near his desk. "And on top of that, he's rebuilding a lodge that will turn the economy of this town around. Doel can't expect to have a private life. If he does, he's a fool!"

"A man who's made several million dollars in five years isn't a fool," Jan argued.

Brian lit up and blew a cloud of smoke. "Look, I want to do several articles, one every other week until snow season. Front page stuff." He glanced at Melanie. "I want to see the workers rebuilding the lodge, the furniture being moved in.

I need photos of the lifts beginning to run, the first snowfall, that sort of thing. Then, find out about the ski school programs and add some schmaltzy stuff, you know, five-year-old kids on skis with their dads helping them, that sort of rot."

"Then you don't really need anything on Doel." she ventured.

"Oh, wrong!" Brian was just warming to his subject. "He's going to open that lodge with a huge celebration of some kind. I want a copy of the guest list. Find out if any of the skiers he's competed against are invited and check to see who will be his personal date. If any of his old flames are going to show up, we have to know about it ahead of time." He stared straight at Melanie, waving his cigarette as he spoke. "And I'll want you at that grand opening with your camera. We'll want every bit of glitz on our front page!"

Melanie's throat went dry as Brian kept talking. "That's not all. I want to know everything about Doel—inside out. His old man is a drunk—why? And didn't he do some time years ago? What happened? And where is he now?"

Melanie said evenly, "I don't see that Jim Doel's tragedies have anything to do with the lodge reopening."

"Like hell. The man raised Gavin alone, didn't he? He shaped the kid. What happened to his mother? Is she still alive? Remarried? Does he have sisters or brothers or an aunt or uncle or cousin around here? You'd be surprised how easy it is to get people to talk about their famous kin. It makes them feel important, as if a little of that fame will rub off on them."

"This series is starting to sound like something you'd find at the checkout counter," Melanie said.

"Why?"

"Because you're more interested in finding out any dirt there is on Doel than reporting about the lodge."

Beside her, Jan drew her breath in sharply, but Brian didn't miss a beat. "I'm not interested in anything of the sort. I just want to sell papers. Period."

"No matter what the price or the standards?"

"I didn't say that, but listen, don't knock the tabloids. They make plenty!"

"And they're always getting sued!"

Brian flipped the ash from his cigarette into the already overflowing tray. "Hey—we won't print anything false. But we've got to generate interest in the lodge, interest in Doel, interest in the *Tribune*! You may as well know that the owners are putting pressure on us. Circulation's down, and we've got to do something about it."

"And that something is throwing Gavin Doel's life open for public inspection?" Melanie challenged.

"You bet it is." Brian took a final drag on his cigarette, then jabbed it out in his ashtray. "Look, he's the one who decided to come back to the small town where he was raised and reopen a resort that had gone bankrupt—a resort that represents a lot to the economy of this town. I can't help it that he's news—in fact, I'm thrilled that he jet-setted around the world and hung out with the rich and famous. All the better for the *Tribune*."

"How would you feel if it were you?"

"Listen, if I had Doel's money and his fame and I was interested in selling lift tickets, you can bet I'd grab all the press I could get my hands on!"

"No matter what?" Melanie asked.

"No matter what! Do you have a problem with that?"

Melanie could feel her color rising. "I'd just like to think that we were working with the man rather than against him."

"His choice. The way I see it, we're doing him a favor." Clasping his hands behind his head, Brian leaned back in his chair and squinted his aquamarine eyes. "So, let's not let

Doel's sensitivity about his privacy bother us too much and get down to business. I'll call his partner, get the go-ahead for the articles and we'll take it from there."

Melanie left the meeting with a sense of impending doom. Brian Michaels could whitewash his intentions all he wanted, but Gavin, when he discovered that his life was going to be thrown open and displayed for every reader of the *Tribune*, would be livid. And Melanie didn't blame him. It occurred to her that she could tell him what was happening, but he'd probably lay the blame at her feet. Besides, nothing had been written yet. Maybe she could help edit the story. Crossing her fingers, she hoped that Brian would have a change of heart.

"Let me get this straight," Gavin said, eyeing his partner angrily. "You agreed to do a *series* of articles about the lodge."

"Sure. Why not?" Rich shrugged, opened the small refrigerator in the office and pulled out a bottle of beer. "I thought we agreed that we could use all the publicity we could get." He shoved the bottle across the coffee table and yanked out another.

"We did," Gavin said, trying to tamp down the restless feeling in his gut. "And I thought you were going to hang around and handle them. Instead you bailed out on me."

"I already apologized. Besides, I had to be at the courthouse—"

"Yeah, yeah, I know," Gavin said grumpily. "I guess I'm just suspicious of reporters."

"They're not all out for blood."

"No—just big stories." He twisted off the cap of the bottle and took a long swallow.

"So?"

"I've been burned before."

"The *Tribune* isn't exactly a national tabloid. It's just a little local paper with ties to the *Portland Daily*. And those ties—" he held up his beer to make his point "—are exactly what we need right now. We have to stir up public awareness and interest in Ridge Resort from Seattle all the way to L.A."

Gavin scowled. There was a chance that Rich was right, of course, but in Gavin's opinion, it was a slim chance at best. In the course of his career, he'd dealt with more than his share of reporters and photographers, but he'd never had to deal with Melanie before.

He took another long swallow and shoved all thoughts of Melanie aside. She'd showed her true colors long ago, and it was just too damned bad that he'd had the bad luck to run into her again.

"So when is the next session?" he asked Rich.

"Next week. They want some pictures of the crew working on the lodge."

He clenched his teeth. "So they're sending up a photographer."

"Mmm-hmm."

Chest tightening, he asked slowly, "Which one?"

"As far as I know they only have one."

"I think we should have our own photos taken."

Rich's brows shot up. "Why?"

"We'll get what we want. No surprises."

"You're the one who wants to stay within budget, remember?" Rich shook his head. "Relax a little and enjoy the free publicity, will ya? This is the best thing that's happened to us so far."

"I doubt it," Gavin growled, feeling suddenly as if he couldn't breathe. Swearing, he reached for his crutches and struggled to his feet. Only one more day of these wretched tools—then, at least, he wouldn't feel like an invalid. Shoving the padded supports under his arms, he moved with surprising agility to the door.

"You know," Rich's voice taunted from behind, "if I didn't know better, I'd say you were all worked up over some woman."

"Well, you don't know better, do you?" Gavin flung over his shoulder, and Rich laughed. Balancing on his good foot, Gavin unlocked the back door and hobbled onto the deck.

Rays of afternoon sunlight filtered through the trees, and the warm air touched the back of his neck where beads of sweat had collected. His hands were slippery on the grips of his crutches and his heart pumped at the thought of coming face-to-face with Melanie again. Melanie. He squeezed his eyes shut and willed her gorgeous, lying Jezebel face from his mind.

Melanie spent the rest of the afternoon in the darkroom developing the pictures she'd taken at Ridge Resort. Most of the shots were of the lodge itself, but a few of the photographs were of Gavin, his jaw hard and set, his mouth tight, his eyes intense as he studiously avoided looking at the camera.

"These are perfect," Jan said, pointing to the most provocative shot on the roll—a profile of Gavin, his hair falling over his face, his features taut, his mouth a thin, sexy line above a thrusting jaw. "Can you blow this one up?"

"Don't you think a shot of the lodge would be better?"

Jan tapped her finger to the side of her mouth and shook her head. "Nope—at least not for the female readers."

"And the male?"

Jan chewed on her lower lip, and her eyes narrowed thoughtfully. "I think even they would be interested in seeing what the enigmatic Mr. Doel looks like up close."

"Maybe we should use an overview of the lodge and a smaller inset of Gavin."

"Maybe," Jan said, but the pucker between her brows didn't go away, and Melanie realized she'd already made up her mind. "Or we could do it the other way around—a large profile of the man behind the lodge and a smaller shot of the resort itself."

"This isn't *People* magazine," Melanie pointed out. "The focus of the story is on the lodge, right?"

"Oh, right, but we'll have plenty of pictures of the construction. No, I think we'd better focus on Doel. He's the public interest."

"He'll have a fit," Melanie predicted.

Jan smiled. "And won't that be interesting?"

"Interesting? You mean like a hurricane or an earthquake is interesting?"

Jan eyed Melanie thoughtfully. "Just how well did you know Gavin Doel? The truth, now."

"I met him a few times."

"So why're you so defensive about him?"

Melanie toyed with the idea of confiding in Jan, but the phone shrilled and Molly, the receptionist, flagged Jan down.

"It's that call you've been waiting for from the mayor's office," Molly whispered loudly.

"I've got it," she said, before turning back to Melanie. "Has anyone ever told you you worry too much?"

"Not for a while."

"Well, you do! Everything's going to work out. For us and for Gavin Doel and his resort."

I hope you're right, Melanie thought, but couldn't shake the feeling that the *Tribune* and everyone on its staff were asking for trouble.

Hours later, she drove home and was greeted at the back door by a thoroughly dusty and burr-covered Sassafras.

"Oh, no, you don't," she said, wedging herself through the door, effectively blocking Sassafras's dodge from the porch into the kitchen. She left her camera case and purse in the kitchen, changed into her faded jeans and an old T-shirt, then squeezed through the door to the porch.

Sassafras whined loudly, scratching at the door.

Melanie plopped onto a small stool. "So, tell me, where've you been?" She laughed, reaching for an old curry comb and ignoring his protests as she combed out his fur. He tried to wriggle free and even clamped his mouth around her wrist when she tugged at a particularly stubborn burr. "Okay, okay, I can take a hint," she said, tossing down the currycomb. She brushed the dog hair from her jeans and held open the door. "Now, Mr. Sassafras, you may enter," she teased.

The old collie dashed inside before she could change her mind, and she followed him. She changed clothes again, throwing on a clean skirt and a cotton sweater before returning to the kitchen. She barely had poured herself a glass of iced tea when the doorbell pealed and Sassafras began to bark loudly.

Glancing at her watch, Melanie groaned inwardly at the thought of the next hour and the Anderson children she was supposed to photograph—four of the most rambunctious kids she'd ever met.

Sassafras growled, then settled in his favorite spot under the kitchen table.

"Coming!" Melanie called, hurrying through the cool rooms of the old log house.

Cynthia Anderson and children were huddled on the wide front porch when Melanie opened the door. In matching red crew-neck sweaters and khaki slacks, the wheat-blond boys, ages two through eleven, dashed past Melanie, down the hall and through wide double doors to her studio.

"Boys! Wait!" Casting Melanie an apologetic look, Cynthia Anderson took off after her brood.

By the time Melanie reached the studio, the boys were already jockeying for position around the single wicker chair Melanie used for inside portraits.

"Maybe we should have this picture taken outdoors," Cynthia suggested as Melanie tried to arrange the siblings—oldest with the youngest on his lap, two middle children standing on either side.

Melanie straightened the two-year-old's sweater, then glanced over her shoulder. "If you want exterior shots, we'll have to schedule another appointment. Right now there's not enough light."

Cynthia rolled her eyes. "No way. They're finally back in the swing of school and soccer practice is just about every night. I barely got them together to come today. Believe me, it's now or never."

Melanie was relieved. Though she loved children, one session with these four was all she could handle. "Okay. Sean, you hold Tim on your knee."

"And turn his face to the right," their mother insisted. "He fell yesterday and he's got a black eye...." She rattled on, talking nonstop about the boys as Melanie worked with them. For the next hour Melanie positioned and repositioned the children, adjusted the light, changed film and cameras and took as many pictures as she could before all four boys started squirming and pushing and shoving.

"Brian kicked me!" Randy cried, fist curled to retaliate.

"Did not!" Brian replied indignantly. "It was Sean!"

Sean was smothering a sly smile, and Melanie wished she could have caught the act on film.

"Boys, stop that!" Cynthia said. "Sean—you and Brian quit it right now! Ms. Walker is trying to take your picture. The least you could is behave!"

"I think that'll do it," Melanie said, snapping the final shot.

"Good!" Sean, the oldest, pushed Tim from his lap. "I'm outta here!" He took off down the hall with his brothers following close behind.

"Thanks a bunch," Cynthia said, hastily writing a check for the sitting fee and handing it to Melanie. She shoved her wallet back into her handbag. "You know, I just heard today that Gavin Doel's back in town."

Melanie managed a smile she didn't feel. "That's right."

"Well, I, for one, am glad someone's doing something with Ridge Resort. This town's been dead ever since it closed."

That much was true. But Melanie wasn't sure that Gavin could bring it back to life.

"Mom!" Outside a horn blared.

"Got to run," Cynthia said, starting for the door. "The natives are restless!"

Later, after developing film in the darkroom, which was adjacent to the studio, and eyeing the strips of the Anderson boys, Melanie soaked in a hot bath, poured herself a cup of tea and relaxed on the couch with a couple of cookies. Sassafras curled on the braided rug at her feet, his ears pricked forward, his eyes on her, hoping for a morsel.

Smiling, she offered the dog a corner of one cookie and he swallowed it without chewing. "Glutton," she teased, and he lifted a paw, scratching her knee for more. "These aren't exactly on your diet." But she let him snatch the remainder of the final cookie from her palm. "Let's not tell the vet—he wouldn't understand."

She picked up the paperback spy thriller she'd been reading for the past week but couldn't concentrate on the intricate plot. Her mind kept wandering. To Gavin.

"Forget him," she chastised herself. "He's obviously forgotten you." Frowning, she tossed down the book, grabbed the remote control and snapped on the television.

A local newscaster, a young dark-haired woman with intelligent blue eyes, was smiling into the camera.

"...and good news for central Oregon," she said. "All those rumors proved true. Gavin Doel and his partner, Rich Johanson, made a public announcement that they plan to reopen Ridge Resort on Mount Prosperity in time for the winter ski season. Our reporter was at Ridge Resort this afternoon...."

The screen changed to footage of Gavin, reflective aviator sunglasses perched on his tanned face, crutches tucked under his arms, standing behind a hefty, steely-haired man whom Melanie assumed was Rich Johanson.

The camera focused on Gavin's features, and Melanie's throat constricted. His face was lean, nearly haggard, partially hidden by the oversized sunglasses. Thin, sensual lips, frozen in an expression of indifference, accentuated his strong, square jaw.

His light brown hair was nearly blond, streaked by days spent bareheaded in the sun. His angled face was as rugged as the slopes he tackled so effortlessly, and there was a reserve to him evident even on the television screen.

Whereas Richard Johanson was dressed in a business suit and couldn't quit answering questions posed by the media, Gavin seemed bored and remote, as if he wanted only for the whole damn thing to be over with.

The screen flickered again, and the image changed to a steep mountain slope in France. A brightly dressed crowd gathered at the bottom of a ski run, and one woman, red-haired and gorgeous international model Aimee LaRoux, glanced at the camera before training her gaze up the hill.

The camera angle changed. Melanie's lungs constricted as another camera singled out a downhill racer. She'd seen this footage over and over again. Her throat went dry as Gavin, tucked low, streaked down the mountain. Seconds passed before one ski caught, flipping him high into the air. Skis and poles exploded. Gavin, in a bone-shattering fall, spun end over end down the icy slope.

Melanie's heart went cold, and she snapped the television off. Her hands trembled so badly she stuffed them into the pockets of her terry robe. She didn't need to be reminded of the accident that may have cost Gavin his career—the accident that had fatefully thrown him back to Taylor's Crossing—the accident that had shoved him back into her life.

No, that wasn't right. He wasn't back in her life. She wouldn't let him! Not even if he wanted back in, which, of course, he didn't.

"And that's the way it's got to be!" she said aloud, as if by saying the words she could convince herself.

Gavin rotated his foot, wincing as the muscles stretched. His leg was pale, thinner than the other and not much to look at. Several scars around his knee and ankle gave evidence to the wonders of medical science, though, according to his doctor, he still had weeks of physical therapy before he could hope to step into a pair of skis.

"Give it time," he told himself as he struggled into his favorite jeans and stood tentatively, placing only part of his weight on the injured leg. "Easy does it." He saw the cane sitting near his bed and ignored it, taking a few tentative steps around the small suite he'd claimed as his.

Located near the office on the first floor of the lodge, the suite boasted worn furniture he'd found in the basement, a small refrigerator, an oven, a fireplace and two closets. He had private access outside to a small deck. He'd added a microwave and coffee maker.

"All the comforts of home," he said with a sarcastic smile as he steadied himself by placing his hands on the bureau. He'd never been one for carrying around extra baggage, never stayed in one place long enough to collect furniture, paintings or memorabilia. Aside from a few special awards, medals and trophies, he didn't keep much, was always ready to move on. Until now, moving along had been easy. But that was before the accident.

And what now?

Settle down? He made a sound of disgust. He'd given up those dreams long ago, when Melanie had showed him the value of love. His finger curled around the edge of the bureau top, and when he glanced in the mirror, he scowled at his half-dressed reflection.

He remembered all too vividly falling in love with Melanie, as if the years of trying to forget her had only etched her more deeply into his mind. Their affair had been short and passionate and filled with dreams that had turned out to be one-sided. Oh, he'd been good enough to experiment with, make love to, whisper meaningless promises to, but as his old man had predicted, in the end she'd decided he wasn't good enough for her. She'd married a wealthy boy from a socially prominent family rather than gamble on a ski bum.

"All for the best," he grumbled, reaching for a T-shirt he'd tossed over the back of a nearby chair and sliding his arms through the cotton sleeves. Just below the knee his leg began to throb, and he sucked in a breath between his teeth. Tucking the shirt into the waistband of his jeans, his wayward mind wandered back to Melanie.

She'd given him some very valuable lessons, though he doubted she realized that she was the single reason he'd become so self-reliant. Her betrayal had taught him and taught him well. Never would he depend upon anyone but himself, and as for women—well, he'd had a few affairs. They hadn't lasted and he didn't care, though it bothered him a little that he'd gained a reputation as a womanizer in some of the tabloids. The rumors of his sizzling one-night-stand dates stemmed more from the overly active imaginations of the press than anything else.

He slid into beat-up Nikes and, with the aid of the cane, walked carefully to the office, where he expected to find Rich.

Instead, rounding the corner and shouldering open the door, he ran smack-dab into the one person he wanted out of his life.

But there she was, in beautiful 3-D. Melanie Walker Brooks.

Chapter Five

Melanie, who had been waiting impatiently in the office of Ridge Resort, reached for the doorknob, only to have the door thrown open in her face. Startled, she drew back just as Gavin, walking with the aid of a cane, pulled up short. A flicker of surprise lighted his eyes, and he drew in a quick breath.

Muttering ungraciously, he glanced rapidly around the room. "You're here—again?" he demanded.

She smiled. "Didn't you miss me?"

His mouth pinched at the corners, and a vein throbbed at his temple. She expected an insult, but he only asked, "Where's Rich?"

"I don't know."

"Are you waiting for him?" His eyes narrowed suspiciously.

"He told me to meet him here."

"When?"

"Today at eleven."

Gavin cast an irritated glance down at his watch, and Melanie had to smother another smile at his obvious frustration. He plowed rigid fingers through his hair, though the rebellious golden strands fell forward again, covering the creases marring his forehead. "What do you want?"

"*I* don't want anything. But, according to my editor, Brian Michaels, the article on Ridge Lodge has been expanded to a series."

"So I heard."

"Brian talked to Rich and sent me up here for more pictures. I was supposed to meet with your partner, that's all. It's no big mystery."

"So now you're my problem."

"I'm no one's problem, Gavin," she replied, surprised at how easily his name rolled off her tongue and how quickly she could be drawn into an argument with him. "And I suspect whatever problems you do have are all of your own making!"

"Not all." Gavin shifted, and his face, beneath his tan, blanched. Instinctively she glanced down at his leg, and he leaned against the door frame for support, effectively blocking all chance of escape. Not that she wanted to, she reminded herself. She could deal with Gavin one-on-one if need be.

"Didn't you get enough pictures the other day?"

"Not quite. But don't worry, I'll try not to get in the way."

He pressed his lips together.

"So why are you so camera shy?" she asked bluntly. "You've been photographed all over the world. Why now, when you can use the publicity, are you backpedaling?"

"Maybe I don't like yellow journalism."

"But the *Tribune*—"

"Peddles sleaze."

"No way!" she sputtered. "It's a small local paper—"

"With big ambitions. Oh, yeah, the *Trib* isn't that what you call it—" at her nod he continued "—is subtle and wraps all its smut in a cozy, folksy format."

"That's ridiculous!" she said, but she was still nervous with the memory of her last meeting with Brian and Jan.

"Is it?" Gavin asked, shaking his head. "I don't think so. I've dealt with Brian Michaels before."

Melanie caught her breath. "You have?"

"That's right."

This was news. Brian had never mentioned knowing Gavin. "When?" she asked suspiciously.

"Years ago. In Colorado."

She started through the door, but Gavin thrust out an arm, stopping her before she crossed the threshold. "What were you doing in here?"

"Rich said to meet him in the office. He wants to discuss some other work, I think. Anyway, that's what Brian said."

"What other work?"

"Your guess is as good as mine."

He frowned, the lines around his mouth tightening. "So when he wasn't here, what did you do?"

Melanie's heart began to pound. What did he think? "I waited."

"And while you were waiting?" he prodded.

Suddenly she understood. He thought she'd been snooping! She could see it in his eyes.

"While I was waiting, which has been all of eight or nine minutes, I sat in that chair—" she hooked a thumb at an overstuffed chair near the window "—and thought about the shots I'll need." Lifting her chin an inch, she said, "Oh, and I did snoop around a little—dug through your things, hoping to come up with some trashy dirt I can use in the paper and maybe sell to the tabloids for a few bucks—"

"I didn't accuse you of—"

"You implied, Gavin, and that's bad enough!" she cut in, unable to stop herself. "For your information, I didn't poke around your desk. I came here to take pictures and talk with your partner! I'm sorry to disappoint you but I don't have any devious plans of skulduggery!"

Gavin, using a cane for support, made his way past her and eyed the top of his desk. He frowned. "I bet your friend would have searched the room, if given the opportunity."

"My friend?"

"The reporter—what's her name? Jane?"

"Jan."

"Didn't like her."

"You don't like much, do you?"

He looked up sharply, and a golden flame leapt in his eyes. "Oh, I like some things," he admitted, his voice low.

"What? Just what is it you like these days?"

"I like expensive Scotch, steep mountains and women who don't ask a lot of questions."

"Dumb and beautiful, right?"

"Right," he said with a sarcastic smile. "It just keeps everything so much simpler."

"And that way you don't have to deal with a real woman, a person with a mind of her own, someone who might not deify you because you're some macho athletic jock!"

Stiffly, he dropped into the desk chair. "Seems to me you didn't mind too much."

"That was a long time ago," she shot back, closing her mind to the fact that she'd loved him. Now he was a stranger, a stranger with a biting cynicism that had the ability to slice deep. "And you've changed."

He leaned back in his chair, and his lips twisted. "I wonder why? It couldn't be because I trusted the wrong person, could it?"

Stunned, she swallowed hard. Pain welled up as if he'd struck her. "It doesn't matter," she replied, refusing to let him know he'd wounded her. "I'm here to do a job. That's all. What you think happened in the past really doesn't matter, does it?"

"It matters a hell of a lot!"

"Not anymore."

One of his golden brows lifted, challenging her, but she ignored it. Instead she picked up her camera case and said, "If you'll excuse me, I'll get to work. When Mr. Johanson shows up, point him in my direction. I'll be outside." Opening the door to the back deck, she flung over her shoulder, "I'll be at the blue chair."

Slamming the door shut, she marched across the deck, rested her palms on the thick weathered plank of the rail and took in three deep breaths.

Damn him, damn him, damn him, she thought, shaking inside.

She brushed her hair from her face and tried to calm down. The mountain air was clear and crisp with the promise of winter. Sunlight dazzled over the rocky cliffs and pine trees while dry grass and wildflowers added the fresh scent of a summer that hadn't quite disappeared. High overhead, against a backdrop of diaphanous clouds, a lonely hawk circled.

Melanie heard the door open behind her and braced herself.

"We don't have a blue chair anymore," he said, his voice soft and caressing. She dug her fingers into the weatherbeaten railing but didn't turn to face him.

"Well, then, whatever you call it. You know the one I mean!"

"The Barbary Coast."

"The what?" Slowly she looked over her shoulder and caught him smiling, his eyes dancing with amusement at her bewilderment. But as quickly as it appeared, that fleeting hint of humor fled. "The runs have been named by the colors of their chairs for as long as there have been lifts."

"Then it's time for a change." He walked up to her and propped his injured leg on the lower rail.

What did she care? She wasn't about to argue with him. He could rename the whole damn mountain for all it mattered to her. She turned again, heading for the Barbary Coast chair.

"So where is that partner of yours?" he asked.

"I don't have one."

"The reporter who was here the other day."

Melanie shrugged. "I'm not Jan's keeper. I told her I'd get the shots we needed and she could arrange for another session with you. I didn't see that I needed to be involved."

His lips twisted. "How long is this going to take?"

She'd had enough of his foul mood. "I guess that depends on you," she said sarcastically. "If you're a good boy and answer all Jan's questions, it'll be over quickly, but if you start baiting her like you're doing with me right now, I guarantee you it'll be long and drawn-out."

"And what about you? How long do you plan to be here?"

"Believe me, I want it over as soon as possible. I plan to take some pictures now, a few more when the reconstruction really gets into swing and then, of course, more when the first snow hits and there are actually skiers up here. We'll probably end with a big spread when the lodge opens. That is," she added, "if you don't disapprove."

"Would it matter?"

"I don't know."

Suddenly she was staring at him as she had years ago—full of honesty and integrity. And she felt a very vital, private need to explain. "You're big-time, Gavin. Whether you want to admit it or not. Of course the press is interested. And it's not just your career, you know. It's your life-style."

His eyes darkened a fraction.

"You've been seen all over the world, in the glitziest resorts with the most gorgeous women, with a very fast, exciting crowd—actors, actresses, models, artists. You know, the beautiful crowd, the people middle-class America has an affair with."

His jaw clamped tight, and for a few long seconds he stared at her.

"Your name will become synonymous with Ridge Lodge Resort. It's only natural that the public will be curious. And face it, you and that partner of yours are counting on it. So why don't you quit fighting me every step of the way and enjoy it?"

"Enjoy it," he repeated on a short laugh.

"Most men would love your fame."

"I'm not most men."

"Lord, don't I know it," she said, hurrying across the deck, down the steps and through the tufts of dry grass. "I still need a few pictures of the interior of the lodge, you, your partner and...I don't know...something spectacular." She was thinking aloud, staring at the chair lift. "Something like a view from the top of the mountain." Her gaze landed at the hut at the base of the Barbary Coast lift. Twin cables, supported by huge black pillars, swept up the rocky terrain. Blue-backed chairs hung from the strong cable.

He followed her gaze. "You're not going up on that thing."

"Is it unsafe?"

"No, but—"

"It would be such a breathtaking view," she said, her mind already spinning ahead to the panorama that would be visible from the top of the lift. She'd been up there many times in winter, but never had she seen the mountains from that height before the snow season. "Oh, Gavin, it would be perfect."

Gavin shook his head. "No way."

"Why not?"

"Too risky."

She cocked a disbelieving brow. "I never thought I'd hear you say that." She started for the hut at the base of the lift and motioned to the cables. "Can't you turn this thing on?"

"Yes, but I don't think it would be a good idea."

"That's no surprise. You haven't thought anything about the *Tribune*'s interest in the resort has been a good idea." She was already climbing down the steps of the deck and heading for the chair.

Gavin, using his cane, was right on her heels. "What're you trying to prove?"

"Nothing. I just want to get my job done. Then I won't bother you for a while."

"Promise?"

Spinning, eyes narrowed, she said, "In blood, if I have to!"

He almost smiled. She could see it in his eyes. But quickly the shutters on his eyes lowered and no hint of emotion showed through.

"Then let's go."

"You don't have to come with me—"

"Like hell."

"Really—"

"Look, Mrs. Brooks, I don't know what kind of liability I have here, but I'm going with you to make sure you don't do something asinine and end up falling off the lift and killing yourself."

"Thanks for your concern," she mocked.

"It's not concern. It's simply covering my backside."

"And what can you do...?" She motioned to his injured leg and wished she hadn't.

His face tightened. "It's with me or without me," he muttered, turning away from her and mulishly crossing the remaining distance to the chair lift.

Telling herself she was about to make a grave error, she tucked the strap of her camera over one shoulder, pocketed a few rolls of film and followed him. "I must be out of my mind," she muttered under her breath but decided he was crazier than she as he struggled up the slight incline.

Gavin walked stiffly, jabbing his cane into the dry earth until he reached the hut, which was little more than a huge metal A frame, open at one end to allow the chairs of the lift to enter, revolve around a huge post, then, after picking up skiers, start back up the hillside. He went into a private glassed-in operator's booth that was positioned on one side of the hut. Inside, visible through the glass, he picked up the receiver of a telephone and punched out a number, then waited, his fingers drumming impatiently on the window.

She watched as he spoke tersely into the phone for a few seconds, then slammed the receiver back into its cradle.

"We're all set," he said, meeting Melanie in the shade of the hut.

"You don't have to—"

"Of course I do," he clipped. "All part of our policy up here at Ridge Lodge to keep the public and the press happy."

"Sure."

A wiry, red-haired man shouted from the lodge, then dashed across the rough ground to the hut.

"This is Erik Link. He's in charge of maintenance of all the equipment," Gavin said as the freckle-faced operator entered the hut. "Erik—Melanie Brooks—"

"Walker," Melanie corrected, extending her hand.

"Nice to meet you," Erik replied.

"Melanie's a photographer for the local paper and she wants some pictures from the summit of this lift." He turned back to Melanie. "Erik will make sure we get up and down in one piece."

"That's encouraging." Melanie said dryly.

Erik grinned. "Piece of cake." He withdrew a key ring from his pocket and went into the lodge.

Sighing, she glanced down at his cane. "Really, Gavin, I can handle this alone. You're still laid up—"

"Temporarily."

"Unless you do something stupid and injure yourself again," she pointed out. "I bet your doctor would have a fit."

He smile then, that same blinding flash of white that had always trapped the breath in her lungs. "My doctor will never know."

"Then let's forget it."

He leaned forward on his cane and surveyed her through hooded eyes. "You've changed, Mel," he said quietly. "There was a time when you'd do anything on a dare. Including being alone with me."

"This has nothing to do with being alone with you."

"Doesn't it?" One eyebrow arched dubiously. "You're the one who wanted the best pictures for that damned paper of yours. I'm just giving you what you wanted."

She was tempted. Lord, it would be great knocking the wind from his sails! She eyed the lift with its tall black poles and hesitated.

"Come on, Melanie. I won't bite. I'll even try to keep a rein on my temper."

"Now you are promising the impossible!"

"We'll see." He motioned to Erik, who positioned himself at the station in the hut. A few seconds later, with a rumbling clang and a groan the chairs started moving slowly up the face of the mountain. Erik, smiling, stood at the attendant's box. "Any time," he yelled over the grind of machinery.

Melanie second-guessed herself. "What if we get stuck?"

"We won't."

"How will you get off?" she asked, eyeing his leg and cane. At the top of the lift, the platform had to be several feet below the chair to allow for snowfall. He couldn't possibly jump off the lift without reinjuring himself, and then there was the problem of climbing back on....

"I won't," he said, edging toward the moving chairs. "You'll have to take your pictures from the chair." Before she could argue, he shoved his cane into one hand, grabbed her fingers tightly, moved in front of the next chair and let the lift sweep them off their feet. Within seconds they were airborne.

"Nothing to it," he said, flicking her a satisfied glance.

"Right," she said, still steaming. "You always were bullheaded."

He frowned. "When I want to do something, I just do it."

"That could be dangerous."

"For me—or you?"

"Give me a break," she murmured, angry at being bullied into the chair but feeling a sense of exhilaration nonetheless. A rush of adrenaline swept through her veins as the chair began it ascent. The mountain air was clear, the sky a brilliant shade of autumn blue, broken only by high, thin clouds. A playful breeze was cool against her neck and cheeks and carried with it the fresh, earthy scent of pine.

Melanie slid a glance at Gavin and told herself firmly that the fact that her heart was beating as rapidly as a hummingbird's had nothing to do with the fact that his shoulder brushed hers or that his thigh was only inches from her leg.

Her throat grew tight, and she forced her gaze back to the view. Uncapping the lens from her camera, she stared through the viewfinder, adjusted the focus and clicked off several quick shots of the mountain looming straight ahead.

The peak was dusted with snow, but the rest of the mountain above the timberline was sheer, craggy rock.

"Why'd you come back to Taylor's Crossing?" she asked as the chair climbed up the final steep grade of bare rock.

"Because the deal was right on the resort and because of this." He kicked up his injured foot and frowned at his leg.

"But that's only temporary."

"Maybe."

"Will you be able to race again?"

"It all depends," he admitted, "on how I've healed." His lips tightened. "Maybe it's time to retire."

"At thirty?"

He laughed, but the sound didn't carry any mirth as it bounced off the mountain face. "Looks that way."

The chair rounded the top of the lift and started downward. Melanie had to grit her teeth. Riding the chair up was one thing, but staring down the sheer mountain was quite another. Her hands began to sweat as she lifted the camera again.

Gavin's fingers clamped over her upper arm. "Be careful."

Melanie's concentration centered on those five strong fingers warm against her bare skin, heating her flesh.

She knew he could feel her pulse, hoped it wouldn't betray her as she forced the camera to her eyes and found breathtaking shots of the mountaintops. With her wide-angled lens, she caught the broken ridge of the Cascades. Thin, lazy clouds drifted between the blue peaks, and tall spires of snow pierced the wispy layer.

As the chair moved downward, past the timberline, she caught rays of morning sunlight. Golden beams sifted through the pine trees to dapple the needle-strewn forest floor.

Lower still, she focused the camera on the lodge, snapping off aerial shots of the weathered shake roof and sprawling wings.

"It is beautiful up here," she admitted, hazarding a glance at Gavin. Their gazes locked, and for a breathless instant Melanie was transported back to a place where things were simple and all that mattered was their love. He felt it, too; she could read it in his gold-colored eyes—a tenderness and love so special it still burned bright.

He swallowed and turned quickly to focus on the pines. His voice, when he spoke, was rough. "Look, Mel, I think we should get some things straight. I didn't know you'd be in Taylor's Crossing when I came back."

"Would it have changed your mind?"

"Probably—I don't know. Rich was hell-bent to reopen this lodge, but . . ." His voice drifted off, lost in the gentle rush of the breeze and the steady whir of the lift. "I—you—we made a lot of mistakes, didn't we?"

Her heart wrenched as she thought of their child—a child who hadn't even had a chance to be born. "More than you know."

"And I was wrong about a lot of things," he said, still avoiding her gaze. "And one of those things was you."

Bracing herself, she decided to try to bridge the horrible abyss that loomed between them, to tell him the truth. She placed her hand on his arm and said, "Look, Gavin, as long as we're talking about the past, there's something you should know—"

"All I know is it's over!" His face grew dark. "The past was just a means to an end. A way to get what I wanted." He stared straight at her. "And what happened didn't really matter. You and I—we were just a couple of kids playing around!"

"And that's why you're carrying this chip the size of Mount Everest on your shoulder," she mocked, "because it 'didn't matter'? Now who're you trying to kid?"

He smiled then, slowly and lazily. "If it makes you feel better to think you're the cause of my discontent, go right ahead. But that's making yourself pretty damned self-important, if you ask me."

"Why wouldn't I think it?" she challenged, angry again. "The minute you set eyes on me again, you went for my throat. There has to be a reason you hate me, Gavin."

A muscle worked in his jaw, and his voice, when he spoke, was barely a whisper. "I've never hated you, Melanie."

Her heart turned over. *Don't,* she thought desperately. *Whatever you do, Gavin, don't be kind!*

She opened her mouth, wanting to say something clever, but couldn't find the words. Besides, what good would it do, dredging it all up again? Instead, she fiddled with her camera, pretended interest in a few more shots and wished the ride would end. Being this close to Gavin, tangled up in old and new emotions, was just too difficult. "You're right," she agreed, forcing a cool, disinterested smile. "We were just a couple of kids. We didn't know what we wanted."

"Oh, I knew what I wanted," he said. "I wanted to be the best damn skier in the world."

"And nothing else?"

"Nothing else really mattered, did it?"

"No, I guess you're right," she replied tightly. "Skiing is all there is in life!"

His shoulders tensed, and the corners of his mouth tightened. At the bottom of the lift he motioned to Erik. The lift slowed, and Gavin helped her off, hopping nimbly on his good leg and swinging her to her feet as the lift stopped.

Leaning heavily on his cane, Gavin started hobbling back to the lodge, and she knew she couldn't leave things unsettled. Not if they were going to work together.

"Gavin..." Reaching forward, she touched his forearm again, and he spun around quickly, his expression stern, his eyes blazing.

"Go home, Melanie. You've got your pictures, though why you're taking them for that rag is beyond me."

"'That rag' is the paper I work for."

He stopped dead in his tracks. "Couldn't you find a better one in Seattle?"

"I moved back here," she said, inching her chin up a fraction. "After the divorce."

He didn't respond as he propelled himself back to the lodge.

"Fool," she muttered, when he'd slammed into the building. "Why do you try?" *Because he has the right to know what really happened eight years ago.*

Drawing in a deep breath, she walked into the lodge and found Jan in the main lobby, chatting with Rich Johanson.

"...then we'll be back in a couple of days," Jan was saying.

Gavin was nowhere in sight. Slowly Melanie let out her breath, and Jan, spying her, waved her over and made hasty introductions.

"Sorry I was late," Rich apologized. "I got held up in court. I tried to call the paper, but you'd already taken off. I hope you weren't inconvenienced."

"No problem," Melanie said, hearing uneven footsteps approach. She stiffened.

"I took care of Ms. Brooks," Gavin said.

"Walker," Melanie corrected. "My name is Walker now."

"Again," he said.

"Yes, again." She forced a cool smile in Gavin's direction, though her fists were clenched so tight they ached.

Jan, delighted to find Gavin available, suggested they continue their interview.

He clenched his jaw but he didn't disagree, and they settled into a table in a corner of the main lobby.

"Looks like he's in a great mood," Rich observed.

"One of his best," Melanie remarked.

"With Gavin it's hard to tell." Rich shoved his hands through his hair. "Did you get everything you need?"

"I think so."

"Good. Good. Let's go outside." He motioned her into one of the chairs on the deck. "I've heard that you're the best photographer in town."

Melanie sat with her back to the sun. "You must've been talking to my Uncle Bart," she said, laughing.

Rich waved off her modesty. "I've seen your pictures in the paper and looked over the work you did for the Conestoga Hotel. The manger couldn't say enough good things about you."

Melanie was pleased. She'd worked long and hard on the brochures for the Conestoga.

"And you did the photographs in the lobby of the hotel, right?"

Melanie nodded.

"Mmm. Look, I talked to several people in town because I need a photographer for the lodge, not only for pamphlets, brochures and posters but also to hang on the walls. We're reopening the resort with a Gold Rush theme and we'll need old pictures, blown up and colored brown—you know what I mean?"

"Sepia tones on old tintypes and daguerreotypes," she said.

"If you say so," he said a little sheepishly. "I don't know all the technical terms, but I do know what I want. We'll need between twenty and thirty for the lobby. Let me show you what I mean." He opened a side door to the main gathering room in the lodge and held it open while Melanie got to her feet and walked inside.

Jan and Gavin were still seated at the table, and from Gavin's body language Melanie guessed the interview wasn't going all that well.

Rich didn't seem to notice. He pointed to the walls where he wanted to hang the old photos. "Over here," he said with a sweeping gesture, "I'd like several mining shots and on the far wall, pictures of the mountain."

Rich rattled on and on. Though she listened to him, she was aware of Gavin talking reluctantly to Jan. She could feel the weight of his gaze on her back, knew he was glowering.

Eventually Rich guided her into the office where she was supposed to have met him two hours before and offered her a cup of coffee. Once they were seated, he said, "Besides the pictures for the lobby, we'll need photographs for brochures and posters. And we'll be selling artwork in one of the shops downstairs. We'd like some of your photographs on consignment." He opened up his palms. "So, if you're interested, I'd like you to become the photographer for Ridge Resort."

"Have you talked this over with Gavin?" she asked. Though a part of her would like to take the job and let Gavin rant and rave all he liked, the sensible side of her nature prevented her from jumping into a situation that was bound to spell trouble.

"I don't have to talk to him," Rich replied with a grin. "This is my decision."

"Maybe you should say something to him," she suggested, gathering her things.

"Look, Ms. Walker, I don't have much time. We plan to open in two months. I need brochures ASAP."

He offered her a generous flat fee and a percentage on all the posters sold, plus extra money for extra work. The job at Ridge Lodge, should she take it, would help establish her studio as well as pay off some of the debts she'd incurred since her divorce and give her a little cushion so that she wasn't quite so dependent on the *Tribune*. In short, Rich Johanson's offer was too good to pass up.

She cast a nervous glance in Gavin's direction, noted the hard, immovable line of his jaw and knew that he would hit the roof. But it didn't matter. She needed all the work she could get. "I'd be glad to work for you," she said, feeling a perverse sense of satisfaction.

Rich grinned and clasped her hand. "Good. I'll draw up a contract and we can get started as soon as it's convenient for you."

"I can work evenings and weekends."

"Will you have enough time?"

She shot another look in Gavin's direction. "Don't worry," she said, ignoring the tight corners of Gavin's mouth and the repressed fury that fairly radiated from him, "I'll make the time." She scrounged in her wallet, handed him her card and added, "You can reach me at my studio or at the office."

"Thanks." Rich stuffed the card in his wallet. "Then I'll see you in a few days." They shook hands again before Melanie, refusing to glance at Gavin one last time, gathered her things and headed for the front doors.

As she made her way down the asphalt path, she heard Jan's quick footsteps behind her. "Hey, Melanie, wait up!"

Melanie turned, watched Jan hurrying to catch her and noticed Gavin, hands braced on the porch rails of the lodge, glaring at her. She couldn't imagine what he'd think when he found out Rich had hired her. With a satisfied grin, she waved at him before turning her attention to a breathless Jan. "How'd it go?" Melanie asked.

"With Doel?" Jan sighed loudly and whispered, "I think it would be easier to interview a monk who's taken a vow of silence."

"Oh?"

Jan glanced over her shoulder,then said softly, "I want details, Melanie, *de*tails."

"About what?"

"You and Doel. I saw the looks he sent you. They were positively sizzling! And when we were up here before, I could've sworn there was something going on between you two. Now, what gives?"

"You're imagining things."

"And you're holding out on me. There's more to what happened to you than the fact that you went to school together." She reached her car and unlocked the door. "I mean it, Melanie. I want to know everything."

"It's not an interesting story," Melanie replied, though she knew sooner or later Jan would find out the truth—or part of it.

"Anything about Gavin Doel is interesting."

"Later," Melanie promised, needing time to sort out just how much she could confide. There was no getting around at least part of the truth. Jan would only discover the information somewhere else, and unfortunately, Taylor's Crossing was a small town. If Jan set her mind to finding out the truth, it wouldn't be too hard to dig up someone who would willingly remember. Only a handful of people had known that she and Gavin had been seeing each other—fewer still guessed they'd been lovers—but the townspeople in Taylor's Crossing had long memories when it came to gossip.

Frowning, Melanie slid into her sun-baked car. She glanced through the dusty windshield to the lodge. Gavin's eyes were narrowed against the sun, his jaw set in granite. How would she ever begin to explain the depth and complexity of her feelings for him? She'd been only seventeen at the time; no one, including Jan, would believe that her romance had been anything but puppy love.

But she knew better. As she slid a pair of sunglasses onto the bridge of her nose and drove out of the lot, she wished she could forget that she'd ever loved him.

Chapter Six

"You did *what*?" Gavin roared, eyeing his partner as if he'd lost his mind.

"I hired Melanie Walker."

"Well, that's just great!" Gavin growled.

"What've you got against her?" Rich asked, his brows drawing together.

"I knew her years ago."

"So?" Sitting at his desk, pen in one hand, Rich stared up at Gavin as if he were the one who had gone mad.

"We dated."

Rich still wasn't getting the point. "I don't understand—"

"While I was gone, she married a guy by the name of Neil Brooks eight years ago."

"Neil Brooks—the lumber broker?"

"You know him?" Gavin growled, rolling his eyes and tossing his hands out as if in supplication to the heavens. "This just gets better and better."

"Of course I know him. Brooks Lumber is our major supplier for the renovation."

"No!" Gavin whispered harshly as he thought of Melanie's ex-husband—the man who had, in a few short weeks, stolen Melanie from him. He told himself he couldn't really blame Brooks. It had been Melanie who had betrayed him. Nonetheless, he loathed anything to do with Neil Brooks. "Find another lumber company."

"No can do," Rich said, assuming a totally innocent air. "Brooks Lumber is one of the few firms that service this area."

"There must be someone else! We're not exactly in Timbuktu, for crying out loud!"

"Brooks offers the best quality for the lowest price."

"I don't give a damn." This was turning into a nightmare! First Melanie and now Neil. Gavin's throat felt suddenly dry. He needed a drink. A double. But he didn't give in to the urge.

"Well, I do. I give a big damn. We don't have a lot of extra cash to throw around. Besides, we had a deal. I handle this end of the business—you help design the runs, bring in the investors and provide the skiing expertise."

"That's exactly what I'm doing. Providing expertise. Don't use Brooks. He's as slippery as a rattler and twice as deadly."

"Are you speaking from personal experience?"

"Yes! Damn it!" Gavin crashed his fist against the corner of Rich's desk, sloshing coffee on a few papers.

"Hey, watch it." Rich, perturbed, grabbed his handkerchief and mopped up the mess. "Look, even if I wanted to change lumber companies—which I don't—I can't. Not now. It's too late. We've already placed our order. Some of it has already been shipped and paid for. We don't have much time, Gavin, so whatever particular personal gripe you've got with Neil Brooks, you may as well shove it aside. And as for Neil's wife—or ex-wife or whatever she is—she's working for us. We both agreed that we'd employ as many local people as we could, remember? It's just good business sense to keep the locals happy!"

"I didn't know Melanie was back in town."

Rich grinned. "You've always had an eye for good-looking women, and that one—she's a knockout."

Gavin clenched his fist, but this time he did no more than shove it into his pocket. "I'm just not too crazy about some of your choices," Gavin muttered. He didn't want Melanie here, couldn't stand the thought of seeing her every day. He'd told himself he was long over her, but now he wasn't so sure. There was a moment up on the lift when he could've sworn that nothing had changed between them. But, of course, that was pure male ego. Everything had changed. "Was working for the lodge her idea?" he asked.

Rich shook his head. "Nope. In fact, I had to do some hard and fast talking to get her to take the job."

"You should have consulted with me first."

"That's what she said."

Gavin was surprised. "But you didn't listen, right?"

"No, I didn't listen. I wanted her. And as for consulting with you, that works both ways."

Gavin's jaw began to work, and he crossed to the window and stared out at the cool late summer day. A few workers dotted the hillside, and down the hall, in the lounge, the pounding of hammers jarred the old building.

"There's something else bothering you," Rich guessed, shoving back his chair and rounding the desk. Crossing his thick arms over his chest, fingers drumming impatiently, he stared at Gavin and waited.

"We don't need any adverse publicity," Gavin said flatly.

"And you think Melanie's going to give us some?"

Gavin hesitated, but only for a second. He trusted Rich, and they were partners. As his business partner, Rich had the right to know the whole story. He probably should have leveled with Rich before. But then, he had no idea he would run into Melanie again. If he had guessed she was back in Taylor's Crossing, he might have balked at the project.

"Well?" Rich was waiting.

"You know that I grew up here," Gavin said, seeing Rich's eyes narrow. "And you know that my father had his problems."

"So you said."

Gavin's muscles tightened as he remembered his youth. "Dad's an alcoholic," he said finally, the words still difficult.

"I know that."

"And he spent some time in prison."

"You said something about it—an accident that was his fault."

"An accident that killed the driver of the other car," he said quietly. "A woman, Brenda Walker. Melanie's mother."

Rich didn't move.

"Dad was legally drunk at the time."

Frowning, Rich said, "I'm sorry."

"So am I, and so was Dad—when he sobered up enough to understand what had happened. He came away with only a few scrapes and bruises, but Melanie's mother's car was forced off the road and down a steep embankment." Gavin relived the nightmare as if it had happened just yesterday. He'd been twelve at the time when the policemen had knocked on the door, the blue and red lights of their cars casting colored shadows on the sides of the trailer that he and his father had called home. He'd thought for certain his father was dead but had been relieved when he'd found out Jim Doel had survived.

However, that night had been just the tip of the iceberg, the start of a life of living with an aunt and uncle who hadn't given a damn about him.

Through it all, Gavin had escaped by testing himself. From the time he could handle a paper route, he'd spent every dime on the thrill of sliding downhill on skis. He'd landed odd jobs—eventually at Ridge Resort itself—and fed his unending appetite for the heart-pounding excitement of racing headlong down a steep mountain at breakneck speed.

In all the years since the night his father had been taken to jail, Gavin's only distraction from the sport he loved had been Melanie.

The only daughter of the woman his father had killed.

Rich asked, "And you think Melanie still holds a grudge?"

"I don't know," Gavin answered. "I thought I knew her, but I didn't. Ten years after the accident, against her father's better judgment, Melanie and I dated for a while." Gavin's gut wrenched at the vivid memories. "But then I had the opportunity to train for the Olympics."

"So you left her."

"I guess that's the way she saw it. I asked her to wait and she foolishly agreed." Gavin's lips twisted at his own naïveté.

"But she didn't."

Gavin felt again the glacial sting of her rejection. His nostrils flared slightly. "Adam Walker—Melanie's father—never approved of me or my old man. And while I was gone, Melanie married Neil Brooks. My guess is that her old man finally convinced her she'd be better off with the son of a wealthy lumber broker than a ski bum whose father was a drunk."

"And now?"

Gavin looked up sharply. "And now what?"

"Melanie and you?"

Gavin let out a short, ugly laugh. "There is no Melanie and me." His insides turned frigid. "There really never was."

Rich let out a sigh. "You should've told me this earlier, you know."

"Didn't see a reason. As far as I knew she was still living the good life up in Seattle."

"She's already agreed to the job, you know," Rich said, rubbing his temple. "I don't see how we can get out of this without causing a lot of hard feelings. Though I didn't sign a contract, if it gets out that we're not as good as our word—"

"Don't worry about it. Keep Melanie Walker," Gavin decided suddenly. He could find ways to avoid her. The lodge was large; the resort covered thousands of acres. Besides, he'd be too busy to run into her often. "Just as long as she does the job," he muttered, and added silently, *and doesn't get in my way.*

Jan wouldn't let up. She'd camped out at Melanie's desk when they returned from the resort and wasn't taking no for an answer. "I saw the way he looked at you, Melanie! You can't convince me that there's nothing going on between you and Gavin Doel," she said, checking her reflection in her compact mirror and touching up her lipstick.

"I haven't seen him in years." Melanie walked into the darkroom and picked up the enlarged photograph of Uncle Bart and his prize colt, Big Money. She slipped the black-and-white photo into an envelope and, returning to her desk, pretended she wasn't really interested in Jan's observations about Gavin.

Sighing in exasperation, Jan tossed her hands into the air. "Okay, okay, I believe that you haven't seen him," she said, ignoring Melanie's efforts at nonchalance. "But what happened all those years ago? The looks he sent you today were hot—I mean, scorching, burning, torrid, you name it!"

Tucking the envelope into her purse, Melanie chuckled. "You're overdramatizing."

"I'm a reporter. I don't go in for melodrama. Just the facts. And the fact is he couldn't keep his eyes off you!"

"You're exaggerating, then." Melanie walked to the coffeepot and poured two cups.

"I'm not exaggerating! Now, what gives?"

Melanie handed Jan one of the cups, took a sip herself and grimaced at the bitter taste. She opened a small packet of sugar and poured it into her cup. "Well, I guess you're going to find out sooner or later, but this is just between you and me."

"Absolutely!" Jan took a sip of her coffee, but over the rim her eyes were bright, eager.

Haltingly, Melanie explained that she and Gavin had dated in high school, glossing over how deep her emotions had run. "And so, when he went to train for the Olympics, we lost touch and I married Neil."

Jan shook her head. "You chose Neil Brooks over Gavin Doel?" she asked incredulously. "No offense, Mel, but there's just no comparison."

"Well, that's what happened."

"And nothing else?"

"Nothing," Melanie lied easily. "But what I told you is strictly off the record, right?"

"Oh, absolutely!" Jan looked positively stricken. "Besides, no one's going to care whom he dated in high school."

Jan slid a look at her watch and frowned. "I gotta run," she said, "but I'll see you tomorrow. When will the proofs of the lodge be ready?"

"I'll have them on your desk first thing in the morning."

"You're a love. Thanks." With a wave, Jan bustled out of the building.

Melanie spent the next few hours in and out of the darkroom, developing the photographs she'd taken at Ridge Lodge. The shots from the chair were spectacular, black-and-white vistas of the rugged Cascade Mountains. A few pictures of the workers, too, showed the manpower needed to give the lodge its new look. But the photographs that took her breath away were the close-ups of Gavin.

In startling black and white, his features seemed more chiseled and angular—as earthy and formidable as the mountains he challenged, his eyes more deeply set, his expression innately sexy and masculine. And though she'd seen little evidence of humor in the time she'd spent with him, the photographs belied his harshness by exposing the tiny beginnings of laugh lines near his mouth and tiny crinkles near the corners of his eyes. She wondered vaguely who had been lucky enough to make him laugh.

She circled the best shots, stuffed them in an envelope and left the packet in Jan's In basket. By the time she was finished, most of the staff had left. Walking into the fading sunlight, she took the time to lock the door behind her, then noticed the cool evening breeze that chilled her bare arms.

The mountain nights had begun to grow cold.

She stopped at the grocery store on the way home and finally turned into her drive a little after seven. The sky was dusky with the coming twilight, shadows stretched across the dry grass of her yard, and a truck she didn't recognize was parked near the garage. Gavin sat behind the wheel.

She stood on the brakes. The Volkswagen screeched to a stop.

Surely he wasn't here.

But as she stared at the truck, her heart slammed into overdrive. Gavin stretched slowly from the cab. *Now what?* she wondered, her throat suddenly dry as she forced herself to appear calm and steeled herself for the upcoming confrontation. It had to be about Rich's offer.

Wearing faded jeans, a black T-shirt, a beat-up leather jacket and scruffy running shoes, he reminded her of the boy she'd once known, the kid from the wrong side of the tracks. No designer labels or fancy ski clothes stated the fact that he was a downhill legend.

Deciding that the best defense was a quick offense, she juggled purse, groceries and camera case as she climbed out of the Volkswagen. "Don't tell me," she said, shoving the car door closed with her hip and forcing a dazzling smile on slightly frozen lips. "You've come racing over here to congratulate me on my new job at the resort."

His jaw slid to the side, and he shoved his sunglasses onto his head. "Not exactly."

She lifted a disdainful eyebrow. "And I thought you'd be thrilled!"

"Rich handles that end of the business."

"Does he? So you didn't come over here to tell me that I'm relieved of my newfound duties?"

"I considered it," he admitted with maddening calm.

"Look, Gavin, let's get one thing straight," she said. "I'm not going to get into a power struggle with you. If you want me to do the job, fine. If not, believe me, I won't starve. So you don't have to feel guilty. If you want someone else to do the work, just say so."

"Rich seems set on you."

"And you?"

Brackets pinched the corners of his mouth. "I don't know. I haven't seen your work. At least, not for a few years."

She ignored that little jab and marched across the side yard to the back door. She kept her back rigid, pretended that she didn't care in the least that he'd shown up at her doorstep. Over her shoulder she called, "Well, if you're interested, come inside. But if you're just here to give me a bad time, then you may as well leave. I'm not in the mood."

Shifting the groceries and camera case, she unlocked the back door. Sassafras, barking and growling, snapping teeth bared, hurtled through. He didn't even pause for a pet but headed straight for Gavin.

"Don't worry," she called to Gavin over her shoulder, "he's all bark—no bite."

But Gavin didn't appear the least bit concerned about Sassafras's exposed fangs or throaty warnings. He flashed a quick glance at the dog and commanded, "Stop!"

Sassafras skidded on the dry grass but the hairs on the back of his neck rose threateningly.

"That's better," Gavin said, slowly following Melanie up the steps. "Damned leg," he grumbled, pausing in the doorway.

"Come on in," Melanie invited. "I don't bite, either—at least, not usually." She placed the bag on the counter. "Now, just give me a minute to get things organized." She kicked her shoes into a corner near the table and stuffed a few sacks of vegetables and a package of meat into the refrigerator.

She felt him watching her, but she didn't even glance in his direction. She pretended not to be aware that he was in the room, managing a fake calm expression that she hoped countered her jackhammering heart and suddenly sweating palms. Now that he was in the house, what was she going to do with him? The house seemed suddenly small, more intimate than ever before.

The fact that he was in her house, alone with her, brought back too many reminders of the past. The rooms felt hot and suffocating, though she expected the temperature couldn't be more than sixty-five degrees.

"Come on, my studio's down the hall," she said, opening the door for Sassafras. Cool mountain air streamed in with the old dog as he eyed Gavin warily, growling and dropping onto his favorite spot beneath the kitchen table. "See, he likes you already," Melanie quipped, suppressing a smile at Sassafras's low growl.

"I'd hate to think how he reacts to someone he doesn't trust."

"Just about the same." Melanie led Gavin to the front of the house and down a short corridor to her studio. He didn't remark on the changes in the house, but maybe he didn't remember. He'd been over only a few times while they'd dated and he hadn't stayed long because of her father's hostility.

As she opened the studio door, Gavin caught her wrist. "I didn't come here to see your work," he said, spinning her around so that she was only inches from him, her upturned face nearly colliding with his chest.

"But I thought—"

"That was just a ruse." He swallowed, his Adam's apple moving slowly up and down in his throat. Melanie forced her eyes to his. "I came her because I wanted to lay out the ground rules, talk some things out."

"What 'things'?" His hand was still wrapped around her wrist, his fingertips hot against the inside of her arm. No doubt he could feel her thundering pulse. The small, dark hallway felt close. It was all she could do to pull her arm from his grasp.

"I just want you to know that I don't want any trouble."

"And you think I'll give it to you?"

"I think that rag you work for might."

She bristled. "The *Tribune*—"

"We've been over this before," he said, cutting her off as she found the doorknob and backed into the studio. She needed some breathing room. With a flick of her wrist she snapped on the overhead light. "I have a feeling that reporter friend of yours would print anything if she thought it would get her a byline."

"Not true."

"If you say so." He didn't seem convinced. Glancing quickly around the studio, he slung his injured leg over a corner of her desk. "But she gets pretty personal."

"You don't have to worry about Jan," Melanie said, instantly defensive. "I told her a little of our history."

"You did *what*?" he thundered, gold eyes suddenly ice-cold.

"It's all off the record."

"You trust her?"

"Of course I trust her. We work together and she's my friend."

He snorted. "And I suppose you trust Michaels, too."

"Yes!" she replied indignantly.

Gavin muttered something unintelligible. "But he hasn't been your boss for long has he?"

"No," she conceded. "The paper changed hands about a year ago. Brian was hired to take charge."

"From where?"

"Chicago, I think. He's worked in publishing for years. Before Chicago, there was a paper in Atlanta."

"Right. Never planted his feet down for long, has he? And I wouldn't think Taylor's Crossing, Oregon is the next natural step up on the ladder of success. Atlanta, Chicago, Taylor's Crossing? Doesn't seem likely, does it?"

"What're you trying to say, Gavin?" she asked, bristling at the unspoken innuendos.

"I've met Michaels before. He was a reporter in Vail. I didn't like him then and I don't trust him now."

Folding her arms across her chest, she said, "You are the most suspicious person I know. You don't trust anyone, do you?"

"I wonder why," he said quietly, his features drawn.

Her heart stopped. "So you're blaming me?"

"No, Melanie, I'm blaming myself," he replied, his words cutting sharply. "I was young and foolish when I met you—naïve. But you taught me how stupid it is to have blind trust. It's a lesson I needed to learn. It's gotten me through some tough times."

"So you're here to thank me, is that it?" she tossed out, though she was dying inside.

"I'm here to make sure that you and I see eye to eye. I want our past to remain buried, and for that to happen, you'd better quit talking to Jan or anyone else at the *Tribune*."

"Is that so?"

"For both our sakes as well as my father's. No matter what happens, I want Dad's name kept out of the paper."

Melanie bit her lower lip. "I don't know if that's possible."

"Well, use your influence."

"I will, of course I will, but I'm only the photographer."

"And the bottom line is Brian Michaels doesn't give a damn whose life he turns inside out!" He stood then, towering over her, his eyes blazing. "My father's paid for what happened over and over again. We all have. There is no reason to dredge it all up again."

"I agree. I just don't know what I can do."

Gavin sighed, raking his fingers through his hair. "Dad's moving back to Taylor's Crossing and I want to see to it that he can start fresh."

"I doubt that anyone will be interested."

"God, are you naïve! You just don't know what kind of an industry you work for, do you?"

"We report the news—"

"And the gossip and the speculation—anything as long as it sells papers!"

"I'm not going to stand here and argue about it with you," she retorted, wishing she felt a little more conviction. "If you're finished—"

"Not quite. Now that we understand each other—"

"I don't think we ever did."

"Doesn't matter. You stay out of my way and I'll stay out of yours. If you have any questions while you're working up at the lodge, you can ask Rich."

"And if he's not there?"

"Then I'll help you."

"But, don't go chasing after you, is that what you're telling me?" she mocked, simmering fury starting to boil deep inside her.

"I just think it's better if you and I keep our distance."

"Don't worry, Gavin," she remarked, her voice edged in cynicism. "Your virtue is safe with me."

He flushed from the back of his neck. "Don't push me, Melanie."

"Wouldn't dream of it," she threw back at him. "I'm not afraid of you, Gavin."

His gaze shifted to her mouth. "Well, maybe you should be," he whispered hoarsely.

"Why?"

He swallowed hard. His expression tightened in his attempt at self-control. "Because, damn it, even though I know it's crazy, even though I tell myself this will never work, I just can't help... Oh, to hell with it."

His arms surrounded her, and his lips slanted over hers.

Surprised, Melanie gasped, and his tongue slipped easily between her teeth, tasting and exploring.

She knew she should push him aside, shove with all her might, and she tried—dear Lord, she tried—but as her hands came up against his chest they seemed powerless, and all she could do was close her eyes and remember, in painful detail, the other kisses they'd shared. He still tasted the same, felt as strong and passionate as before.

Her lips softened, and she kissed him back. All the lies and the accusations died away. She was lost in the smell and feel of him, in the power of his embrace, the thundering beat of her heart.

Slowly, his tongue stopped its wonderful exploration, and a low groan escaped from him. "God, Melanie!" he whispered against her hair, his arms strong bands holding her close. "Why?"

She tried to find her voice, but words failed her.

Slowly he released her, stepping backward and shoving shaking fingers through his hair. She watched as he visibly strained for control.

"Gavin, I think we should talk."

"We've said everything that has to be said," he replied. "This isn't going to work, you know."

"We'll... we'll make it work."

His gaze slid to her lips again, and she swallowed with difficulty. "No."

"I need to explain about Neil," she said.

His features hardened. "You don't have to explain about anything, Melanie. Let's just forget this ever happened."

"I don't think I can."

"Well, try," he said, turning on his heel and striding out the door.

She didn't move for a full minute, and only after she heard his pickup spark to life, tires squeal and gravel spray, did she sag against the door.

The next few weeks promised to be hell.

"Damn! Damn! Damn!" Gavin pounded on the steering wheel with his fist. What had gotten into him? He'd kissed her! *Kissed* her—and she'd responded. Suddenly, in those few moments, all time and space had disappeared, and

Gavin was left with the naked truth that she wasn't out of his blood.

He cranked on the wheel and gunned the accelerator as he left the city lights behind and his truck started climbing the dark road leading to the mountain.

He couldn't hide from her. Not now. As a photographer for the resort, she'd be at the lodge more often than not. And then what? Would he kiss her again? Seduce her next time? Delicious possibilities filled his mind, and he remembered how the curve of her spine fit so neatly against the flat of his stomach, or the way her breasts, young and firm, had nestled so softly into his hands, or how her hips had brushed eagerly against his in the dim light of the hayloft.

"Stop it!" he commanded, as if he could will her image out of his mind. He flicked on the radio and tried to concentrate on the weather report. Temperatures were due to drop in the area, a weatherman reported, but Gavin's lips curved cynically. He decided that in the next month or two, his temperature would probably be soaring. All because of Melanie.

Chapter Seven

Ridge Lodge and Gavin were plastered over the front page of the *Tribune*. There were several pictures of the resort, including a panoramic shot Melanie had taken from the lift, showing the lodge sprawling at the base of the runs, and there was one photograph of Gavin—a thoughtful pose that showed off his hard-edged profile as he talked with the reporter.

He didn't like the picture. It showed too much of his personality and captured the fact that he felt uncomfortable and suspicious while being interviewed. Melanie obviously had a photographer's knack for making a flat black-and-white photograph show character and depth.

"Damn her," he muttered, forcing his eyes to the story. Bold headlines proclaimed: Doel to Reopen Ridge Resort. The byline credited Jan Freemont with the story.

Gavin's jaw clenched as he scanned the columns. But the article was straightforward, and aside from mentioning the fact that Gavin had grown up around Taylor's Crossing, his personal life wasn't included. His skiing awards and professional life were touched on, but the focus of the article was the resort.

So maybe Brian Michaels was playing by the rules this time. Perhaps the *Tribune* was a local newspaper that wasn't interested in trashing everyone's personal life.

Gavin didn't believe it for a minute. He'd met Michaels before; the man's instincts usually centered on gossip and speculation. Unless Michaels had mellowed or developed some sense of conscience.

"No way," Gavin told himself as Rich, several newspapers tucked under his arm, a wide grin stretched across his jaw, strode into the office.

He dropped the papers onto Gavin's desk. "Looks like you were worried for nothing," he said, thumping a finger on the front page.

"We'll see."

"I told you, this is the best source of free publicity, and the story's been picked up by the *Portland Daily* as well as several papers in Washington, Idaho and northern California."

"If you say so," Gavin said, unable to concede the fact that he was wrong.

"And now the *Tribune* is doing a series on the resort with a final full-page article scheduled for the grand opening. What could be better?"

"Can't think of a thing," Gavin drawled, sarcasm heavy in his words.

"Well, neither can I." Rich stuffed his hands into his pockets and walked to the windows, looking out at a cloudy afternoon sky. "So, you be good to the reporters who start showing up."

"Wouldn't dream of anything else."

Rich sighed theatrically. "I know you gave Ms. Freemont a bad time."

"I was good as gold," Gavin mocked.

"It's your attitude, Doel. It's way beyond bad."

"I'll try to improve."

"Do that."

"Won't have to. You're the one going to handle the press from now on."

"I know, I know. But I'm not always here. In fact, I'm taking off for Portland today, hopefully to settle a case. I need to check on my practice for a couple of days—make sure that legal assistant I hired is handling everything. I'll be back by the weekend."

"And in the meantime, you expect me to deal with—" he glanced at the byline again "—Jan Freemont."

"And anyone else who strolls in here looking for a story or pictures—and that includes Melanie Walker."

Gavin frowned. He'd already decided to try to work things out with Melanie. Bury the past. Forget it. Just treat her like anyone else. If that were possible. After kissing her, he wasn't convinced he could pull it off. One kiss and he'd been spinning—just like a horny high school kid. Disgusting. "I'll do my best," he told Rich, and flashed a cynical smile.

"Oh, God, Gavin, try harder than that," Rich said with a laugh as he stuffed some papers into his briefcase.

"Not funny, Johanson."

"Sure it was. That's your problem, you know. No sense of humor."

"As long as I've only got one problem, I guess I'm doing all right. Now, get outta here."

Rich snapped his briefcase closed. "Seriously, Gavin, try not to antagonize too many people—especially reporters—while I'm gone."

Gavin assumed his most innocent expression. "You've got my word. Unless the questions get too personal or way out of line, I'll be—"

"I know, 'good as gold.' God help us," Rich muttered, waving a quick goodbye as he left.

Gavin glanced again at the opened newspaper, his gaze landing on his profile. No doubt Melanie would return within the next couple of days. Well, he'd find a way to be nice to her. Even if it killed him.

Melanie had every intention of dealing with Rich Johanson and staying clear of Gavin. She'd already spent three sleepless nights thinking of Gavin and how easily she'd responded to him.

And he'd responded, too. Whether he admitted it or not. Her foolish heart soared at the thought, but she quickly brought it back to the ground. No matter how Gavin responded to her, that response was purely sexual. His emotions were far different from hers. He'd kissed her as he'd kissed a dozen women in the past year. She'd kissed him as she'd kissed only him. No other man, including Neil, had ever been able to cause her blood to thunder, her pulse to race out of control.

And that's why Gavin was off-limits, she told herself as she shoved open the door of Ridge Lodge three days after Gavin's visit.

Unfortunately, the first person she ran into was Gavin.

Thankfully, they weren't alone. A work crew was busy hammering and sawing, stripping old wood and refinishing. Men with sagging leather belts filled with hammers, chisels, nails, planers and files moved throughout the interior and scrambled up on scaffolding that reached to the joists and beams of the ceiling three stories overhead. Though it was late afternoon, the lodge wasn't dark or intimate because of the huge lights the construction workers had mounted to aid them in their restoration of the rustic old inn.

Blueprints, anchored by half-filled bottles, were spread upon the bar while power saws screamed and dust swirled in pale clouds. A radio blared country music, but Melanie was sure no one could hear it over the din.

"I'm, uh, looking for Rich," she shouted over the noise, aware that a blush had stained her neck. Gavin was standing near the bar, eyeing the ceiling. Wearing jeans and a loose Notre Dame sweatshirt, he seemed to be supervising the restoration.

He frowned, dusted off his hands and moved closer so they wouldn't have to shout. "Rich isn't here. He left me in charge."

Great, Melanie thought, bracing herself for an inevitable confrontation.

"And I promised I'd be on my best behavior."

"I wasn't aware you had one."

His lips twitched. "It's buried deep. But you're in luck today. I'm going to try my level best to be charming and helpful."

"Bull," she replied, caught up in his teasing banter.

"Hey, look." He opened his palms. "Either you deal with me or you come back later."

"I thought you didn't want anything to do with me."

His eyes darkened. "Sometimes fate works against us."

Amen, she thought, but held her tongue. No reason to antagonize him. At least, not while he was trying to be affable.

"Rich left a contract for you on his desk," Gavin was saying, as if the other night hadn't existed—as if nothing had changed. "I'll get it for you. Come on."

Wondering how long his gracious manner would last, she followed him down a short hall and into the office.

Slamming the door behind him, he actually grinned. "Sorry about the mess."

"Doesn't bother me. In fact, I'd like to take a few pictures."

Nodding, he rummaged through the papers on the desk, found the typewritten contract and handed it to her.

Taking the document, she observed, "You're in a better mood today."

"Why not?" he tossed back, leaning over the desk. A few pale rays of afternoon sunlight streamed through the window to catch in the golden strands of his hair. Melanie's heart flipped over. "You and I got everything straight the other night, right?"

"Right," she agreed, not sure she was any more comfortable with this affable Gavin than she had been with the jaded, cynical man who had left her only three nights before—a man who had kissed her with a passion that had cut to her soul.

Gavin shoved his hands into the back pockets of his jeans. "And now that the construction's moving along, I feel that I'm not just spinning my wheels any longer."

"And so now everything is just wonderful?" she asked, unable to keep the disbelief from her voice.

He glanced up sharply, but a precision-practiced smile curved his lips. "Until something goes wrong."

She didn't believe him for a minute. This was all just an act, but she didn't argue with him. If he was going to be agreeable, it would make her job that much easier.

"Here's the contract. Take it home, look it over, have a lawyer look at it if you want to, but Rich wants it signed by the end of the week."

"No problem," she said as he handed her a stiff white envelope with the name and address of Rich's legal firm printed in the upper left-hand corner. She tucked the envelope into her purse, then settled down to business. "I've got some ideas for the brochure, but what I'd like are old pictures of the lodge and of you for background."

"I don't see why—" He stopped himself short. His sunny disposition clouded for a minute, and small lines etched his forehead. For the first time she understood how difficult it was for him to appear easygoing. "Sure. Why not?" he said. "Everything you'll need is in my suite." With a muttered oath, he grabbed his cane. "This way. Come on."

She followed him down a narrow hallway to a door near the back of the lodge.

Twisting the knob, he said with more than a trace of cynicism, "Home sweet home." He held the door open for her, and she walked into his living quarters.

She'd expected a grand suite with lavish furnishings for a man as wealthy and famous as Gavin, a man who had desperately wanted to shed his poor roots.

Instead, she found the suite comfortable and sparse. A rock fireplace filled one wall. Nearby a bookcase was crammed with books, magazines, a stereo and a television. A faded rug covered the worn wood floor, and a few pieces of furniture were grouped haphazardly around the room.

Wincing, Gavin bent down to the bottom shelf of the bookcase, rummaged around and pulled out a couple of battered photograph albums and a box. He tossed everything onto a nearby table. "I think that should do it," he said, forcing a smile as he straightened. "If you need anything else, just whistle. I'll be supervising the renovation or working out in the weight room." He cast an impatient glance at his injured leg. "Physical therapy."

"It shouldn't take long," Melanie replied, trying to be polite, though her voice sounded strained.

"Good."

"I'll try not to bother you."

Oh, woman, if you only knew, Gavin thought, trying his damnedest to be civil. But every time he looked at her, gazed into her wide hazel eyes, he was reminded of how much he'd loved her, how deeply she'd touched his soul.

"Damn crazy fool," he muttered, leaving the room as quickly as he could. Just being around her made him restless. And though he knew rationally that he was through with her forever, there was a wayward side of his nature that wanted to flirt with danger, a wayward side that kept reminding him of their last kiss and the feel and smell of her yielding against him. What would it hurt to spend time with her—get a little back? Now that he was over her, he could handle any situation that arose—or could he? The other night hadn't gone exactly as planned. However, he was trying to keep the promise he'd made to Rich and himself, trying not to antagonize her. But it was hell.

In the lobby, he spent nearly an hour with the foreman and was relieved that the remodeling, though only a few days old, was still on schedule. Then, because he didn't want to run into Melanie again, he hobbled down the short flight of steps to the pool and the weight room.

Fortunately, this area needed very little work, and the long, rectangular pool was operational.

He stripped out of his work clothes, stepped into a pair of swim trunks and took a position at the weight machine. Slowly, he started working his leg, stretching the muscles with only a little resistance and weight and adding more pounds as he began to work up a sweat.

"Take it easy," Dr. Hodges had said. "Don't push yourself." Yet that was exactly what he felt compelled to do. Cooped up in this damned lodge with Melanie poking through old photographs upstairs while the upcoming ski season, which could make or break the resort, loomed ahead, Gavin had no choice but to push himself to release tension and nervous energy.

He pressed relentlessly on the foot bar of the thigh machine. Sweat trickled down his back.

The pain in his leg started to burn. He ignored it, pushing again on the weight, stretching out his knee and calf only to release the tension and hear the weights clang down. Gritting his teeth, he shoved again. Sweat dripped from his temples to his chin.

How the hell would he get through the next few weeks, unable to participate in the sport he loved, unable to trust a woman he'd treasured?

"Don't even think about it," he growled to himself, his muscles bulging as he pressed relentlessly on the weights, his thigh muscles quivering. He slammed his eyes shut, but even in his concentration, Melanie appeared—a vision with a gorgeous body and seductive smile. She was older now, a little jaded in her own way. Yet he found her sarcastic remarks interesting, her sense of humor refreshing. The fact that she had the nerve to stand up to him was beguiling—or would have been if it wasn't so damned maddening. The nerve of her actually baiting him when she'd left him high and dry all those years before.

He wondered if she ever thought of him—of those nights they'd shared. God, with his eyes closed, he could still smell the scent of hay on her skin, see the seductive light in her hazel eyes, hear the sound of her pleasured cries as he...

He dropped the weights, and they slammed together, the noise ringing to the rafters. Climbing off the damned machine, he shoved his sweaty hair from his eyes and noticed he felt an uncomfortable swelling between his legs. "Damn it, Doel, you're a first-class idiot," he said, swearing beneath his breath.

Embarrassed at a reaction he would have expected from a teenager, he dived into the warm water of the pool and began swimming laps. Stroke after stroke, he knifed through the water, determined to push Melanie from his mind. With supreme concentration he counted his laps, losing track somewhere after thirty and not really caring. The water was refreshing, loosening his muscles, and he stopped only when he felt his ankle begin to throb. He glanced at the clock on the wall. Six-thirty. Nearly three hours had passed since she'd shown up. Surely she was long gone.

Dripping water across the aggregate floor, he snapped a clean towel from the closet and wiped his face. He was still breathing deeply, but at least his ridiculous state of sexual arousal had passed and he felt near exhaustion.

Towel drying his hair, he headed upstairs. The lodge was quiet and nearly dark. He'd go back to his room, change, then head into town for dinner.

With Melanie? a voice inside his head suggested.

"Not a chance." The only way he was safe from her was to keep his distance.

Melanie lost all track of time. Poring over the photographs of Ridge Lodge was fascinating. The old pictures created a visual and unique history of the lodge and Taylor's Crossing. She spent hours choosing those photographs she thought might enhance the brochure, and she'd had trouble deciding which shots she wanted to enlarge for the lobby and restaurant. She finally picked thirty pictures that had the right feel as well as clarity. She would let Rich and Gavin choose from these.

She should have quit then, but she picked up the second photograph album. The pages fell open to a picture of Gavin barely out of his teens, poised on the crest of a snow-covered hill. His face was tanned, his skin unlined, his hair blowing in the wind, his smile as brilliantly white as the snow surrounding him. She swallowed hard. She recognized the picture. She'd taken it herself on the upper slopes of Mount Prosperity.

Gavin had been an instructor at the time, paying for his skiing by earning his keep at the resort. And she'd spent every minute she could with him.

Her throat ached, and she pressed her lips together as she stared at the image. Memory after memory flashed in her mind, colliding in vital, soul-jarring images that she'd kept buried for eight years.

"Don't do this," she whispered, but she couldn't help herself and she slowly turned the pages, each slickly bound photograph a chronicle of Gavin's professional life. She saw pictures of breath-stoppingly steep runs, dazzling snow-covered canyons cut into narrow runs that sliced through the rugged slopes, and always Gavin, tucked tightly, skimming across the snow, throwing a wake of powder behind him.

And there were other photographs, as well: pictures of Gavin accepting awards or trophies or standing beside any number of gorgeous women, the most often photographed being Aimee LaRoux.

Melanie had composed herself and her heartbeat had nearly slowed to normal when she lifted the album and a single picture fluttered facedown to the table.

She flipped it over, and time seemed to stand still as she stared at a picture of herself with Gavin, laughing gaily into the camera. Seated at a booth near the huge fireplace in this very lodge, they snuggled together, their faces flushed from the last run of the day, their hair mussed, their eyes bright with love for each other. Gavin's arm was thrown carelessly across her shoulders, and he looked as if he had the world on a string. And he did. It was the night he'd learned that he was to train for the Olympic team.

Melanie took in a shuddering breath and released it slowly. "Oh, Lord," she whispered when she heard the creak of old floorboards and looked up to find Gavin standing woodenly in the doorway.

Wearing only swimming trunks and a towel looped casually around his neck, he didn't say a word. But his eyes were filled with a thousand questions.

She tried not to notice the corded muscles of his shoulders or the provocative way his golden hair swirled over his chest. Lowering her eyes, she noticed the thick, muscular thighs and a series of thin scars around his ankle.

"I thought you'd be gone," he finally said.

Oh, God, he'd caught her looking at the picture! Wishing she could slam the album shut, she forced her eyes upward again. He was already crossing the room, and his gaze was focused on the desk and the photograph still clutched in her fingers.

She searched for the right words, but they wouldn't form in her cotton-dry throat.

Stopping at the table, he stared at the photograph, and his lips curved down at the corners. "Reliving the past?" he growled.

"No, I—" She dropped the picture as if it were hot, then was instantly furious with herself for being so self-conscious. Inching her chin upward, she said, "It fell out of the album. I was just putting it back."

"Don't bother."

"Wh-what?"

"Just toss it."

To her horror, he snatched the picture from her fingers, crumpled it and dropped it into a wastebasket.

"No!" she cried, feeling as if a part of her past had just been wrenched from her soul.

"You want it?"

"No, but—"

"Then let's just leave it where it belongs, okay? It was just an oversight. I got rid of all those pictures a long time ago."

Inside, she was shaking. From rage? Or something else, a deeper, more primal emotion? She didn't know and she didn't care. But her voice was steady as she stood. "You can't just erase what happened between us, Gavin."

"*Nothing* happened."

"We loved each other."

"I thought you agreed we were just two kids fooling around."

"I lied."

His eyes narrowed. "Not the first time, is it?"

She sucked in her breath, feeling as if she'd been slapped. "I think I'd better go."

"Good idea."

She started gathering her things, picking out the photographs she needed and scooping them into a pocket of her case, but he grabbed her arm, forcing her to spin around and face him again.

She swallowed hard.

"Just explain one thing," he ground out.

"Name it."

"If you loved me," he said quietly, every feature on his face tense, "then why didn't you wait for me?"

"I didn't want to be a burden," she said quickly, thinking for a second that the truth was better than the lies they'd both been living with for years.

"A burden?"

"You had a future—a chance for a berth on an Olympic team. You didn't need a wife tying you down."

His eyes narrowed suspiciously and his nostrils flared, but his hard mouth relaxed slightly. "We could have waited until the Olympics were over and I had started my career."

She licked her lips. Could she tell him about the baby? Now, when honesty seemed so vital? Would he understand? Instinctively, she reached for his forearms, her fingers touching rock-hard muscles. "There's something else—"

But before she could finish, he lowered his head and his mouth slanted over hers in a kiss as familiar as a soft summer breeze. His arms surrounded her, crushing her against him. He tasted of chlorine and salt and whiskey, and she felt his thighs press intimately into the folds of her skirt.

She offered no resistance and kissed him back. Being held by him seemed so natural and right, and all the wasted years between then and now melted away. Once again she was seventeen, caught in the embrace of the man she loved.

Groaning, he shifted, his wet trunks dampening her dress, his fingers catching in the long strands of her hair. Her head lolled back, and her mouth opened to the insistent pressure of his tongue. Quick, moist touches of his tongue against the inside of her mouth caused her blood to boil, her knees to weaken.

He kissed her lips, her cheeks and her throat. Closing her eyes, she ignored the warning bells clanging wildly in her head. His touch was erotic, the hand against the small of her back moving deliciously.

"Melanie," he whispered hoarsely. With his weight, he lowered her to the floor and pinned her against the carpet. Still kissing her, he found the buttons of her blouse, and the thin fabric gave way to expose her breasts covered in lace.

Stop him! Stop him now! But when his palm glided over her breast, she could only moan and writhe as his fingers dipped beneath the lace, gently prodding, touching and withdrawing until her nipple strained tight against the bra and her breasts ached for more—so much more.

With agonizing slowness his tongue moved along her cheek and neck and rimmed the circle of bones at the base of her throat. Her own hands were busy touching and exploring the corded strength of his chest and the fine, furry mat of hair that covered suntanned skin. His shoulder muscles were hard as she reached around him, and her fingers dug into his back as he continued to kiss her, moving downward.

"Oh, Gavin," she cried as his mouth fit hot and wet over her nipple. His tongue touched her in supple, sure strokes that caused her blood to burn and wiped out any further thoughts she had of stopping him.

He suckled through the lace and moved one free hand to cup her buttocks, bringing her body so close to his that she could feel his thighs and hips straining against the fabric that separated him from her.

Lord, how she wanted him. Nothing else mattered but the smell, taste and feel of him.

Finally, he unhooked her bra; the lace gave way, and she felt cool air against her bare skin before his mouth covered one breast and teased and laved the taut nipple.

She cradled his head against her, wanting more, knowing that only he could fill the ache that was beginning to yearn deep inside.

"Oh, God," he whispered, drawing up and away from her, staring down at her dishabille and groaning low in his throat. He squeezed his eyes shut for a few heart-stopping moments, and when he finally lifted his eyelids again, the passion burning so brightly in his gaze had died. "What're you doing to me?"

He rolled away from her and sat with his back to her, his rigid arms supporting him as he drew in deep, ragged breaths. "Damn it, woman, why can't you just leave me alone?" His voice was rough, the hand he plowed through his hair trembling.

"I didn't start this, Gavin."

"Well, you sure as hell didn't stop it!"

Humiliated, Melanie sat up and started working on her clothes. "This wasn't my fault," she said, still buttoning her blouse.

"Wasn't it?" he flung back at her, glancing over his shoulder before pushing himself upright. His features twisted in pain for just a second as he strained his ankle.

"Of course not!" she declared hotly. "And I'm tired of you always throwing the blame at my feet!"

"Maybe that's where it belongs."

She swept in a long breath. "You really can be a bastard when you want to be."

"Yeah, well, you don't seem to mind sometimes," he threw back at her.

"Maybe that's because sometimes, when you're not trying out for boor of the year, you're wonderful."

He stopped, his eyes locking with hers. Time stood still. His throat worked, and his face gentled for just a second. Warring emotions strained his features. "You're dreaming! Living in a past that didn't exist!"

"Gavin—"

Swearing roundly under his breath, he hobbled toward the bookcase. He opened an upper cabinet, withdrew a bottle and glass, then poured himself a quick drink. "Why didn't you leave a couple of hours ago?" he asked suddenly. "What were you doing hanging around?"

"I wasn't finished sorting through the pictures."

He tossed back half his drink and stood rigidly near the windows. "Or you were waiting for me—because of that," he said, cocking his head toward the now ruined snapshot of the two of them.

"No, I just stumbled across it. But don't worry, I'm leaving now."

"Not quite yet," he said, slowly drawing the back of his hand across his mouth, as if he were wiping off excess whiskey—or the feel of her kiss.

Furious with him, she grabbed her camera bag and slung the strap over her shoulder.

Gavin set his unfinished drink on the window ledge and closed the distance between them. "There's something I have to know," he said quietly, though his anger was still evident in his uncompromising expression.

"It's too late for this discussion."

"Just one thing," he said again, his features set.

"What?"

"Why did you marry a bastard like Brooks?"

"It's none of your business," she lied.

"Like hell. Why, Melanie?" he thundered.

She slowly counted to ten. "There were reasons…." But they wouldn't come to mind. Melanie grappled with the truth, wishing she could just tell him about the baby they'd never shared.

"I'm waiting," he said, his voice low. "Was it because of his money, hmm? Is that what you found so attractive?"

"No!"

"God, I hope not," he muttered, shaking his head. "But I can't help wondering why you're hanging around here, lingering in my room, more than willing to seduce me."

"What?" she gasped. "I wasn't lingering and I had no intention of seducing anyone!"

"You could've left."

"I told you, I wasn't finished."

"Well, you are now."

"You got that right." She grabbed her purse and swung toward the door, but one of Gavin's arms snaked out and surrounded her waist.

"You haven't answered my question yet."

There was nothing she could say to change the past. With a sinking sensation, she realized that telling Gavin the truth about the baby would only increase the tension between them, making it impossible for her to work with him. "I don't think your question merits an answer."

"You walked out on me—"

"Correction, Gavin. You did the walking—or to be more precise, the skiing," she charged, unable to hide the bitterness in her tone. "You just skied your way out of my life and I fell in love with someone else."

The corners of his mouth twitched, as if he found her reason bordering on the ridiculous. "You loved Brooks? After me?"

"Yes!"

His eyes narrowed. "Save that for someone who'll believe it. You sold out, Melanie, to the almighty buck."

Without thinking, she slapped him with a smack that echoed through the room. Gavin's teeth set, and he clamped both hands over her arms. "Don't ever do that again."

"I'll try never to get that close!" Her voice shook with anger.

"Then you'd better stay out of my bedroom."

"You're what? Oh, God, Gavin, don't flatter yourself!"

His eyes blazed, and his fingers dug into her flesh. For a few seconds they glared at each other, breathing deeply, fury and other, more dangerous, emotions tangling between them.

Gavin sighed finally. "You make me crazy," he admitted.

"Same here. It's a bad combination."

Something flickered in his gaze, and then his mouth crashed down on hers. She wanted to fight him, to stop this insanity, but when his lips molded over hers intimately, she couldn't resist.

Closing her eyes, Melanie willed herself not to respond. Though her heart was thudding wildly, her blood on fire, she set her jaw and acted as if she could barely endure the kiss.

But Gavin didn't give up. His lips coaxed, his hands moved magically across her back, and at last she gave into her weak knees and leaned against him.

"Oh, God, Melanie, why do we always have to hurt each other?" he whispered raggedly.

"I don't know." Her heart felt as if it might break all over again. Slowly Gavin released her.

"I don't believe you ever loved Neil Brooks," he said quietly.

"It doesn't matter what you believe," she lied. Reaching behind her, she found the door handle and yanked it open. As quickly as her legs would carry her, she walked through the dark lodge and outside, where she took in deep breaths of fresh air.

Her legs were unsteady as she walked to her car, but she held her chin up and decided that Gavin Doel, damn his black-hearted soul, was going to be harder to deal with than she'd ever imagined.

She tried to start her car, flooded it and swore. Slowly counting to ten, she tried again. This time the old engine sputtered and caught. She didn't waste any time. Shoving the Volkswagen into first, she barely noticed the battered old pickup that pulled into the lot. She had other things on her mind.

"Oh, Melanie, don't be a fool," she told herself as she turned on her headlights, but she had the sinking sensation that she was falling in love with him all over again.

Gavin grabbed his drink, almost tossed it back but at the last second chucked the whiskey down the drain. He didn't usually drink—at least, not the way he had in the past few weeks. Having lived with an alcoholic father, he had always been careful with liquor.

Until he'd seen Melanie again. Just being with her, gazing into her intelligent eyes, seeing glimpses of her sense of humor, touching the slope of her jaw or burying his face into the clean scent of her hair, made him crazy.

"Get a grip on yourself," he said, knowing that alcohol didn't solve any problems. He twisted the cap on the bottle just as he heard footsteps in the outer lobby.

He froze. Melanie? Back? God, how was he ever going to keep his hands off her? He'd intended to kiss her to prove that he could kiss her without his emotions getting in the way, to prove that he really didn't care about her....

"Gavin?" a rough male voice called out.

"In here," he replied. So his old man had made it back to Taylor's Crossing. Ignoring his cane, Gavin crossed the room and held open the door, letting the light from his apartment spill into the hallway.

"Oh, there you are! This place is a goddamn maze!" Jim Doel, tall and gaunt, his hair snow-white, strode down the hallway to Gavin's apartment.

"It just takes awhile to get to know your way around."

Casting a critical eye on the rooms his son now called home, Jim took a seat on the raised hearth of the fireplace. "Quite a comedown from what you're used to, isn't it?"

"It's all right."

"And you're already fixin' it up. I saw the rigging." He rubbed his hands on the faded knees of his jeans.

"It should be finished by the time ski season opens."

"That's not so far away." Jim noticed the bottle of whiskey on the table and glanced meaningfully at Gavin. "I saw you had a visitor."

Gavin braced himself.

"That Walker girl still sniffin' around?"

"She's a photographer for the paper."

"So what was she doin' here so late?"

"Rich hired her to do some publicity for us. Brochures, maps, that sort of thing."

Jim raised an interested eyebrow. "And where is Rich?"

"In Portland."

"Convenient." Jim reached into his pocket for a pack of cigarettes.

"I think it'll work out."

"You thought that before," Jim observed. He lit up and clicked his lighter shut.

"What're you trying to say, Dad?"

"Nothin', nothin'." Jim drew hard on his cigarette. Gavin waited as his father blew smoke to the ceiling. "I'm just a little concerned, that's all. That girl hurt you once before."

"Water under the bridge," Gavin lied.

"Is it, now? I wonder. But then, I guess I don't have to point out to you that she didn't bother to wait for you when you took off for Colorado. No siree, she just up and married Neil Brooks within weeks after you left."

"What're you getting at?"

"That she's fickle, that one. Can't stick with one man. First you, then the minute you're gone, she puts the richest boy in town in her sights, marries him, then when she gets bored, divorces him. Now she's back here, making herself available because you're back in town—and now you're probably the richest man in town."

"Not by a long shot."

Jim shrugged. "Well, she does seem to be developin' a pattern, doesn't she?"

"What do you know about her marriage?"

"Nothin' except it was short. Six years or so, I think, and then she comes back when her dad gets sick." Jim's face grew tense. "I never did like old Adam Walker, you know. He never forgave me for what happened to his wife."

"That was a long time ago," Gavin said, hoping to ease some of his father's pain.

Jim sighed. "But it's something that will stick with me until the day I die." He cleared his throat and tossed his cigarette into the grate. "You don't know how many times I prayed I could've changed things."

"Probably just about as many times as I did," Gavin admitted.

Scowling, Jim looked his son straight in the eye. "Don't get mixed up with Melanie, son. She'll only hurt you again."

Gavin bristled. "I survived."

"If that's what you call it."

"Look, I can make my own decisions. Now tell me, what else is on your mind?"

"I thought maybe you'd give your old man a job." Seeing that Gavin was about to protest, he held up one hand. "Hey, you've been good to me. If it hadn't been for you, I probably never would've dried out. And for that I owe you, son, I owe you big. But I'm tired of being a charity case. This time I want a job—a real, bona fide job. I'm not old enough to be sent out to pasture yet, and I'm handy with a hammer and nails. What d'ya say?"

Chapter Eight

The next three weeks went by in a blur. Indian summer waned, and the air turned brisk and chilly. Gray clouds lingered over the Cascades, promising early snow.

Melanie barely had time to notice the change in the weather, let alone eat or sleep. When she wasn't at the newspaper office, she was working in her studio or at the lodge, where she tried to keep her distance from Gavin. She wasn't always successful.

Fortunately, he, too, was working day and night. They spoke to each other only when absolutely necessary. She dealt primarily with Rich Johanson, unless he was out of town, and somehow managed to keep her relationship with Gavin strictly professional.

She was friendly, businesslike and cheerful, hiding her innermost feelings. Gavin was cordial but reserved, and glared at her suspiciously whenever she seemed in a particularly good mood.

The tension hovered between them, gnawing at her insides while all the time she plastered a smile on her face.

She was lucky on one count. Gavin and Rich had no trouble agreeing on pictures for the brochure. When she showed them her favorite shots, they weeded out the ones that didn't fit their image of the resort.

Rich slipped the good shots he needed into an envelope and said he'd take them, along with the copy he'd written for the brochure, to a printer in Portland.

Gavin handed Melanie a sealed envelope with a check inside and said, "Good job."

The words sounded hollow, and Melanie, despite her fake smile, was miserable. She couldn't wait to get through the charade and regretted taking the job.

As for the resort, the renovation of Ridge Lodge was on schedule, and the parking lot, lodge and lifts teemed with construction workers. A handful of employees had already been hired for the operation of the lodge and lifts, and a chef, a doctor, building supervisor and an equipment manager were already on staff.

Jim Doel, who had recently returned to Taylor's Crossing, had been hired as a handyman, and Melanie had kept her distance from him as well as from his son. Though Jim never was openly hostile, Melanie sensed his animosity whenever she dealt with him. And she, too, hadn't resolved all her feelings toward him. As much as she wanted to rise above it, the simple fact was that he'd killed her mother and robbed her of a normal childhood. Maybe that was Adam Walker's fault. Her father had spent years bad-mouthing the man.

"So, how're things going up at the lodge?" Jan asked late one Friday afternoon as Melanie handed her some pictures of people gathered at a city council meeting in city hall.

"I think everything's on schedule."

"Good. I've got another interview with our friend Mr. Doel next week and I wanted to be prepared. If there's any trouble at the lodge, I'd like to know about it. But everything's okay, right?" Jan asked, perching on the corner of Melanie's desk.

"No trouble," Melanie replied, carrying the pictures to the layout editor's desk. "In fact, when you go up to the lodge, I think you'll be surprised how smoothly everything's running."

"Is it?" Jan's eyebrows drew together, and she made a point of studying her nails.

"Uh-huh. Looks as if the resort will be a huge success," Melanie added, wondering why she felt compelled to defend Gavin.

Constance, who had overheard the tail end of the conversation, made her way to the coffeepot and asked, "So, do you know who'll be invited to the grand opening?"

Jan mumbled, "I wish."

Melanie shook her head. "I haven't the foggiest. It's not as if I'm on the inside, you know. I'm just doing some freelance work for the resort."

Constance sighed. "I'd give my right arm for a look at that guest list."

"Why don't you just ask?"

"I have. I got Doel on the phone yesterday, but he told me very succinctly that it was none of my business. I just thought maybe you had some idea."

"Not a clue," Melanie replied.

"Well, I'm going up there Monday and I'll have a look around," Jan said, filled with confidence as usual. "Maybe I can convince Mr. Doel that a copy of the list would add public interest. He might just sell a few more lift tickets if people thought some celebrities were staying at the lodge."

"I wouldn't bet on getting anything more from him," Melanie said.

Constance agreed. Refilling her coffee cup, she said, "He's impossible. It's almost as if he resents the free publicity we're handing him."

"You were the one who pointed out that he was publicity shy," Melanie observed as Constance's phone jangled loudly from her desk.

With a dramatic sigh, Constance, said, "Jan, see what you can do." She hurried back to her desk. "Beg, borrow or steal that guest list."

"I doubt if I'll burglarize Gavin Doel's office all for the sake of a few names."

"Not just any names. We're talking names of the famous," Constance reminded her as the phone rang impatiently. "There's a difference. A big difference." Frowning, she picked up the receiver and plopped down at her desk, immediately absorbed in the conversation.

Jan turned her attention back to Melanie. "What do you think her chances are of getting the names of the invited?"

"From Gavin? Zero. From Rich Johanson?" Melanie lifted her hand and tilted it side to side. "About fifty-fifty."

Jan nodded. "Yeah, Johanson's always been more interested in publicity than Doel. And speaking of our local infamous professional skier, how're things going with you two?"

"Fine, I guess. We work together. That's it."

"That's it? Really?" Jan arched a skeptical brow. "Come on, Melanie, you can talk to me. I saw how he looked at you, and you said yourself that you'd been serious with him."

"I think I said I'd dated him."

"You said you were serious."

"Did I? Well, if I did, I meant I was serious for seventeen." Dear Lord, why had she ever brought it up?

"I know, but I read between the lines," Jan replied. "You two act as if you've never gotten over each other."

"That's ridiculous."

"Is it?"

"Of course it is," Melanie said, pretending to study an enlarged photograph of wheat fields to the south of town. "Gavin's not interested in me," she added tightly.

Jan laughed. "Yeah, right, and I'm the Queen of England! Don't try to convince me that you can't see the signs. That man is interested—whether he wants to be or not."

Melanie didn't comment and went back to work when Brian called Jan into his office.

The rest of the day she heard snatches of conversation in the office and most of it centered around Gavin. As she drove home, she wondered if there was any way to escape from him.

Unfortunately, Taylor's Crossing was a small town and Gavin was highly visible and extremely gossip-worthy. She heard about him and the lodge everywhere she went. And it didn't end when she stopped by her Uncle Bart's and Aunt Lila's house that evening.

"The weather service predicts snow in the mountains by Friday," Bart said, squinting through his kitchen window to the night-blackened sky. Melanie dropped into a chair near the table, and Bart followed suit. "That should be good news for Doel."

Melanie, tired of all the talk about Gavin, took a swallow from the steaming mug of coffee Aunt Lila handed her.

"Now, Bart," her aunt said, "you quit fishing."

"Is that what I'm doing?" Bart asked, one side of his mouth lifting at the corner.

"Of course it is. She's barely been here ten minutes and you've brought up Gavin twice."

Bart lifted a stockinged foot and placed it on an empty chair. "I was just making an observation about the weather."

"Sure."

"And it wouldn't kill me to know how Melanie and Gavin are doing working so close together."

"You're worse than a gossiping old woman," Lila muttered, but smiled good-naturedly.

"Oh, for God's sake, I am not. I'm just interested in Melanie's welfare, that's all."

"She's old enough to make her own decisions without any help from you."

Melanie couldn't help but grin. Lila's and Bart's lighthearted banter had always been a source of amusement to her, and since she'd lost her mother at a young age, Aunt Lila had stepped in and filled a very deep void. "Well, if you must know," Melanie said, deciding to end the speculation about Gavin once and for all, "Gavin and I get along all right. We don't see a lot of each other, though. I deal primarily with Rich Johanson."

"That stuffed shirt!" Bart muttered.

"He's okay," Melanie said. "In fact, I like him. He keeps Gavin in line."

Bart smoothed his white hair with the flat of his hand. His faded eyes twinkled. "Does he need keeping in line?"

"All the time," Melanie said.

"And I heard he hired his old man, too."

This was dangerous ground. Melanie felt her equilibrium slipping a little. "That's right. Jim does fix-it jobs for the resort—things that the general contractor didn't bid on, I guess."

"How long is he staying on?"

"I don't know," Melanie said honestly. "We don't talk much."

"I'll bet," Bart said. "But Gavin can't be all bad if he takes care of his kin."

For once Aunt Lila agreed. "He's helped Jim more than any son should have to." Then, as if realizing she'd said to much, she added, "You're staying for dinner, aren't you?"

Melanie finished her coffee. "Another time. I've got an appointment later tonight. Cynthia Anderson is coming over to choose some pictures I took of her boys a few weeks ago, but I had something I wanted to give you." She reached into her purse and pulled out a small package wrapped in tissue paper.

"What's this?" Bart asked as she handed it to him.

"Open it and see," Lila prodded.

Bart didn't need any further encouragement. He unfolded the paper and exposed a framed picture of himself and Big Money taken on the day of the fair over a month before. Bart was grinning proudly, while the nervous colt tugged hard on his lead and tried to rear.

"Why, Melanie," Bart whispered, touched, "you didn't need to—"

"I know, but I wanted to. This was my favorite shot, but my editor preferred the one that ended up in the paper. I picked it out weeks ago, but it took a while to find the right frame."

"I have just the place for this," Lila said, eyeing the picture lovingly. "Oh, Melanie, thank you."

Melanie felt a lump in her throat as she finished her coffee and pushed back her chair. "You're welcome. Now I'd better run home before the Anderson boys show up and terrorize Sassafras."

Uncle Bart walked with her out the back door. Rain had started to fall, but the temperature had dropped. Goose bumps rose on Melanie's arms.

"Despite what your aunt said in there," Bart said, squaring an old Stetson on his head, "you know she thinks the world of Gavin. He used to do odd jobs around here, you know, and Lila's pretty soft where he's concerned."

Melanie eyed him in the darkness. "You already told me I should be chasing after him."

"I didn't say that." Bart's teeth flashed and his breath fogged. "But if he decides to do the chasing, I wouldn't run too fast if I were you."

"I'll remember that," she said dryly as she slid into the car.

Bart slammed the door shut for her, then paused on the step to light a cigarette. Melanie waved as she drove away. So now everyone thought she should try to start a new romance with Gavin. Jan, Uncle Bart and even Aunt Lila. It was enough to make a body sick.

And yet, falling in love with Gavin again held a distinct appeal. "You're hopeless," she told herself as she wheeled into her driveway and recognized Cynthia Anderson's gray van parked in front of the house. "And you're late."

As she climbed out of her own car, the side door of the van flew open and the boisterous Anderson brood, dressed in blue and white soccer outfits, scrambled out.

Cynthia herded them toward the front porch. "I know I didn't say anything when I made this appointment," she said quickly, "but do you have time to take a couple of shots of them in their soccer gear?"

Groaning inwardly, Melanie nodded. "I suppose."

"Good, good. Because Gerald would just love a picture of them like this—oh, but, boys, we mustn't tell Daddy, okay? It'll be a surprise. For Christmas."

Melanie wondered how the four boys could keep a secret for ten minutes let alone nearly two months. "Let's get started."

"Oh, thanks, Melanie," Cynthia said, whipping her comb from her purse and pouncing on the youngest one. "Okay, Tim, hold still while I fix your hair."

"No!" the boy howled. "No, no, no!"

"Aw, knock it off, Mom," Sean, the oldest, chided. "We look good enough. Besides, I'm freezin' my tail off out here. Let's go inside!"

Steeling herself, Melanie opened the front door, the boys thundered down the hall and Sassafras bolted outside, splashing through puddles as he headed around the corner of the house.

Melanie followed the Andersons through the door and hung her coat on the hall tree near the stairs. She didn't have time to think about Gavin for the rest of the evening.

The first snow arrived on Saturday in early November. Large powdery flakes, driven by gusty winds, fell from a leaden sky. Storm warnings had been posted, but Melanie decided to chance the storm, hoping that it would hold off for a few hours. She tossed her chains into her car and carefully placed five huge portfolios in her car.

The drive was tedious. Already tired from spending most of the previous night putting the finishing touches on the sepia-toned prints, she was anxious to take the pictures to the lodge and finish that part of her employment.

Because you want to see Gavin again, her mind tormented, but she pushed that unpleasant thought aside and ignored the fact that her heart was beating much too quickly as she drove through a fine layer of snow to Mount Prosperity.

Aside from half a dozen cars and a few trucks marked Gamble Construction and the snowplow, the freshly plowed parking lot was relatively empty.

Melanie drove straight to the lodge, and because she wanted to protect the prints as well as her car, she pulled into a parking shed that connected with the side entrance to the lodge. Grabbing her largest portfolio, she steeled herself for another cool meeting with Gavin. *You can handle this,* she told herself as she trudged up the stairs and opened the door.

Inside, the lodge was quiet. The screaming saws, pounding hammers and country music were gone. Only the few workers finishing the molding remained.

Most of the renovation was complete. The high wood ceilings had been polished, the oak floors refinished and new recessed lighting installed in the lobby and bar. Two snack bars boasted gleaming new equipment, and the restaurant had been recarpeted.

Fresh paint gleamed, and new blinds were fitted to the windows. An Oriental rug had been stretched in front of the fireplace, and several couches and lamps had been placed strategically around the room.

Melanie propped her portfolio against a post and eyed the renovations. Tugging off her gloves, she walked over to the bar to admire the polished, inlaid brass.

"Something I can do for you?"

She nearly jumped out of her skin at the sound of Jim Doel's voice. She whipped around. Tall and lined, Jim settled a cap on his head and waited, his face tense, his eyes never wavering.

She and Gavin's father had never gotten along. Working at the lodge together hadn't made things any easier. She pointed to her portfolio. "I'm here to meet Rich. I have those old pictures he was interested in."

"He's busy."

"Then Gavin."

The older man's lips tightened. "He's busy, too."

"Are they here?"

Nodding, he motioned toward the back of the lodge. "Got some bigwigs with them. Don't know when they'll be through."

"It's okay," she said, forcing a smile. "I'll wait in the north wing."

"It may be awhile."

"I've got plenty of time," she replied, not letting him dissuade her. Jim Doel had never said why he didn't like her, but she assumed it was a combination of feelings—guilt for the death of her mother and anger that she, at least in Gavin's father's opinion, had betrayed his only son. He'd never know the truth, so she would have to get used to his glacial glances and furrowed frowns until she was finished with her job here.

Inching her chin up a fraction, she hauled her heavy portfolio off the floor and said, "Please let Rich know where he can find me."

Jim nodded grudgingly, and Melanie, rather than ask for his help, made two more trips to the car to pick up the bulky pictures. It took nearly half an hour to carry them into the north wing, and as she paused to catch her breath on her final trip, she heard the sound of voices coming from the banquet room.

The door was ajar, and her curiosity got the better of her. She looked into the crack and caught a glimpse of several men, all dressed in crisp business suits, clustered around the huge, round table. Smoke rose in a gentle cloud to the ceiling.

Gavin sat across from the door, and he looked bored to tears. His hair was combed neatly and he was wearing a blue suit, but his gaze lacked its usual life and he tugged at his tie and stuck his fingers under his collar.

Melanie couldn't help but grin. Where were the beat-up leather jacket and aviator glasses? she wondered, wishing she dared linger and watch him a little longer. She'd never thought of him as an entrepreneur, and she found it amusing to catch a glimpse of him in a starched white shirt and crisp tie, dealing with lawyers or accountants or investors or whoever the other men happened to be.

She made her way to the end of the hall and the north wing. As wide as the lodge itself, the huge room was vacant, aside from some chairs stacked in a corner and a few bifold tables shoved against the windows.

Melanie shrugged out of her coat, then began setting out the photographs that she'd selected for the sepia-colored pictures that were to decorate the main lobby. There were pictures of miners with pickaxes, wagon trains and mule teams, crusty old-timers panning for gold and younger men gathered around a mine shaft. There was a shot of a steaming locomotive and another of a nineteenth-century picnic by a river. She laid them out carefully, proud of her work.

She didn't hear Gavin walk into the room, nor did she notice when he stopped short and sucked in his breath.

Gavin hadn't expected to find her here, leaning over the table, her hips thrust in his direction and her black glossy hair braided into a rope that was pinned tightly to the back of her head.

Her lips were pursed, her eyebrows knitted in concentration, and her hips, beneath her denim skirt, shifted seductively as she arranged photograph after photograph on the table.

As if feeling the weight of his gaze, she glanced over her shoulder, and for a fleeting second her eyes warmed and her lips moved into a ghost of a smile.

Gavin's breath caught in his lungs for a heart-stopping moment, and he had trouble finding his voice. "Are you waiting for Rich?"

He noticed her shoulders tighten. Turning, she eyed him suspiciously. "Isn't he here?"

"Not now. He had business in Portland."

Her lips turned down. "But I just saw him—"

"I know. He got a call. There's some emergency with a case of his. He just took off."

"Well, that's great," Melanie said, motioning to the windows. "I hoped to get out of here before the storm really hit."

"What's keeping you?" he baited, and saw a spark flash in her eyes.

"My job. We have a contract, remember?"

"Rich's idea."

"Well, it doesn't matter whose idea it was, does it? Because, like it or not, you and I are stuck with it!"

"You could always leave," he suggested, and the look she shot him was positively murderous.

"I came here to do a job, Gavin, and I intend to finish it. The sooner it's done, the sooner I'm out of here." She placed her hands on her hips.

"Then let's get to it."

"Okay, first you need to figure out exactly where you want these hung. For what it's worth, I think you should hang them in chronological sequence...." Impatiently he listened as she explained about each of the pictures and how each shot had a particular meaning to the forty-niner theme of the lodge. Though she spoke with enthusiasm, he had trouble concentrating and was constantly distracted by the slope of her cheek, the way her teeth flashed as she spoke, or how her sweater stretched across her breasts.

"...and that picnic, it's my favorite," she was saying. "It took place at the base of Mount Prosperity sometime in the eighteen-eighties, I think, much later than forty-nine, but it still has a certain flavor...." Her voice drifted off, and her face angled up to his. "You haven't heard a word I've said, have you?" she charged, lips pursing angrily.

"Does it matter?"

Her eyes flashed. "No, I suppose it doesn't. I just thought since you were the owner of this place, you might be interested. I guess I was wrong."

"Go on," he suggested. His thoughts had taken him far from the photographs on the table. He knew that he and Melanie were virtually alone in the lodge. Rich had left with the accountant and investors, the workers had the day off, the carpenters who had come in were now gone, and even his father, after gruffly announcing that someone was waiting for Rich in the north wing, had left the premises.

Vexed, she placed her hands on her hips and tilted her head to the ceiling. "I don't know why I try," she muttered as if conversing with the rafters in the vault high overhead.

Gavin motioned impatiently at the table. "Look, they're all fine. You just tell me where to hang them and we'll do it."

"You and me?" she asked.

He felt one side of his lip curve up. "Face it, Melanie, we're stuck with each other."

She paled slightly. "But you're still laid up—"

"My ankle's fine."

"And you don't mind risking breaking it by falling off a ladder?" she said, sarcasm tainting her words.

"Won't happen," he replied, noticing how anger intensified the streaks of jade in her eyes. "Just give me a minute to change."

She didn't have time to protest. He dashed off, leaving her with the photographs. *Don't argue with him,* she told herself. *Take advantage of his good mood.* But she glanced through the windows to see the snow begin to drift around the lodge. Most of the mountain was now obscured from her view. They'd have to work fast. The railing of the deck showed three inches of new snow, and the wind had begun to pick up. Maybe she should just forget this and come back when the storm had passed.

Not yet, she decided. She had too much to do to let a little snow bother her. She'd grown up around here and she knew how to drive in the snow. She'd be fine. She hazarded another glance outside and decided she didn't have any time to lose.

By the time she'd hauled the photographs back to the main lobby, placing each matted print on the floor near the appropriate wall space, Gavin reappeared, tucking the tail of his blue cambric shirt into faded jeans. He strode quickly, without the use of a cane, to the huge fireplace on the far wall. Bending on one knee, he began stacking logs on the huge grate.

"Do we really need a fire?" she asked, glancing at her watch.

"Probably not."

"It'll go to waste."

Ignoring her, he struck a match. The dry kindling ignited quickly, sizzling and popping as yellow flames discovered moss-laden oak. His injury didn't seem to bother him, and when he straightened and surveyed his work, he nodded to himself.

"Now that we're all cozy," she mocked, hoping to sound put out, "let's get started."

"You're the boss," he quipped, gesturing to the stack of prints she had started positioning around the main lobby.

"Remember that," she teased back.

"Always." His eyelids dropped a little, and Melanie's breath caught in her throat as he stared at her.

Clearing her throat, she pointed to a picture of a grizzly old miner and two burros. "You can start with this one," she said. "It should go near the door. And then, I think, the picture of the locomotive on the trestle. Next the mine shaft..." She walked around the large, cavernous room, shuffling and reshuffling the prints. Gavin was with her every step of the way, and her nerves were stretched tight. She felt the weight of his gaze, smelled the musky scent of his after-shave and saw the set angle of his jaw. *Dear God, let me get through this.*

When she finally decided on the placement of each picture, he took off in search of a ladder. Melanie sank against the windows and felt the cold panes against her back. *Just a few more hours.* She glanced anxiously through the window and noticed the storm had turned worse. The higher branches of the pines surrounding the lodge danced wildly in the wind, and the snow was blowing in sheets.

When Gavin returned with the ladder, his face was grim. "I just listened to the weather report," he informed her. "The storm isn't going to let up for hours."

Melanie's heart sank. Nervously, she shoved her bangs from her eyes. "Then I should leave now."

"No way."

"What?" She looked up sharply.

"It's nearly a whiteout, Mel. Winds are being measured at over forty miles an hour. I'm not going to let you leave until it's safe."

"It's safe now. Not that you have a whole lot of say in the matter."

"Just wait. We've got a lot of work to do. Maybe by the time we're done, the winds will have died down."

"Is that what the weather service said?"

Tiny brackets surrounded his mouth, and he shook his head. "Afraid not. In fact, they predict it'll last through the night."

"Then I've got to leave now!"

"Hold on," he said firmly, one hand clamping over her arm. "If there's a lull, I'll drive you out of here in one of the trucks with four-wheel drive."

"I've got my car here. I'll—"

"You'll stay put!" he said, his eyes gleaming with determination. "Until it's safe."

"Oh, so now you're the one giving orders."

"While you're up here in my lodge, you're my responsibility," he said quietly.

"I'm my own person. I don't need you or anyone else telling me what to do!"

A muscle worked in his jaw. "Then use your head, Melanie. You know how dangerous a storm like this can be. Just wait it out. We can finish here."

"And then what?"

"I don't know," he admitted, "but at least you won't be in the ditch somewhere, freezing to death!"

"No, I'll just be suffocating in here while you keep ordering me around."

He couldn't help but smile. "Is that what I'm doing?"

"Damn right!"

He laughed then, and Melanie was taken aback at the richness of the sound. "So be it," he muttered. "Now, come on, quit complaining and let's get to work."

She hated to knuckle under to him, but the thought of driving out in a near blizzard wasn't all that inviting. "All right," she finally agreed, "but I'm leaving the minute the winds die down."

He didn't comment, just started up the ladder. She was afraid his ankle wouldn't support him, but he didn't once lose his balance, and slowly, as they hung picture after picture, the rust-tone prints began to add flavor to the lobby.

As she watched him adjust a picture of oxen pulling a covered wagon, she noticed how quiet the lodge had become. The only sounds were the scrape of the ladder, their soft conversation and the whistle of the wind outside. "Where is everyone?" she asked.

"Gone." he replied, glancing down at her from the top of the ladder.

"Gone?"

"That's right. We're here all alone. Just you and me."

He was still staring down at her as she shifted uncomfortably from one foot to the other.

"Does that bother you?" he asked, one foot lower on the ladder than the other, his denim-clad legs at her eye level.

"No," she lied. "Why should it? As long as I've got one self-centered egotistical male bossing me around, I'm happy as a clam."

"Good." Gavin struggled to keep from smiling. He stepped up, and she tried not to watch the way his buttocks moved beneath the tight denim. "I figured the sooner this was done—"

"The sooner I'd be out of your hair."

He made a disgusted sound. "I was going to say, the sooner you'd be happy. If that's possible."

She didn't bother responding. And she tried to drag her gaze away from him to keep from noticing the way his shirt pulled across his broad shoulders and the lean lines of his waist as he reached upward. His hips, too, under tight jeans, moved easily as he shifted his weight from one rung to the next.

Without warning, the lights in the lodge flickered.

Gavin froze on the ladder. "What's going on..." But before he could say anything else, the only illumination in the entire building came from the fireplace. "Son of a bitch!" He shoved his hands through his hair, then climbed down the final rungs of the ladder. "Stay here," he ordered. "We've got an emergency generator, but I don't think it's operational yet." He started down the hall, his footsteps echoing through the huge old building.

Melanie watched him disappear into the darkness, then walked anxiously to a window. Snow, driven by a gusty wind, fell from the black sky to blanket the mountain. It peppered against the window in icy flakes.

Now what? she wondered, shivering. Rubbing her arms, she walked back to the fireplace and checked her watch in the firelight. Gavin had been gone nearly fifteen minutes.

The old empty lodge seemed larger in the darkness. The windows rose to cathedral spires and reflected gold in the firelight, and the ceilings were so high overhead they were lost in the darkness.

She heard the clip of Gavin's footsteps and saw the bob of a flashlight. "Well, so much for the generator," he said, his lips thin in frustration.

"What's wrong with it?"

"Nothing that some new parts won't fix, but that's not the bad news. We have a ham radio in the back, and I listened for a few minutes while I found these." He held up several kerosene lamps and a couple of flashlights. "The storm is worse than they expected. High winds have knocked down power poles and some of the roads are impassable."

With a mounting sense of dread, Melanie said, "Then I'd better leave now, before things get worse."

"Too late," he replied. "The road to the lodge is closed. I called the highway department. A falling tree took out several electricity poles and has the road blocked. This storm is more than the electric company can handle right now. The sheriff's department and state police are asking everyone to stay inside. The weather service now seems to think that this storm won't let up until sometime tomorrow at the earliest."

Her stomach dropped. "You mean—"

"I mean it looks like you and I are stuck here for the night, maybe longer."

"But I can't be. I've got work and my dog's locked in the house and..." Her voice drifted off as she saw the glint of determination in his eyes.

"You're staying here, Melanie," he said, his voice edged in steel. "You don't have any choice."

Chapter Nine

"I can't spend the night here," Melanie stated, stunned. "That's a crazy idea."

"You have a better one?" Anger crept into his voice. So he didn't like the arrangements any better than she did. Good.

"No, but—"

"I don't have time to stand around and argue with you. Since we don't have any power, I've got to make sure that the pipes don't freeze, that the building is secure and that you and I find a way to keep warm tonight!"

"But—"

"Listen, Melanie, we just have to accept this," he said, his fingers gripping her shoulder.

"I can't."

He muttered an oath. "Can I count on you to help me, or are you going to spend the rest of the night complaining?"

She started to argue but clamped her mouth shut.

"That's better."

"I just want to go on record as being opposed to this."

"Fine. Consider it duly recorded. Now let's get on to business, okay?"

Ignoring the hackles rising on the back of her neck, she silently counted to ten. He did have a point, she grudgingly admitted to herself. There wasn't much she could do but make the best of the situation. Even if it killed her. "Okay," she finally agreed. "Let's start by being practical. Are the phone lines still working?"

"They were fifteen minutes ago."

"Good." She pushed her hair from her face and ignored the fact that he was staring at her. "I need to call someone to check on Sassafras and I'd better let Bart and Lila know where I am."

"You sure that's a good idea?" he asked, his face a hard mask.

She bristled. "Would you rather they send out a search party? No one knows I'm up here, and believe me, I'd like to keep it that way, but I can't."

Gavin crossed to the bar, yanked the phone from underneath and slammed it onto the polished mahogany. "Suit yourself."

Ignoring his black temper, Melanie picked up the receiver and dialed. "Come on, come on," she whispered as the phone rang and Gavin, blast him, stared at her in the mirror's reflection. Finally Aunt Lila picked up on the sixth ring.

"Mellie!" the older woman exclaimed, her voice crackly with the bad connection. "I was worried to death! Bart went over to check on you and brought Sassafras over here, but we didn't know where you were."

Melanie squirmed. She caught Gavin's tawny gaze in the mirror and turned her back on his image. "I brought the photographs for the lodge up to the resort," she said, trying to concentrate on anything other than the man glowering at her in the glass. Quickly, she explained how she'd lost track of time and the storm had turned so wild. "I just should have paid more attention and left before it got so bad outside."

"Well, thank goodness you're safe. Now, you just stay put until the roads are clear."

"That could be several days," Melanie said.

"I know, but at least you're safe."

Safe? Melanie doubted it. She cast a sidelong glance at Gavin. His features were pulled into a thoughtful scowl, his lips thin.

She hung up and let out a long breath. "Okay, get a grip on yourself," she muttered.

"What?"

She shook her head. "Nothing."

He was standing at the end of the bar, lighting the wicks of several kerosene lanterns. He glanced up at her and nearly burned his fingers. "That's the first sign that you're losing it."

"I always talk to myself."

"I know," he said quietly. "I remember." He looked up at her again, his eyes warm in the firelight, the angles of his face highlighted by the flame of the lantern. Melanie's heart turned over, and she looked away quickly, before her gaze betrayed her.

He cleared his throat. "I'll go check on the pipes and you can see if there's anything for us to eat in the kitchen."

"Is that what I'm reduced to—cook?"

Gavin smiled. "Gee, and I figured that was a promotion."

"You're the most insufferable—"

"I've heard it all before," he said, striding down the hall.

"Cook, eh?" Indignantly, she grabbed a lantern and headed past the bar to the restaurant and the kitchen beyond.

Stainless steel gleamed in the light of the lantern. The refrigerators, freezers and pantry weren't completely stocked for the season, but there were enough staples to get through several meals. They might not dine on gourmet cuisine, but they wouldn't starve. And if she didn't decide to poison Gavin, he might be in for a rude awakening!

She found a Thermos and saved the rest of the coffee, then pulled a bottle of wine from the wine cellar. *This is dangerous,* she thought, eyeing the bottle of claret. Wine had been known to go to her head, and tonight, she knew instinctively, she should keep her wits about her. But what the hell? She intended to show Gavin up, and if a little claret could help, why not?

She couldn't resist the temptation and placed the wine and Thermos on a serving cart along with a huge copper-bottomed pot and some utensils.

Water presented another problem. Without electricity, the pumps wouldn't work. No problem, Melanie thought, refusing to come up with any excuses. She'd prove to Gavin that she could bloody well take care of herself—and him, if need be!

Melanie threw on her jacket and gloves and braved the elements long enough to scoop up snow in several huge soup kettles. She gritted her teeth against the wind that ripped through her clothes and pressed icy snowflakes against her cheeks. Even through her gloves, her fingers felt frozen as she lugged the filled kettles into the kitchen and placed them on the cart.

She pushed the cart to the lobby and placed the kettles in the huge fireplace, then headed back to the kitchen, where she grabbed spices, bouillon mix, tomato juice and all the vegetables she could find. Thinking ahead, she added bowls, utensils and a loaf of bread. She'd never considered herself a great cook—in fact, Neil had thought she was "hopeless," but she figured, as she shoved the cart back to the lobby, it really didn't matter. Haute cuisine wasn't the issue. Survival was—and, of course, showing Gavin up.

Once she was back in the lobby, she poured the juice into a huge pot, added bouillon and canned vegetables, then peeled and cut potatoes. She tossed the thick chunks into the simmering mixture and kept warm by staying close to the fire.

When Gavin returned half-frozen an hour later, he was greeted by the scent of hot soup heating on the grate. Candles and lanterns flickered on nearby tables.

He brushed the snow from the shoulders of his sheepskin jacket, then warmed his hands by the fire. His eyes narrowed at the sight of the simmering pots. "What's this?"

"Oh, just a little something I whipped up," she tossed back.

"Sure."

He lifted a lid, and scented steam rose to greet the suspicious expression on his face. "You outdid yourself."

"I just aim to please, sir," she replied, smiling falsely.

"Okay, Melanie—what's up?"

"Oh, Mr. Doel, sir, I hope you're pleased," she said, her lips twitching at the way his eyebrows drew together. Served him right! "Here, take this." She handed him a cup of coffee, and he wrapped his chilled fingers around the warm ceramic and sipped. "What's your game, Melanie?"

"Game? No game."

"Oh, sure. Right."

She couldn't keep a straight face. "I just got tired of you barking commands at me and telling me what to do."

"As if you've ever listened." He frowned into his cup.

"I listen."

One of his brows lifted skeptically. "You do a lot of things, Melanie. And," he acknowledged, pointing to the kettles in the fire, "most of them very well. But listening isn't high on the list."

"And how would you know?"

"I remember more than the mere fact that you talk to yourself, Melanie." He paused, looking deep into her eyes. "In fact, I remember too much."

Her throat suddenly started to ache. She swallowed hard and whispered, "We'd better eat now."

Ladling the soup into bowls, she tried to ignore him. But she saw the snowflakes melting in his hair, the nervous way one fist clenched and opened, the manner in which he tugged thoughtfully on his full lower lip.

They ate in silence, both lost in their own thoughts as they sat on the floor in front of the fire. Melanie pretended interest in her soup and coffee, wishing she was anywhere but here, alone with the one man who could ignite her temper with a single word, the man who could turn her inside out with a mere look.

It's only for a few hours, she told herself, but the wind continued to moan and mock her.

It seemed to take her forever to finish her soup. She set her bowl aside, then, sipping her coffee, slid a glance at Gavin from the corner of her eye. She wondered what would have happened if, all those years ago, she'd told him the truth about the baby, if they had married, if their child had survived....

"What's this?" he asked, spying the bottle of claret for the first time.

"A mistake," she said.

"Oh?" He picked the bottle up by its neck, found the cork on the cart and slid her a knowing look. "Don't tell me, you were planning to get me tipsy, then, when I wasn't thinking properly, you were going to strip off all my clothes and have your way with me."

Blanching, she could barely speak. But when she found her tongue, she threw back at him, "Sure. That's exactly what I planned. Right after we both took a midnight swim in the pool, then ran naked through the blizzard."

His eyes darkened, and her throat closed. "There are worse fantasies."

"That's not my fantasy!"

"Isn't it?"

"Oh, Gavin, you're giving yourself way too much credit."

"Am I?"

"Yes!" she cried, the sound strangled. *Don't let him get to you,* she told herself, but couldn't stop the knocking of her heart.

"If you say so."

Good Lord, was there ever a more maddening man born?

He poured them each a glass of wine, then clicked the rim of his to hers. "To blizzards," he mocked.

She laughed. "Blizzards?"

"And running naked through the snow."

Melanie's pulse leaped, but she tried to appear calm. "Right. And running naked through the snow."

His mouth twisted wryly, but his eyes gleamed, and as he swallowed his wine, Melanie couldn't help but notice the way his throat worked.

The fire hissed and popped as a chunk of wood split. Outside, the storm raged, and Melanie, drinking slowly, caught alone in the lodge with Gavin, found that life outside the lodge seemed remote.

Don't let the night get to you.... But Gavin was so close, pouring more of the clear red claret, his hand touching hers as he steadied her glass, his gaze lingering on her mouth as she licked a drop on her lips. She remembered him as he used to be—so loving and kind. Their love had been simple and pure . . . and doomed.

"It's been a long time," he said quietly, his brows beetling, his thoughts apparently taking the same path as hers.

"We were children."

He shook his head. "I don't think so." His eyes held hers, and in that instant, she knew he intended to kiss her.

"Gavin, I don't—"

His mouth silenced the rest of her words, and her blood heated slowly. He tasted of wine, and the feelings he evoked were as violent as they had been years before. A thrill of excitement crept up her spine. Her heart began to pound, and she parted her lips willingly, moving close to him, feeling the contour of his body against hers.

"You don't what?" he asked, lifting his head and regarding her with slumberous golden eyes.

"I don't want to make love to you."

"Good. Because I don't want to make love to you." But his lips found hers again, and she yielded.

Gentle at first but more insistent as he felt her respond, his mouth moved over hers. Melanie's blood burned like wildfire as he clasped a hand around her neck, lacing his fingers in the loose knot pinned to the back of her head.

His heart thudded a rapid cadence, matched only by her own. She felt the pins slip from her hair, one by one, to fall on the floor as his kiss intensified and his tongue slipped familiarly through her teeth.

His weight carried them both to the carpet in front of the fire. Melanie's breasts pressed against the hard wall of his chest, and her arms circled his neck.

"Melanie," he whispered against the shell of her ear, and she shivered in anticipation. He pulled the final pin from her hair, and her thick braid fell over her shoulder.

Gavin touched the dark curls, his fingers grazing her breast. Beneath her sweater her nipples grew taut, and heat began to swirl deep inside.

Melanie knew the wine was going to her head, and even worse, the intoxication of being close to him was creating havoc with her self-control. She should stop him now, while she could still think, but the words couldn't fight their way past her tongue.

When he reached beneath her sweater and his hand touched her skin, the same old warning bells went off in her mind, but she didn't listen.

Instead she moaned and curved her spine, fitting herself perfectly against him. His breathing grew ragged as he lifted the sweater from over her head and gazed down at her.

"This is crazy," he muttered, as if his self-control, too, had been stripped from him.

He placed the flat of his hand between her breasts, his long, warm fingers feeling her heartbeat. His eyes closed for a second. "I want you, Melanie," he said, as if the words caused him pain. "I want you as much as I've ever wanted a woman."

Melanie's throat went dry. She didn't want to hear about his other women. This wasn't the moment for confession. "Shh...."

"But this could be dangerous."

More than dangerous, she thought, gazing up at his powerful features and focusing on the sensual line of his lips held tight with failing self-restraint. Making love to him was an emotional maelstrom. "I—I know."

"I wouldn't want to hurt you."

"Hurt me?"

"By getting you pregnant."

Tears threatened the corners of her eyes. "It's okay...."

"You're safe?"

"Neil and I couldn't have children."

He stared down at her for a long second.

Her throat ached, and she blinked as he lowered his head and kissed her with all the passion that had fired his blood years before.

Melanie lifted her hands, her fingers nimbly unbuttoning his shirt, her hands impatient as she shoved the fabric over his shoulders. In the glow from the fire, his skin took on a golden hue.

Her fingers swirled around his nipple, and he sucked in his breath, his abdomen concaving, his muscles a sexy washboard beneath his tight skin. Sweat dotted his brow, and she wondered vaguely if he was arguing with himself, listening to voices of denial screaming in his head.

She touched his waistband, and his eyes leaped with an inner fire. "Oh, God, you always could make me go out of my mind." Then his lips crashed down on hers, and gone was any trace of hesitation. His tongue pushed into her mouth, parrying and thrusting, exploring and claiming.

Melanie wrapped her arms around him, felt the fluid movement of his muscles as he shifted, lowering his lips down the slope of her cheeks, brushing across her skin. He kissed her eyes, her cheeks, her ears and lower, to her neck and the small circle of bones at her throat. His tongue tickled the pulse that was thundering in that hollow, and one hand moved in delicious circles on her abdomen.

Her breasts ached, and she moved impatiently.

"Slow down, Mel," he whispered hoarsely. "We've got all night."

His promise should have been a final signal for her to stop, before it was too late. But Melanie was well past turning back. And when he slid the strap of her bra over her shoulder, she moaned, her nipples strained upward, and he stared down at her. "God, I missed you," he admitted as he tugged on the ribbon and her breast spilled out of its lacy bonds, the dark nipple puckering under his perusal.

He touched a finger to his tongue, then to her breast. Melanie writhed at the sweet torture, wanting more, aching deep inside as he cupped her breast and kissed the hard nipple.

His tongue caressed her as his mouth closed over her. His arms wrapped around her torso, and his fingers splayed across the small of her back, pulling her urgently against him.

He kissed her again. Melanie exploded in her mind, memories of love and trust, passion and promises.

Quickly, he removed her bra and skirt, then kicked off his jeans and lay next to her, his naked body, bronze in the firelight, pressed intimately to hers. No words were spoken as he lay upon her, finding a path he'd forged long ago. Their bodies joined and fit, moving rhythmically, heating together, fusing into one.

Melanie gazed up at him, and her heart, pounding a thousand times a minute, swelled. His tempo increased, and she dug her fingers into the sleek muscles of his back, her body arching, her mind spinning out of control.

"Melanie, oh, Melanie," he cried hoarsely.

The earth shattered into a million fragments of light.

He collapsed against her, and she clung to him, holding on to this special moment, feeling his weight as a welcome burden as afterglow enveloped them.

I love you stuck in her throat, but she didn't say the words, nor did she hear them. The only sounds in the darkness were the gentle hiss of the fire and the moan of the wind outside.

When he finally rose on one elbow, looking down at her through warm tawny eyes, one side of his mouth lifted and white teeth flashed against his skin. "You know," he said, tracing the slope of her jaw with one finger, "I think we'd better go."

"Go? But I thought we had to stay here," she said dazedly. Shoving her hair from her eyes, she wondered what she was doing here, naked, still feeling the warmth of afterglow invade her.

"To my suite." He glanced to the shadowed rafters and sighed. "There's no way I can keep this room warm—not until the power comes back on. There's just too much space. But we'd be warm in my room."

And in your bed, Melanie thought. The thought of sleeping with Gavin, waking up in his arms, was inviting—but dangerous. Falling victim to him spontaneously was one thing; making love to him again was just plain foolish. "I don't think this is such a good idea."

"I know it isn't, but I'll be damned if I'm going to sleep alone tonight. We'd both freeze."

"Oh, so this is just a matter of convenience."

"No—pleasure."

"Stop this," she cried as he started to carry her. "Gavin, your leg!"

"My leg's fine."

"No, I mean it." She started to squirm out of his arms, then realized that she was probably doing more damage than good. "I'm perfectly capable of walking."

He chuckled deep in his throat. "Believe me, I'm not underestimating your capabilities."

"And I could carry things."

"We don't need anything."

"But the flashlight and the lanterns—"

"Unnecessary," he replied, carrying her down the dark hallway without once stumbling. He kicked open the door to his room. Red embers glowed from the fireplace, and a lantern, flickering quietly, had been placed on a bedside table.

"You planned this," she accused as he laid her onto the bed. The sheets were cold against her bare skin.

"No...well, yeah, maybe I did." He covered her with an antique quilt and crawled into bed with her.

"You're wicked!" she rasped, wishing she had the strength to climb off his bed and stomp back to the lobby.

"Absolutely."

"And beyond redemption."

"God, I hope so."

"And—"

His mouth found hers, and his hands wrapped around her waist, drawing her naked body to his. It was incredible, he thought, how perfectly she fit against him, how her curves molded to his muscles, how she seemed to melt into him. He'd stupidly thought that making love to her would purge her from his system, but he'd never been more wrong in his life.

It had been only minutes since they'd joined and he'd felt the wonder of her flesh wrapped around his, and yet he was ready again, his body fevered, his mouth hungry.

And she responded. Her breasts felt heavy in his hands, her nipples willing buds that he brushed with his thumbs. And when he took her into his mouth, tracing those dark points with his tongue, she moaned, her body arching up to his, her moist heat enveloping him.

He rolled her onto him, suckling at her breasts, his hand firm on her buttocks. The windows rattled with the wind, and he thought vaguely that he hoped the storm would never end.

With the morning came regret. What had she been thinking about? Making love to Gavin was asking for trouble. And yet, lying in his arms, she found it impossible to roll away from him and pretend that a one-night stand with him meant nothing to her.

Once a fool, always a fool, she thought, a willing prisoner in Gavin's arms. The storm had subsided, and the day promised to be clear and cold. Soon she would have to leave him.

She rested her cheek against his chest and fell back into a dreamless sleep.

Gavin, however, was very much awake. As he lay in the bed, gazing through the window, watching the sunrise blaze against the snow-covered mountain, the bedside phone rang loudly.

He groaned, unwilling to move. Melanie's cheek rested on his chest, and one of her arms was flung around his abdomen. Her skin was creamy white, her tousled black hair in sharp contrast to the white pillow case and sheets. His heart warmed at the sight of her tucked so close and lovingly beside him.

He wanted to protect her and cherish her and love her—

The phone rang again, and she stirred, lifting her head and shaking the hair from her slumberous eyes.

"Uh-oh," Gavin growled. "Looks like someone found us."

"Bound to happen sooner or later," she said, yawning through a smile.

"I suppose. Go back to sleep." He grabbed the jangling receiver with his left hand while still holding Melanie with his right.

"Ridge Lodge."

"About time you answered! I've been trying to reach you all night," Rich grumbled.

"I've been here."

"Well, you didn't answer!"

"The phones must've been out," Gavin replied, not really interested.

"What's going on up there? No, don't tell me. You've probably got some beautiful woman waiting for you in bed."

"Get real, Rich," Gavin replied, smothering a smile. "The electricity has been out since last night."

"What about the backup generator?"

"Not yet fully operational."

"Oh, God," Rich groaned. "Any damage?"

"Nothing severe." Gavin stretched lazily. For the first time since he'd agreed to this project, he wasn't really interested in the resort.

"Listen, we've got a million things to do. Now that there's snow, we're wasting big bucks every day we're not open. So I called all our suppliers and the trucks will deliver as soon as the roads are clear. Get ready. Make sure the lot is plowed and that Erik and some of the other boys are there when the shipment of rental gear arrives...." He rattled on and on, giving instructions, though he expected—and got—no answers. Gavin just grinned, and when Melanie tried to roll out of bed, he pinned her hard against him. He hadn't felt this good in years and he wasn't about to give it up.

He harbored no illusions that he and Melanie could ever get back together—not really. She hadn't wanted him when he was dirt poor and she probably didn't want him now. But while they were locked away from the rest of the world, he was going to spend every second with her. She was warm, willing and...and, damn it, she was the one woman who could make love to him as no other had ever...

"So I've called the ski patrol, and a group of would-be instructors will be at the lodge as soon as they can get through. Take their applications, talk to them, and for God's sake, make sure you see them on a pair of skis. Put them through their paces."

"I'll handle it," Gavin said, glancing down as Melanie looked up at him through the sweep of dark lashes.

"Right. And check on the—"

Gavin dropped the receiver back in its cradle and rolled over, giving her the full attention she deserved.

"Problems?" she asked.

"Nothing that won't wait." He fingered a strand of black hair that curled deliciously around her face, neck and breasts. Her eyes flashed silvery green in coy delight.

The phone began to ring again, and Gavin reached to the bottom of the bed and yanked on the cord. There was still a faint jangle from the phones in the lobby and bar, but Gavin didn't pay any attention. Instead, he wrapped his arms around her. "I think we have more important things to think about."

"More important than opening the lodge?"

"Mmm." He nuzzled her neck. "Definitely more important." And, kissing her, he proved it.

Later, while Gavin was working elsewhere in the lodge, Melanie dialed the newspaper.

The receptionist answered on the second ring. "Taylor's Crossing *Tribune*."

"Hi, Molly, it's Melanie."

"Melanie! Where've you been?" Molly asked, her voice breathless. "Brian's been looking everywhere for you!"

"I got stuck up at Ridge Lodge when the storm hit last night," Melanie said, feeling more than a trifle guilty as she glanced at the still-rumpled bed. "The road's been closed. Is Brian there?"

"Yeah, I'll connect you."

Molly clicked off, and a few seconds later, Brian Michaels's voice boomed over the wires. "Where the hell are you?"

"Ridge Lodge," she said, repeating everything she'd just told Molly.

"And you were up there all night?" Brian asked.

"That's right."

"Hell, Melanie, I need you down here! We need pictures of the downed lines and the road crews and God only knows what else."

"I'll be there as soon as the roads are clear," she promised. "And I've got some great shots of the lodge."

"Good, good. According to the state police and the highway department, the road to the lodge will be open this afternoon."

A twinge of regret tugged at Melanie's heart. "I'll make a beeline to the office." she promised.

"Good. I'll be in all afternoon." His voice lowered. "And, since you're up on the hill anyway, there is something I'd like you to check into for me."

The hairs on the back of Melanie's neck rose. "What's that?"

"I want you to nose around. See if the resort is experiencing any financial trouble."

"Financial trouble," she repeated, her temper starting to rise.

"Right. There's a rumor circulating that an investor is backing out, that Doel's sunk all his personal fortune into this place and unless it opens and opens big, he's in trouble."

"I doubt it," Melanie replied tightly.

"Where there's smoke there's fire."

"I think that depends on who set up the smoke screen." She kept her voice low, hoping Gavin wouldn't walk in on her. Clenching her fingers around the receiver, she felt trapped. To think she'd defended Brian to Gavin!

"Well, Rich Johanson spends a hell of a lot of time in Portland trying to keep that legal practice of his alive."

"So what?"

"Seems strange to me."

"You're fishing, Brian."

"Maybe, but you keep looking around. As long as you're there, you may as well keep your eyes and ears open."

"Listen, Brian, I'm the photographer for the *Tribune*. That's all. I'll take all the pictures you need, but that's as far as it goes! I'm not going to run around here trying to ferret out some dirt."

She hung up and slowly counted to ten. She'd gotten only as far as seven when the door to the apartment opened and Gavin strode in.

"Road crews are already working between here and Taylor's Crossing."

"So I heard," she admitted, motioning to the telephone. "I just called the office."

A lazy, self-deprecating grin stretched across Gavin's jaw. "And what did good old Brian have to say?"

"He misses me."

Gavin lifted a lofty brow. "Anything else?"

"Well, he did mention that I should poke around here and find out if you were financially stable."

"You're kidding." Gavin swore loudly.

"Nope."

"Then he was."

"I don't think so."

Gavin shoved his hands into his back pockets. "Michaels will stoop to anything," he said, disgusted. "The financial situation at the lodge is none of his business. You know, I wouldn't be surprised if he sent you up here just to find out what was going on."

Melanie hardly dared breathe. He wasn't serious, was he? Here, in this room, the bed still warm from lovemaking—how could he even say anything so cruel? "Brian didn't send me, Gavin."

"Of course he didn't," Gavin agreed. "But I wouldn't put it past him."

"And me?"

He snorted contemptuously. "I don't think you sleep with men to get the kind of story or pictures or whatever it is you want from them."

"I don't sleep with men, period. Except for you," She picked up a pen from the table and twisted it nervously.

His face lost all expression. "What about Neil?"

"Only while we were married."

He blanched.

"And there's something I should explain about that," she said quietly, her voice shaking as she struggled for the right words. "I married Neil because of the baby."

The room went still. Melanie heard her own heart thud painfully. She lifted her eyes to meet the questions in Gavin's gaze.

"I thought you said you didn't sleep with Neil until you were married."

"I didn't."

"And just last night—didn't you tell me you couldn't get pregnant?"

"I couldn't—I mean, I can't, not now, not with Neil—I mean... Oh, God." Her hands were shaking and her throat was cotton dry. She forced herself to stare straight into his eyes. "What I'm trying to say, Gavin, is that the reason I married Neil was because I was pregnant." She couldn't help the tears clogging her throat. It was all she could do to stand there, keeping her knees from buckling.

The air in the room was suddenly hot, the glare in Gavin's gaze positively murderous. "Pregnant?" he repeated slowly, quietly.

"Yes."

"But you said..."

She squeezed her eyes shut. "I know what I said. But I did get pregnant once, Gavin. And the baby was yours."

Chapter Ten

"Mine? The baby was mine?" he whispered hoarsely, his face devoid of color, his lips bloodless.

"Yes. I was pregnant when you left, but I didn't know it. When I found out you were already trying out for the ski team and—"

"Lies!"

"No! Oh, Gavin, why would I lie?" she cried.

"I don't know," he growled, stepping forward, his eyes gleaming menacingly. "But you must have a reason."

"I just thought you'd want to know."

"Now? After eight years?" His voice was so low and threatening that her skin crawled. "When it's so convenient? How stupid do you think I am?"

"I don't—"

He grabbed her upper arm, his fingers digging deep. "Just last night you told me you couldn't conceive. That's right, isn't it? Or has that story changed, too?"

She didn't blame him for being angry, but the explosion of emotion on his face scared her. She tried to jerk her arm away but he clamped down all the harder.

"I'm not lying, Gavin!"

"Oh, no? So where's the kid? Hmm? The son—or daughter, was it?—that I fathered?"

She crumbled inside. "Oh, God, Gavin, don't. Can't you see how hard this is for me?"

"I see that you lied eight years ago and you're doing it still."

"No—please, you've got to believe me."

"Why?"

"Because it's the truth!" she cried, desperation ringing in her voice. "The truth!"

"You don't know the meaning of the word!"

"How would you know? You never stuck around long enough to find out!"

He winced. "All right, Melanie. If you want to go on spinning your little tale, go right ahead." He released her suddenly, as if the mere touch of her made him ill. Crossing his arms over his chest, he muttered, "Go on. I'm all ears!"

Melanie lifted her chin and fought the tears that kept threatening to spill. "I was pregnant with your child, and my father talked me into not telling you."

"Wonderful guy."

"He was thinking of you."

"Sure."

"He said you weren't ready to be burdened with a wife and child, that you'd only grow to resent me because you'd have to give up your dream."

"Are you expecting me to buy any of this?"

"Only if you remember how much I loved you," she said, fighting fire with fire. His eyes betrayed him. Emotions, long hidden and tortured, showed for one instant, and he was again the vulnerable boy from the wrong side of the tracks. Her heart felt as if it were breaking into a thousand pieces. "I did love you, Gavin. All I thought about was loving you and living with you for the rest of my life. I—I didn't mean to get pregnant. It just happened."

"So you married another man. And Neil was more than happy to play daddy to my kid. Oh, come on, Melanie. This just doesn't wash."

"Why else would I marry a man I didn't love?"

"Money," he said cruelly, his voice filled with conviction.

"I didn't care about money. But I wanted a good life for the baby."

"The baby." He lifted his hands. "Where is he?"

She swallowed the hot, painful lump in her throat, "I miscarried. Six weeks after I married Neil."

"Now didn't that work out fine and dandy?" he mocked, his words cutting to the bone.

She shook her head at the memory. "No, it was awful—"

"It was a lie. Either you're lying to me now, or Neil Brooks is a bigger fool than I am for believing you."

"You think I made this up?"

"I don't know what to think, Melanie. But you just told me yourself that you couldn't get pregnant. How do you expect me to believe something as outrageous as this?"

"I didn't lie. Neil and I couldn't have children. I—we—after I lost the baby, we never used birth control. And, even though we hoped, there never was another baby."

"And how does medical science explain this incredible phenomenon?"

"It doesn't. Neil wouldn't go to the doctor and . . . well, I didn't bother. Things started falling apart, and we started sleeping in different rooms."

"So you're expecting me to believe that I got you pregnant and you, out of some convoluted sense of nobility, refused to tell me about it but you convinced Neil to marry you and raise another man's child as his own. Only, lo and behold, before the blessed event occurs, you lose the baby and never, ever conceive again?"

She fought the urge to snap back at him. Instead, curling her fists, she blinked against tears of frustration. "Yes."

"Well, Melanie, you missed your calling. You shouldn't have become a photographer. You should be an actress. You've just given one helluva performance!"

Melanie's temper exploded. How could he have become so cruel? So callous? So jaded?

She thought of their recent lovemaking; the scent still lingered in the air. He'd been tender and kind—and now, so heartless. Sick inside, she knew she had to leave. Now. Before whatever they'd shared turned ugly. Without a word, she started gathering her things.

"What're you doing?"

"Leaving."

"You can't leave."

"Watch me."

"But it's freezing, the roads are blocked and—"

"I don't give a damn about the roads or the weather!" she flung out as she found her camera and purse.

"You're angry."

"Try *furious*!"

"Just because I didn't believe your story."

"Forget it." She started for the door, but he grabbed her arm, spinning her around.

"You can't leave," he said again.

"Let go of me, Gavin."

"Your car won't make it."

"What do you care?" She peeled his fingers from her arm. "I'll walk if I have to."

"Melanie—"

She ran out the door and through the now familiar hallways.

The lodge was empty; her footsteps rang on the hardwood. She heard Gavin behind her, but she shoved open the front doors and was blasted with the rush of bitterly cold air.

Snow glistened and still fell in tiny flakes. She nearly slipped on the icy front steps and he caught up with her. "Melanie, listen, I'm sorry."

"No reason to be!" she snapped, plowing through the snow that nearly hit her at the knees. "You think I'm a liar or worse. Fine. At least I know where I stand." She plunged on, determined to find a way to leave him.

"For crying out loud, Melanie..."

Her Volkswagen, even parked under cover, was under a pile of snow. Ignoring the wind, she brushed the icy flakes from the windshield, climbed into the car and turned the key. The engine ground slowly as she pumped on the gas. "Come on, come on," she whispered, sending up a silent prayer. She couldn't stay here a minute longer—she wouldn't!

Gavin opened the car door as the engine sputtered, coughed and died. "Now, just a minute—"

"Drop dead!"

"Look, I didn't mean to ridicule you."

"Well, you did!"

"It's just that your story is so unbelievable."

"So you said!" She stomped on the accelerator and twisted the key again. "Come on, come on," she muttered to the car. *Oh, please start! Please!*

His jaw worked. He was obviously struggling with his own temper. "Come back into the lodge. I'll make some coffee and we can talk this over civilly."

"Impossible! Just leave me alone! That's what you're good at—leaving!"

His lips tightened. "I'm trying, Melanie. Now the least you can do is meet me halfway."

"After what you said to me? After being accused of being a liar?" She turned furious hazel eyes up to him. "You know me, Gavin. You know I wouldn't lie about something like this. What would be the point?"

"I thought you needed an excuse for marrying Neil. Something I might understand."

The car gave a last sickening cough and died. When she turned the key again, all she heard was a series of clicks. Gavin's hand touched her shoulder. She shrank away.

"I'll buy you a cup of coffee and I'll listen to what you have to say. Besides, this car isn't going anywhere. Even if it did start, you'd never make it through the lot."

He was right about that. The lot was covered with nearly two feet of snow. The Volkswagen wouldn't get out of the shed before stopping dead—that was, if she ever could get it started.

"Come on, Mel," he insisted.

"Forget it! You won't believe me."

"I'll try." His voice turned gentle. "Melanie, you threw me for a helluva loop."

"Then you believe me?" she asked, her features tormented.

He glanced up at the sky, and snow collected in his hair and on his collar. Lines bracketed his mouth and eyes. "I don't know what to believe."

"Fine." She yanked hard on the door, but he wedged himself between the handle and the interior.

"As I said before, you're not going anywhere in this," he ordered tautly, taking hold of her and hauling her from the car.

She tried to climb back inside, but he pulled her out, bodily carrying her back to the lodge.

She wriggled and kicked, trying desperately to get back on her feet and find her rapidly escaping dignity. "Put me down! You'll slip and ruin your ankle and—"

"Oh, be quiet!" he growled, trudging through the snow, following the trail she'd broken only minutes before. "We're going back inside and you're going to start over, slowly, from the beginning."

"If you think I'm going through this again, you're out of your mind!"

"Probably," he said. "But I think you owe it to me to—"

"*I owe you*? Oh, give me a break. I owe you nothing! Nothing! I shouldn't have opened my mouth in the first place."

"But you did," he reminded her, slowly climbing the steps and kicking open the front door. He didn't stop until he'd carried her all the way into his apartment. Plopping her onto the couch, he said, "Now let's start over."

"I've told you everything."

"A little late, isn't it?"

"I explained that I didn't want to burden you."

"Oh, yes, noble of you," he mocked, trying and failing to keep his temper under control. "So you, pregnant with my child, married Neil Brooks?"

"Yes."

"And he agreed to go along with your scheme?" he asked dubiously.

"It wasn't a scheme!"

He shoved shaking hands through his hair. "What I don't understand, Melanie, is, if this is true, why you didn't at least have the courage to tell me about it. Didn't you think I'd want to know?"

"I didn't want you to feel trapped," she said, her hands curling into fists of frustration.

"But if I was the father—"

"You know you were!"

"Then the child was my responsibility."

"A child you didn't want."

"You don't know that!" He crossed to the window, and anger fairly radiated from him. "If the baby had lived, would you have ever told me the truth?"

She opened her mouth, closed it again and struggled with the truth. When her words came, they sounded strangled. "I—I don't think so."

"And why the hell not?" He whirled, facing her again, his temper skyrocketing. His nostrils flared and his eyes blazed.

"Because I wouldn't want a scene like this one!"

Something flickered in his eyes, something dark and dangerous. "Or because I wasn't good enough for you?"

"What?"

"Is that why you ran to Neil instead of me? Because you wanted to raise your child—*our* child—by a rich man instead of the son of the town drunk?"

She couldn't believe it. Not now. Not after he'd sworn that he would listen to her. "I don't have to listen to this, Gavin. I loved you. I loved you so much I was out of my mind with wanting you. But I didn't want to make you hate me for the rest of your life!"

"So you married Brooks in order to pass off my child as his," he said, disgust heavy in his voice.

"No!"

"God, Melanie, this is one for the books—"

"You said you'd listen!"

The sound of footsteps rang through the hall. Someone had made it up to the lodge! The roads were clear! She could leave.

"Mr. Doel? Are you here? Mr. Doel?" Erik Link's voice echoed through the corridors, and Gavin's lips pursed.

He muttered an oath, then called over his shoulder, "In here."

The door flew open. "I just wanted to say that the roads are clear and—" Erik's voice fell away at the sight of Melanie, and she realized how she must look, her hair in tangles, her cheeks burning, her chin thrust forward like a recalcitrant child getting the lecture of her life. "I—uh, I didn't mean to interrupt."

"You didn't," Melanie informed him. She jumped to her feet and grabbed her things. "In fact, I'd really appreciate it if you'd give me a ride back to town. My car's given up the ghost."

"Sure." Erik's gaze moved from Melanie to Gavin.

"I'll drive you home," Gavin said. "If the roads are passable—"

Melanie tossed her hair over her shoulder. "Oh, I wouldn't want to bother you, Mr. Doel. You must have a thousand and one things to do before the resort opens."

"That's right, and the first one is to get you safely home." He grabbed his keys from a hook near the door, gave Erik quick instructions about plowing the lot and keeping the lodge warm, then followed Melanie, who was walking briskly toward the back lot.

"You shouldn't have bothered," she shot at him when they were once again outside.

"I'd feel better about this if I made sure you were all right."

"I can handle myself. I don't need you bossing me around," she flung back, wishing she could hurt him as he'd hurt her. All his horrid accusations filled her head and she ached inside. Well, she'd done her duty, told him the truth. Now she couldn't wait to get away from him, from the lodge—from Taylor's Crossing if she had to!

They walked to the garage, and she climbed into a huge four-wheel-drive truck and waited while he turned the ignition. The engine caught immediately.

Gavin slid behind the wheel. Melanie didn't so much as glance in his direction. But he didn't shift out of park. Instead, he drummed his fingers impatiently on the steering wheel, jaw set, as if struggling for just the right words.

Well, she wasn't about to help him. He'd been wretched and he deserved to squirm.

He sighed, shifting uncomfortably, and the bench seat moved beneath her. If she could only get through this!

The cab of the truck was warm, the windows fogged, and Melanie, against her best judgment, sneaked a glance his way. He was staring at her, lips tight, eyes narrowed, as if he were trying to size her up. One wayward strand of honey-blond hair fell over his forehead.

The air between them fairly crackled.

Melanie broke the silence first. "I just wish you'd remember that you trusted me once," she said.

"That's the problem. I remember all too well."

"And you think I betrayed you."

"You did."

"Fine. Think what you want. Can't you start this thing?"

He shoved the truck into gear and let the wheels grab. The truck lurched, and he tromped on the accelerator, plowing through the unbroken snow until he was on the path that Erik's truck had broken through the parking lot.

The trip down the mountain took nearly an hour. Melanie turned an ostracizing shoulder to Gavin and stared out the window at the aftermath of the storm. Pine boughs drooped under a blanket of thick snow. The sky was gray, the clouds high, the air frosty and clean.

But inside the truck the atmosphere was thick. The miles rolled slowly by. At the sight of a road crew, Melanie yanked her camera out of its case and, asking Gavin to slow down, clicked off several shots of workers sawing through fallen trees and restringing electrical cable.

She didn't say another word until he reached her house. It took all of her willpower not to throw open the door and run up the front steps.

He ground the truck to a stop. "Melanie—"

She didn't want to hear it. Opening the door, she climbed out. "Thanks for the ride and all the hospitality," she said, her tone scathing. "Believe me, I won't forget this morning for the rest of my life."

And neither will I, Gavin thought as she slammed the door of the truck shut and stomped through the snow to the back door. He waited a few seconds, until he was sure she was inside, then he threw the truck in reverse.

He wanted to believe her. In his heart he desperately wished he could trust her again. But how could he? And this cock-and-bull story about the baby—his baby... Why the hell would she lie? Why now? It would have been easier for her to keep quiet.

There was obviously some truth to the tale. He knew her well enough to recognize her pain. And her private agony was matched by his when he thought about a child he would never know, a child he'd created with Melanie.

His hands gripped the wheel tightly, and an angry horn blared as the truck moved too close to the center line. Teeth clenched, he focused on his driving, but a thousand emotions tore at his soul.

He could have been a father—the father of a seven-year-old. For God's sake, he didn't even know what a seven-year-old was like!

And Melanie could have been his wife—not Neil's. If only she'd been honest with him way back when.

What kind of life could he have given her? Would he have given up his chances for glory on the Olympic team? Would he have forced Melanie and the kid to travel from one ski resort to the next while he tried to scratch out a living as a pro? Without the catapult to fame from the Olympics, would he have had the backing to race professionally, to get on his feet? Or would he have returned to Taylor's Crossing and become a ranch hand or a logger or given lessons to children during the weekends at Ridge Resort?

But there was no baby. An unfamiliar pain, raw and cutting, seared straight to his soul. If he'd stayed in Taylor's Crossing and married Melanie, would the child have survived? Hell, he didn't even know why a woman miscarried, but he felt tremendous guilt that he hadn't been around to offer support and comfort to Melanie for a child they would never share.

"Son of a bitch," he muttered, driving straight to the lodge. He parked near Erik's truck and noticed that several other vehicles had arrived. Two plows were working to clear the lot. Rich must have gotten through to the crew.

He walked into the lodge and made a beeline for the bar. Ignoring the looks cast his way by some of the workers, he grabbed a bottle of Scotch, twisted open the cap and took a long swig right from the bottle. It burned like hell.

"What's eatin' you?" his father asked. He glanced up, and in the mirror over the bar he saw Jim Doel's florid, lined face, an older version of his own.

"You wouldn't believe it."

"Try me."

Gavin shook his head and took another tug on the bottle.

His father approached and, laying an arm over Gavin's shoulders, said, "I don't know what you're fightin', son, but believe me, this—" he touched the bottle with his free hand "—isn't gonna help."

"Nothing will," Gavin agreed.

"It's that Walker woman again, isn't it?" his father guessed. "Don't you know it's time you got her out of your blood once and for all?"

"I wish I could," Gavin admitted. "But I don't think it's possible."

"Anything's possible."

"What I don't need right now is a lecture," Gavin grumbled.

"No. What you need is another woman."

Scenes of lovemaking filled Gavin's mind. He remembered Melanie snuggled tight against him, her hair brushing his bare skin. "I don't think another woman's the answer."

"'Course it is," his father countered. "I know that model has called you."

"I'm not interested."

"Well, maybe you should be." His father's eyes met his in the glass. "There's no reason for this girl to tear you apart."

Gavin clenched his teeth. What he felt for Melanie went way beyond the bonds of reason.

"So the lost lamb has found her way back to the fold," Guy remarked when Melanie shoved open the door and walked briskly past his desk.

Melanie, in no mood for humor, replied, "Since when was I a lamb?"

Guy held up his hands in surrender. "Only a figure of speech."

She unwrapped her scarf, shrugged out of her coat and hung them both in the employee closet near the darkroom. "Was I the only one who didn't make it in?"

"Are you kidding? The county was literally shut down. Constance and Molly were both out yesterday." He retrieved Melanie's Garfield mug from her desk, rinsed it out and poured her a cup of fresh coffee. "Even Brian's place lost power for a few hours. He came in late yesterday, and boy, was he fit to be tied."

"So things were just like usual," Melanie remarked.

Guy grinned. "I guess. Anyway, he's on a real kick to sell more papers."

"Isn't he always?"

"Yeah," Guy muttered, fidgeting with his watch and avoiding her eyes. "But this is different. I don't know what happened, but my guess is he got the word from the powers that be to increase circulation or—" Guy rotated his palms to the ceiling "*—sayonara!*"

At that moment Brian Michaels himself burst into the newsroom. His face was flushed from the cold, and he saw Melanie instantly. "So you're back," he said, yanking off his gloves and hanging his felt hat in the closet near the front door. "Good. We've got work to do. Come into my office."

"Be right there." Melanie grabbed a notebook from the top of her desk and, ignoring Guy's worried glance, followed Brian into his private office. "Now listen," Brian said before she'd even had a chance to sit down, "I'm serious about the rumors about the lodge being in financial trouble. I want to know all about it. You were up there—what's going on?"

"Nothing out of the ordinary. Because of the storm, they're hoping to open early."

"That's it?" he asked skeptically.

"That's it." She eased into one of the uncomfortable chairs near his desk.

Brian's brow furrowed, and he reached into his top drawer for a new pack of cigarettes. "No sign of any financial difficulty?"

"None. They were expecting delivery of the supplies and equipment as soon as the roads were clear."

Frowning, Brian tapped his cigarette pack on the edge of the desk. "You wouldn't keep anything from me, would you, Melanie?"

"No."

"But if you thought I was prying into someone's personal life, especially if that person happened to be someone you cared about, you wouldn't give up private information easily."

She felt heat climb up her back. "You're right. I wouldn't."

"Not even if it was news?"

"No."

He opened the pack and shook out a cigarette. "This job is important to me, Melanie. And it should be important to you. We owe it to our readers to report the truth, no matter how... uncomfortable... it might be."

"I didn't see anything at the lodge. As a matter of fact, I've been there when Rich Johanson has been paying bills." She leaned across his desk as he lit his cigarette and snapped his lighter closed. "I think you're barking up the wrong tree. The lodge looks solid as a rock. And if they can open earlier than planned, I would think there's a better chance then ever that they'll make it work."

Squinting through the smoke, he said, "How long were you at the lodge?"

"Less than twenty-four hours," she said uneasily. "I got there just before the storm hit."

"Who else was there?"

"Just Gavin Doel."

"Just Doel?" One sharp eyebrow arched. "How was that?"

"Cold," she lied. "The lodge lost power."

"And phone lines?"

"They were down—at least for a while in the middle of the night."

"So what did you and Doel do all that time?" he asked.

Was he suggesting something? She couldn't be sure. With effort she kept her voice steady. "We tried to keep the pipes from freezing, attempted to start the backup generator... that sort of thing."

"And in all that time Doel never once said anything that might indicate that things weren't running smoothly at the lodge?"

"Well, he wasn't too pleased about the lack of electricity."

"I mean financially."

"No." She leaned back in her chair. "What's this all about?"

"Just a rumor I heard."

"From whom?"

He grinned. "You know I won't reveal my sources."

"Well, I think your sources are all wet."

"But you won't mind checking into it when you're back up at the lodge doing whatever it is you do there."

Melanie's temper snapped. "Of course I'll mind!" she said, standing and glaring down at him as if he'd lost his mind. "I can't go creeping around spying on Gavin and Rich, and I wouldn't even if I could. I don't know why it is that all of a sudden you want to do some big smear campaign against Ridge Lodge, but I won't be a part of it!"

"This isn't a smear campaign. Think of it as investigative journalism."

Melanie's sound of disgust eloquently voiced her feelings.

"You don't have a choice," Brian added calmly.

"Of course I do...."

But his meaning was clear, and his face had hardened. "Not if you want to keep your job. Let's be straight with each other. Circulation hasn't picked up and I've got to make some cuts in expenses around here. I'm going to trim some people from the staff."

"Are you saying you're going to fire me?"

"Not yet, but I expect you to be a team player, Melanie. Now, why don't you develop the shots you've already taken up there, then go up with Jan and find out what's going on at the lodge?"

His intercom buzzed, and Melanie walked out of the office. She couldn't afford to lose this job, not yet. She still had debts to pay off from her father's illness and the addition to her house. But she'd be damned if she was going to help Brian ruin Ridge Lodge or Gavin Doel!

Brian Michaels stubbed out his cigarette and watched as Melanie marched stiffly into the darkroom. Something had happened to her while she was up at the lodge, and his reporter's instincts told him she'd gotten herself mixed up with Doel.

Now *that* was interesting. Gavin Doel, internationally famous athlete, involved with a local woman?

For the first time all week, Brian smiled to himself. Maybe he was going for the wrong angle on Doel. Sure the man was newsworthy, but the readers just might be more interested in his love life than his lodge.

And Melanie Walker was beautiful as well as spirited. Exactly what was going on?

Jan had mentioned that Doel and Melanie had known each other way back when. Brian wondered just how well.

It wouldn't take much to find out. He had microfiche and old newspapers that went clear back to the fifties. There was also a town library filled with high school yearbooks and a lot of people who had lived here all their lives.

Surely someone would remember if Gavin and Melanie were involved before. Maybe it was nothing, just a passing friendship—or maybe not even that. But Brian wasn't convinced.

No, there was a spark that leaped to life in Melanie's eyes every time Doel's name was mentioned. He could see through her feigned nonchalance. And she'd been defensive as hell.

Oh, yes, it was time to do some checking on Gavin Doel. And this time, he'd put Jan on the story. Jan didn't have the same overrated sense of values that Melanie clung to.

In fact, he might even do some digging himself. He'd never liked Gavin Doel. Doel had once cost him his job, and from that point on, his career had gone downhill until he'd landed in this two-bit town. Well, maybe now Gavin Doel was his ticket out!

The guy had everything, Brian thought jealously. It was high time Doel was knocked down a few pegs, even if it cost Melanie Walker.

It was too bad about Melanie. Brian liked her. She worked hard, was nice to look at and was smart. Except when it came to Gavin Doel. Yep, it was too bad about Melanie. Brian felt an abnormal twinge of conscience and hoped she didn't get hurt—at least, not too badly.

But if she did, it was her fault. She was better off without an arrogant bastard like Gavin Doel. The sooner she knew it, the better for everyone.

Chapter Eleven

Melanie returned to Ridge Lodge, determined that the next story in the *Tribune* would reflect the excitement of reopening the resort.

As she parked in the lot, she realized that the story would nearly write itself—if Jan would let it.

Ridge Lodge was frenetic.

Delivery trucks brought skis, boots, fashion skiwear, food, snacks, light fixtures, paper products, tourist information, utensils, medical supplies, souvenirs and on and on.

The ski patrol had already started checking the runs, and an area had been cleared near the Nugget Rope Tow for the ski school to meet. Chairs and gondolas moved up the hill as the newly named lifts became operational. Grooming machines chugged up the snow-covered slopes, while snowplows kept the parking lot clear.

A rainbow of triangular flags snapped in the wind, and the snow continued to fall, bringing with it hopes for a long and prosperous season.

Inside, the lodge was hectic. Employees manned the phones as the resort geared up for an early season. Others were briefed on the way the lodge worked, dishes were stacked, beds were made in the rooms, the bar was stocked and a new sound system was turned on.

Melanie smiled as she saw her sepia-toned pictures hanging near mining equipment, adding to the Gold Rush atmosphere of the lobby.

In the huge stone fireplace a fire crackled and burned invitingly. Workers arranged furniture in the bar and lobby, and the Oriental rug where she and Gavin had made love was still stretched across the floor. A pang of regret tore through her.

Her smile disappeared. Hadn't she learned anything? Chiding herself for being a fool, she loaded a new roll of film into the camera and made her way past the bustling workers.

"Well, how do you like this?" Jan asked, breezing in the front door and stamping the snow from her boots.

"What—oh, the lodge?" Melanie glanced around. "Looks a little different, doesn't it?"

"*Very* different." Tucking her gloves in her purse, Jan eyed the walls. "Those your pictures?" she asked, moving closer to a print of miners panning for gold.

"Yes."

"They're not bad."

"Thanks."

Jan's mouth tightened. "You know I hate this, don't you?"

"Hate what?"

"Being the bad guy. I wouldn't be surprised if Doel and Johanson tried to kick me out of here."

Melanie was skeptical. "Would you blame them? You keep asking all sorts of personal questions."

She lifted a shoulder. "Brian wants a more personal story. I try to give him one." Jan's eyes clouded a minute. "Melanie, I think I should warn you…" She let the sentence trail off.

"Warn me about what?" Melanie demanded, then understood. "About Gavin?" When Jan didn't reply, she added, "Come on, Jan. Weren't you the one who thought I should chase after him?"

"Maybe that wasn't such a hot idea," Jan replied nervously. She looked as if she were about to say something else when she spotted Rich Johanson. "Look, just be careful," she said cryptically. "Don't do anything foolish."

Too late for that, Melanie thought as Jan, following Rich, took off in search of her story.

Melanie wandered down a long corridor to the shops. Mannequins were already dressed in neon and black jumpsuits. Sweatshirts, imprinted with the resort's logo or simply saying Ski the Ridge!, were displayed in a window case.

All around her, employees chatted and laughed, stocking the shelves or waxing skis or adjusting bindings on rental skis.

In the exercise room machines stood ready, and nearby, steam rose from the aquamarine water in the pool. Yes, Ridge Lodge was nearly ready for its guests. Despite Brian Michaels's arguments to the contrary, Ridge Lodge was destined to be a success. She could feel it. And the photographs she snapped off reflected that success—smiling employees, gleaming equipment, well-stocked shops….

She worked her way outside and changed film and lenses. Then she clicked off shot after shot of the moving lifts, a group of instructors in matching gold jackets as they practiced together, an operator in the cage at the bottom of

Daredevil run, and above it all, Mount Prosperity stood proudly, a regal giant in a mantle of white.

She didn't notice Gavin for nearly two hours, then, as she trained her lens on a group of instructors making their way through the moguls at the bottom of Rocky Ridge run, she spied him in the lead, blond hair flying, skis so close together they nearly touched, his form perfect.

Her throat went dry as the camera zoomed in for a closer shot. She noticed the concentration in his face, the natural grace with which he planted his poles, the way he turned effortlessly, as if he'd never been injured.

"The man is awesome," Jan said as she stepped through the snow to reach Melanie. Her eyes were trained on Gavin, as well. "Looks like he's good as new."

"I suppose." Melanie turned her camera on another instructor, a woman who was gamely trying to keep up with Gavin and losing ground with every turn.

"I wonder if he'll race again."

"I hope so," Melanie muttered, still adjusting the focus.

"You do?" Jan said. "Why?"

"Because he loves it. It's his life. He's not happy unless he's tearing down some mountain at breakneck speed."

Jan sighed wistfully as Gavin, flying over the last of the moguls, twisted in midair, tucked his skis together and cut into the hillside, stopping quickly and sending a spray of snow to one side.

"So you think once this lodge is up and running, he'll take off for the ski circuit?"

Melanie stiffened. "I don't know," she said honestly. "You'll have to ask him."

"Oh, I intend to." Jan's eyes darkened thoughtfully. "There's a lot more I'd like to know about Mr. Doel."

At that moment Gavin looked up. His gaze scanned the lodge before landing on Melanie. Through the lens, Melanie noticed his jaw tighten.

With a quick word to the instructors, he planted his poles and skied, using his arms and a skating motion with his legs, as he crossed the relatively flat terrain from the base of the run to the lodge.

Melanie's stomach knotted.

"Well, if it isn't the *Tribune*'s finest," he said, eyeing Melanie's camera and Jan's ever-present notebook.

Melanie ignored the jab and decided to try her damnedest to be professional. She would put what happened between Gavin and her behind her if it took all of her willpower. "You agreed to the series of articles, remember?"

"Yep," he said flatly, but his lips twisted. "What's the angle—isn't that what you call it?—for this week's edition?"

"Financial impact," Jan said as Gavin leaned over and shoved on his bindings with the heel of his hand. With a snap, he was free of his skis. "The *Trib*'s interested in the economic impact on the community, as well as how you keep a lodge resort this size out of the red."

"It takes some doing," he replied.

"Mmm. I'll bet."

"But we have backing."

"Investors?"

He straightened, his expression menacing. "Where're you heading with this?"

"Nowhere," Jan said guilelessly, but Melanie decided to step in.

"I thought I already mentioned that there've been rumors that the resort is failing financially," she said, warning Gavin.

Gavin's jaw set. His eyes turned as cool as the early winter day. "And I thought I explained that there are no problems, financial or otherwise."

"Then none of your investors is bowing out?" Jan asked.

Gavin whirled on her. "Not unless you know something I don't." His eyes narrowed threateningly. "Oh, I get it. Michaels is fishing again. Well, give him a reminder for me, will you? If he prints anything the least bit libelous about this lodge or me, I'll sue. Now, if you don't mind, I'd like to speak with Melanie. In private. And don't print that!" Lips compressed angrily, he took hold of Melanie's arm and, without a backward glance at the reporter, propelled Melanie up the few steps to the back deck.

"What the hell's going on?" he demanded once they were out of earshot.

"You know as much as I do," she replied, glancing over his shoulder. Fortunately, Jan, after casting them a questioning look, had turned back toward the main lobby.

"What's Brian Michaels's game?"

Melanie yanked her arm away from him. "All I know is he's looking for dirt. Any kind of dirt."

"On me?"

"Yes. Or the lodge."

"Then that brings him right back to you, doesn't it?" he countered, his expression hard. "Does he know about you and me?"

Melanie caught her breath. How could Gavin talk about their past without so much as a hint of emotion? "No," she replied levelly.

"You're sure?"

"Positive. A few weeks ago he asked me to look into your past—you know, dig through the files—and I told him I came up empty, that you walked the straight and narrow while you lived in Taylor's Crossing."

The lines near his mouth tightened, and he muttered a nearly inaudible oath. "And he doesn't know about Dad?"

Melanie shook her head, thinking about the pictures she'd lifted from the file cabinet. "There isn't a file on your father—at least, not at the *Trib*."

Gavin's brows shot up. "But—"

"Don't ask. Just don't worry about your father."

He studied her face for a second, and her breath seemed trapped in her lungs.

With all the effort she could muster, she inched her chin up a fraction. "Is that all you want? Because I've got work to do—"

He exploded, pounding a gloved fist on the top rail of the deck. "No, damn it." His voice lowered, and he grappled for control of his emotions. "No, Melanie, it's not all I want."

"I don't think I want to hear this—"

"Just listen. I've been thinking. A lot." His gaze touched hers, and she quivered inside. It took all her grit to hide the fact that he was getting to her. "Look, I know I came on a little strong the other day."

"A little strong? You mean your impersonation of Genghis Khan? Is that what you call a little strong?"

He shook his head and let out an exasperated sigh. "You shocked me, Melanie. And you threw me for one helluva loop!"

"I didn't mean to. I just thought you should know the truth."

"It came a little late."

Melanie had heard enough. She tried to storm away, but he grabbed her arms again and his face became tender. "Let me go, Gavin," she insisted, "before we cause a scene we'll both regret!"

He ignored her. "How did you expect me to act?"

As if you cared. As if you remembered how much we loved each other. "I didn't expect anything, Gavin. And I still don't!"

"I'm sorry," he said softly, his gloved hands still gripping her arms. "Really. But you dropped a bomb on me the other day, and it's all I've thought about ever since. I made some mistakes. We both did. I'm just sorry you thought I was too irresponsible to handle fatherhood."

"Not irresponsible," she said tightly. "But I just didn't want to be the one to destroy your dreams."

He dropped his hand and yanked off his gloves. "You don't understand, do you? Eight years ago you were part of that dream," he admitted, his eyes narrowing on her. "The skiing was great, don't get me wrong. But it wasn't the same after you married Neil."

Melanie froze. She could hardly believe him. Though the pain etched across his face seemed real enough, she didn't trust him. Couldn't. "Believe it or not, Gavin, I just tried to do the right thing."

"But it wasn't right, was it?" he said softly.

"I don't think there was a right or wrong."

His eyes searched her face. She thought he might kiss her. His gaze centered on her lips for a heartbeat, but, as if he had a sixth sense, he glanced over his shoulder and furrows lined his brow. "Oh, great," he grumbled.

Melanie looked past him and spied Jan heading for the deck.

Gavin touched her shoulder. "You and I need to talk somewhere quiet, somewhere without your friend." His mouth curved down as Jan climbed onto the deck.

"I don't mean to interrupt," she said, eyeing them with interest, "but I do have a few more questions and a deadline."

"Just a minute." He turned back to Melanie. "When things slow down here, I'll call."

Melanie shook her head. "You don't have to."

"I know. But I want to."

Their gazes held for just a second, and Melanie melted inside. Quickly, she squared her shoulders. "You do that," she quipped.

Gavin cleared his throat, took in a deep breath and, folding his arms over his chest, turned his full attention back to Jan. "All right, Ms. Freemont. What is it you want to know?"

Melanie didn't stick around for the rest of the interview. She took two rolls of film, then, trying to forget that Gavin wanted to see her again, returned to the office.

Two days later, all hell broke loose.

Melanie caught her first glance of page one of the *Tribune*. With a sinking heart, she read the headline that screamed: Financial Problems Plague Ridge Resort.

"This is outrageous!" she sputtered, skimming the article and feeling sick. How could Jan have reported anything so blatantly false? The article stated that Gavin himself was in serious financial trouble, that since his injury he'd become a recluse, not giving any ski clinics, not endorsing any skiwear, not making a dime.

He'd sunk his personal fortune, according to the story, into Ridge Lodge, and when he and his partner had run out of money, they'd sought private funds from investors, who were rumored to be upset with the way their money was handled.

By the time Melanie finished reading the article, her insides were in shreds.

The pictures she'd taken of the workers readying for the opening of the resort were sadly missing. The shots that were included were some she'd shoved aside—a worried profile of Gavin, a picture of an empty lift, another shot of chairs stacked on tables in the empty bar, a photograph of Rich and Gavin talking, their faces set and grim.

Anger burned her cheeks, and her fingers clenched the thin newsprint. "That bastard," she hissed.

Guy Reardon looked up from his desk. He seemed paler than usual. "I was afraid of something like this." He dropped his pencil and sighed. "I think it's only going to get worse."

"How can it get worse?"

Guy's eyes were troubled. "Believe me, it can."

"Do you know something I don't?" she asked.

He lifted a shoulder but avoided her gaze. "It's just a feeling I've got, Mel."

"Well, it's got to stop!" Brandishing the newspaper as if it were a sword, she walked swiftly between the desks to the editor's door. She didn't even bother knocking but shoved open the door and cornered Brian. He was just hanging up the phone.

"I can't believe you published this!" she said, tossing the paper onto his cluttered desk. The headline fairly leaped from the page.

"Why not?"

"Because it's not true! I've been up to the resort!" She thumped her fingers on the front page. "There's not a shred of truth in that story!"

"Maybe you're biased."

"What?"

"Close the door, Melanie," Brian said, lowering his voice. Her skin crawled, but she yanked the door shut and stood glowering down at him while he lit a cigarette. "Let's not pull any punches, okay?" he suggested.

"Fine with me. Why the smear job on the lodge?"

"Reader interest."

"And if readers are interested in gossip, in pure speculation, in anything no matter how damaging or incorrect, the *Trib* will print it, right?"

"This has never bothered you before."

"Because it hasn't happened before. I thought this newspaper had some pride, some integrity, some sound journalism behind it!" Melanie's blood was beginning to boil. "And what about libel? Aren't you afraid of being sued?"

He thought about that and shook his head. "I think you're too personally involved."

"I'm *what*?"

His eyes behind his glasses squinted. "I know about you and Doel, Melanie. I know you dated him in high school." He reached into the top drawer of his desk and withdrew an envelope.

Melanie's stomach turned over as Brian dumped the contents of the envelope onto the newspaper she'd dropped on his desk. She recognized her own face as well as Gavin's in the black-and-white shots. They were younger, obviously in love, and seated together at Ridge Lodge long before it closed. Eight years ago.

"Where did you get these?" she whispered.

"I had Jan dig through the files. When she came up empty, I had her look through the high school records and check with people around town." He shook his head. "It seems that all the *Tribune*'s personal history on Gavin Doel is missing. As for Gavin's old man, Jim Doel, he doesn't even have a file here. Isn't that strange?"

"Not so strange. I took them, Brian."

"Big surprise. You know that's stealing, don't you?"

"I was just trying to protect my personal life."

He waved off her explanation and pointed to the prints on the desk. "It doesn't matter, does it?"

Her insides shredding, she said, "I just don't think any of our readers would be interested in this."

"And I think you're wrong. I think the readers will find everything about your...well, for lack of a better word, *affair* with Gavin Doel interesting reading."

"No!" she said vehemently.

"It'll be great. The angle will be The Girl He Left Behind But Never Forgot."

"It'll never sell, Brian. Too much schmaltz."

"I don't think so."

Desperate, she whispered, "You can't be serious."

Brian frowned. "Look, Melanie, I've got a problem. If I don't increase circulation, I'm out of a job. Now, from my experience, I can tell you what will sell papers."

"My life?"

"Not yours. Doel's."

"My private life is none of your business, none of the readers' business."

"Unless you're involved with a celebrity."

"Not even then!"

"Anyway, I know, for whatever reason, you broke off with Doel and married your ex."

Melanie's face drained of color. Sweat dotted her back. He couldn't know about the baby—or could he? Her knees were suddenly weak, but she forced herself to stand, her fists tightening, her fingernails pressing painfully into her palms. "My life is not open for inspection," she said quietly. "And neither is Gavin's!"

He studied the tip of his cigarette. "You know, this can work to our advantage. Mine, yours and the *Tribune*'s."

"How's that?" she asked suspiciously, not entirely sure she wanted to hear his rationale.

"I want you to get close to Doel again, see what you can find out."

"You're not serious," she whispered.

"Why not?"

Her eyes narrowed on the man she had once respected. "If you don't know, I'm not about to tell you."

"Hey, this is business—"

"Not to me, Brian. I quit!"

His eyes grew round. "You don't know what you're saying!"

"Oh, yes, I do," Melanie flung back with newfound conviction. "And you know what? It feels good. I should've done this the first time you suggested I dig up some dirt on Gavin!"

"I'm just doing my job, Melanie."

"Well, you can do it without my help!" With all the dignity she could muster, she turned on her heel and marched out of the office, letting the door bang closed behind her. More than one interested glance was cast in her direction, but she was too angry to meet anyone's eyes. She crossed the room to her desk. Grabbing her purse, briefcase, mug, camera case and coat, she took one final look at the newspaper office and started for the doors.

"What happened?" Constance asked, biting on her lower lip nervously.

"Ask Brian."

"You're leaving?"

"For good."

"But . . ." Constance glanced quickly to Brian's glassed-in office. "I'll call you."

"Do that."

As she headed through the front doors, Melanie ran into Jan and couldn't help saying, "I don't think Barbara Walters has too much to worry about."

"What?"

"Your story, Jan. It's garbage."

"You're the one who was holding out," Jan reminded her. "You knew a lot about Doel and then you took the damned files—"

"Wouldn't you, if you were in my shoes?" With that Melanie swung outside, not feeling the cold wind as it blew from the east.

"I told you that girl was trouble!" Jim Doel flung a copy of the *Tribune* onto the empty bench in the weight room.

"What girl?" Gavin, working on strengthening his thigh muscles, let the weights drop with a clang.

"You know which one." Jim's face was florid, his mouth a firm, uncompromising line.

"You must be talking about Melanie."

"That's right."

Grabbing a towel, Gavin wiped the sweat from his face and ignored the churning in his gut. "What happened?"

"See for yourself!" Jim growled, motioning toward the newspaper.

The headline nearly jumped off the front page. "Son of a..." He bit off the oath as he saw that the article was written by Jan Freemont. "How do you know Melanie's involved?"

"She works for that rag, doesn't she?"

"Yeah, but she already told me that Brian Michaels was up to something. I doubt that she would tip me off, then be a part of it."

"Why not? That way she looks innocent."

"She *is* innocent," he retorted vehemently, wanting to believe his own words, instantly defending her.

"If you ask me, you've got it all wrong. If she works for the paper, she's part of the problem." Jim sank onto the empty bench, lifted his wool cap and scratched his head. "I know you've always been soft when it comes to Melanie," he said quietly, "but it seems to me she causes you nothin' but grief."

If you only knew, Gavin thought, reading the article and slowly seething. Though no concrete evidence was given, the story suggested that Ridge Lodge would close soon after it opened, leaving its investors, and anyone foolish enough to pay in advance for lift tickets and lodging, high and dry.

Gavin stripped the towel from his neck. "This is probably my fault," he admitted.

"Your fault?"

"For not playing the game."

"What game?"

"Years ago I met Brian Michaels. He was a reporter with the paper in Colorado. He wanted dirt on the ski team and then personal stuff on me and my teammates. I not only told him to get lost, I called the paper he worked for and complained. So did my coach. Michaels lost his job."

"And you think he'd hold a grudge?"

A corner of Gavin's lip lifted cynically. "I don't think he'd chase me down to get back at me, but since he's here and I'm here and I've got something to lose, I'd bet he can't resist a chance to get even."

"And so he's payin' you back?"

"Not for long," he muttered, his eyes narrowing. He wasn't about to take all the bad publicity lying down. Rich was a lawyer; he could deal with the legalities of libel. As for Michaels, he intended to talk to the owners of the paper.

But first he had to deal with Melanie.

Leaving his father sitting on the bench, Gavin walked through the shower, then threw on a pair of jeans, a sweater and a battered pair of running shoes. On his way out of the lodge, he spied the manager and left some quick instructions.

He couldn't wait to hear Melanie's side of the story.

Newspaper tucked under his arm, he shouldered open the door of the lodge. A blast of cold mountain air swirled in. Outside, dusk was settling around the mountain, shading the snow-covered landscape in shades of lavender and blue. He barely noticed.

As he climbed into his truck, Gavin told himself that Melanie wasn't involved in this—she wouldn't have used him for a story. But he couldn't ignore the seeds of doubt his father had planted.

After all, hadn't she lied to him, kept the secret of their child from him? If there really had been a pregnancy. His lips pursed in a grim line as he shoved the truck into gear and accelerated. The pickup lurched forward. She wouldn't have lied about the baby. There was no reason. No, he decided, his jaw clamped, her story was genuine—at least to a point. He still wasn't convinced that she'd kept the secret for altruistic purposes. No, she probably wanted to snag rich Neil Brooks all along.

Or had the baby been Neil's? Was there a chance she'd been sleeping with Neil at the same time she was having an affair with him? That made more sense. Neil would much rather claim his own child than a bastard of Gavin's.

"Stop it," he ground out, his fingers tight on the wheel.

His chest constricted, but he forced his thoughts back eight years to the hayloft where they had met, to the moonlight that had streamed through the window to cast her black hair in a silver sheen, to the look of sweet, vulnerable innocence that had lingered in her eyes.

No, he couldn't believe that she had lain with him one night and the next with Neil Brooks. No matter what had happened between them, he wouldn't believe that she was that emotionally cold and calculating. "Get over it," he growled at himself as he cranked the wheel. The truck skidded around the corner, then straightened.

In the distance, through the pines, the city lights of Taylor's Crossing winked in the darkness. It would take twenty minutes to get to Melanie's house. He only hoped that she was home—and alone.

Chapter Twelve

Melanie finished matting some photographs in her studio, returned a couple of calls on her answering machine and tentatively planned two portrait shoots for the next couple of days. Since she was officially out of a job, she needed all the work she could get—and that included working at Ridge Lodge. With Gavin.

She dialed the resort's number and was told by a foreman that Gavin and Rich were out.

"Terrific!" she muttered, wondering about their reaction to the article as she fixed herself a meager dinner made from leftover chicken, vegetables and gravy. "Use your imagination, Mel," she told herself as she rolled premixed pie dough and laid it over the top of a casserole dish. Gavin would be furious—and hell-bent to avenge the article. "It's going to be trouble. Big trouble," she predicted, switching on the radio and adjusting the volume. The disk jockey reported that another storm was about to hit the central Oregon Cascades. More snow for the lodge, she thought. At least some news was positive!

Sassafras, hoping for a morsel of chicken, stood at attention near the stove. "Later," she promised, then eyed her creation. "We'll both have some—to celebrate."

Though not working for the *Tribune* created a score of financial problems, she felt a sense of relief.

Shoving the dish of chicken pot pie into the oven, she winked at the old dog. "Tonight, we dine like kings," she announced, then wrinkled her nose. "Well, not really kings, maybe more like dukes or squires or...well, peasants would probably be more appropriate. But we're celebrating nonetheless."

To prove her point, she pulled out the bottle of champagne she'd had in the refrigerator since her birthday and popped the cork. She found a glass high in the cupboard over the stove.

"Here's to freedom," she said, pouring the champagne. It frothed over the side of the glass, and she laughed. "I guess I won't get a job pouring drinks down at the Peg and Platter, hmm?"

Sassafras whined and lowered his head between his paws, still staring up at her with wide brown eyes as the doorbell pealed.

With a loud growl, the dog leaped to his feet and raced, toenails clicking on the old hardwood floor, to the front door. Melanie set her glass on the counter and followed.

Through the narrow window near the front door, she saw Gavin, collar turned against the wind, blond hair dark and wet, snow on the shoulders of his leather jacket, jaw set and stern.

A newspaper was folded neatly under his arm. Today's edition of the *Tribune*.

"Give me strength," she whispered prayerfully as she unlocked the door and swung it open.

"What the hell is this?" he demanded, shaking the paper in front of her nose.

"It's good to see you, too," she tossed back at him, the hackles on the back of her neck instantly rising.

He strode in without an invitation. "Whose smear job is this?"

Melanie closed the door behind him and braced herself. "Brian Michaels's."

"And what did you have to do with it?"

"Nothing."

His sensual lips compressed. "You're sure?"

"Absolutely. I didn't see the front page until this morning."

"Helluva way to bring tourists into town." He flung the newspaper onto a nearby table.

"Did you come over here to accuse me of something?" Melanie asked, unable to keep the irritation out of her voice. "Because if you did, let's get down to it."

"What would I accuse you of?"

"I don't know. It sounds like you think I was part of some conspiracy on the paper."

"No, I don't believe that," he said quietly, though he was still angry. White lines bracketed his mouth, and his jaw was clenched so hard a muscle worked beneath his cheek.

"Oh, so this is just a social call," she said, unable to resist baiting him.

"I just want to know what's going on. You work for the paper—"

"Worked. As in past tense."

His eyes narrowed. "What happened?"

She motioned to the newspaper. "That happened and . . . well, it's probably going to get worse."

"How?"

"Brian's not about to let up. Come on into the kitchen. I've got something in the oven and I've got to keep my eye on it.'' He followed her through the hallway by the stairs. The scent of stewing chicken and warm spices wafted through the air. ''Join me?'' she asked, holding onto the neck of the champagne bottle.

He lifted a shoulder.

''I'll take that as a yes.'' She poured his glass and handed it to him. ''I'm celebrating.''

Lifting an eyebrow, he took a sip from his glass. ''Celebrating what?''

''My emancipation. I quit the *Tribune*.''

He frowned. ''You said things would get worse.''

''They will. Brian found out that we dated in high school, Gavin. He plans to use it. He even asked me to get close to you again, get you to confide in me.''

''Great guy, your boss.''

''Ex-boss,'' she reminded him. ''That's when I quit.''

''How much does he know?''

She shook her head. ''I don't know.''

''About the baby?''

His words sliced through the air like a sharp knife. ''I don't think so,'' she replied, shivering.

''Who does?''

Shaking her head, she frowned. ''My dad did and Uncle Bart and Aunt Lila.'' She closed her eyes and rubbed her temple. ''And of course Neil and the doctor.''

''No one else?''

''I don't think so.'' Drawing in a shuddering breath she opened her eyes again and, grateful for something to do with her hands, lifted the glass to her lips. ''I lost the baby before I'd started to show—before Neil or I had said anything to our friends.''

Gavin's nostrils flared. ''And you didn't mention it to your 'friend' Jan?''

''Of course not!'' Melanie replied guiltily. She knew now that she should never have confided anything to Jan. ''I told her we dated so she'd stop asking questions. I didn't think it would backfire.'' She finished her drink in one gulp.

''When reporters can't find news, they create it.''

''Not usually,'' Melanie replied, noticing that Gavin's glass had been drained. She poured them each another glass and asked, ''So why is it that Brian has it in for you?''

''You think he does?''

She nodded. ''Don't you?''

''Probably. I met him a long time ago in Colorado. He started sticking his nose in where it didn't belong, and I complained. He was fired shortly thereafter.''

''He never mentioned it,'' Melanie said thoughtfully. ''In fact, when your name was first linked with the lodge, Brian was interested, very interested. But I don't think it was because he wanted to dig up some scandal. At least, I hope not.'' She sipped from her glass again and stared over the rim at Gavin.

He was tense, his features hard, the muscles beneath his shirt bunched, but his gaze, when it touched hers, was warm and seductive. His tawny eyes were as they had always been, erotic and male, knowing.

Her mouth grew dry, and she quickly finished her second glass of champagne.

He stood near the windows of the nook, one shoulder resting on the door frame, large fingers wrapped around the slim stem of his fragile wineglass.

The soft noises in the house filled the room—the slow tick of the clock in the front hall, the steady rumble of the furnace, the muted strains of a love song from the radio, a creak of ancient timbers and the old collie's whispering breath as he slept under the table.

''So what're we going to do about this?'' he finally said, his eyes searching her face.

''About what?''

''Us.''

That single word caused her heart to start thumping. "I don't know if there is an 'us.' I'm not sure there ever was."

"Sure there was," he said easily, finishing his champagne and setting the empty glass on the counter.

"It was a long time ago."

"What about last week, when you were up at the lodge?"

Yes. What about those precious hours we spent together? "As I remember, it didn't end well."

"You shocked me." He let out a long, slow breath, but his gaze never wavered. "If I'd known about the baby..."

"What, Gavin? What would you have done?"

"Come home."

Her heart wrenched. "But that would have been no good," she whispered, her words difficult. "You didn't stay for me. You couldn't come back for a baby. You would've felt trapped." She saw the denial on his lips and held up a palm. "You would have, Gavin. Someday, sometime. You would have wondered, 'what if?' "

"And you weren't willing to gamble that I would decide it didn't matter?"

"No."

He crossed the room slowly, his gaze moving deliberately from her eyes to her lips. "You didn't give me enough credit, Melanie."

"I just wanted you to be happy—"

Wrapping strong arms around her waist, he drew her against him. "Happiness is elusive," he whispered before he kissed her, his lips molding over hers. He smelled of snowflakes and tasted of champagne.

Knowing she shouldn't give in, Melanie closed her eyes and leaned against him, content to feel his hands splayed possessively against her back. She welcomed the feel of his tongue as it slid easily between her teeth, his hard body pressed so intimately to hers. His thighs moved, pinning her legs to his. Her pulse leaped, and her heart thundered.

When at last he lifted his head, his eyes were glazed. He touched her wet lips with one finger, tracing her pout, his gaze searching hers. "I thought that if I ever saw you again, it wouldn't matter," he confessed. "I told myself that I was over you, that you'd been a boyhood fascination, nothing more." Disgust filtered through his words. "Obviously I was wrong."

The timer on the stove buzzed so loudly Melanie jumped.

"What's that?" Gavin asked.

"Dinner."

"It'll wait." In a quick motion, he turned off the stove and the buzzer. Noticing the coat rack near the back door, he tossed a long denim coat in her direction, grabbed her hand and tugged, pulling her outside.

"Hey, what're you doing?" she said, laughing as he led her down the back steps and through the snow. "I'm not dressed for this."

"Don't worry about your clothes," he said, sliding a hard look over his shoulder.

"Gavin . . . ?"

He didn't answer but just tugged on her arm, leading her across the yard. The sky had turned black, in stark contrast to the white earth. Snow covered tree branches, roofs, eaves and ground, drifting against the fence and piling onto the stack of wood near the barn.

The barn.

The air was suddenly trapped in her lungs.

With a tingling sense of déjà vu, she knew where he was taking her. Her throat went dry, and time seemed to spin backward.

He tugged on the handle of the door, and it slid to the side on rusted rollers, creaking and groaning. Inside, the dark interior smelled of dust and old hay. There were no more cattle or horses, and the barn itself was in sad need of repair.

Melanie balked. Her breath fogged. "You're not seriously thinking of—"

"Let's go," he insisted, leaving the barn door open, letting in a pale stream of illumination from the security lamp near the garage and the silvery reflection of the snow.

He paused at the bottom of the ladder to the hayloft, and Melanie stopped, yanking her hand from his. "They say you can never go back, Gavin."

"I'm not going back."

"This might not be a good idea."

"Why not?"

"Eight years."

His arms surrounded her, and his mouth closed over hers. Memories rushed through her mind, yet they paled to the here and now, to the rough feel of his jacket against her cheek, the smell of his cologne mingling with the dust, the warmth of his hand pressing hard against the small of her back. She'd been kidding herself, she realized, when she'd made love to him before and thought she could remain emotionally detached.

Groaning, he half pushed her up toward the loft. Melanie's throat went dry, but a thrill of anticipation skittered up her spine and she stepped onto the ladder.

With each rung, she wondered if she were making a mistake she would never be able to undo, but she kept climbing, one step at a time, until she stood in the cold, darkened loft and Gavin was beside her, his breath stirring her hair as he slid the coat from her shoulders and tossed it onto the old straw. Then, holding her chin between both his palms, he ground a kiss against her lips that made her shiver from head to toe.

A tremor passed through Melanie, and she was sure he could feel it as his tongue pressed insistently against her teeth and into her mouth, searching, tasting, plundering.

His hands held her tight against him, his thighs pressing against hers, her breasts crushed to his chest.

"I never forgot you Melanie," he admitted, his voice rough. "Never." His hands slid lower, cupping her buttocks, pulling full against him. Through their clothes, she felt the hardness between his legs, the urgency in his touch.

"I tried. God, I tried. And there were other women—women I hoped would make me forget."

"Shh," she whispered, the breath torn from her lungs. She touched his lips with the tip of one finger. "I don't want to hear about them."

He drew her finger into his mouth and sucked, his tongue playing havoc with her nerve endings as it tickled and toyed.

Melanie's abdomen tightened. Liquid heat scorched her veins, and she couldn't stop the moan that slipped through her lips.

Kissing her again, he pulled her closer, forcing one of her legs to move upward and rest against his hip. Her head lolled backward, and her arms wrapped around his neck as they fell to the hay. The old denim coat was a meager blanket against the cold air and the rough hay, but Melanie didn't notice. She was on fire inside, and the scratch of the straw only heightened her already tingling senses.

Gavin's mouth found hers again. Hot, anxious lips pressed hard against hers in a kiss that was as punishing as it was filled with promise.

"Gavin," she cried wantonly. She arched upward, closer, closer. He stripped away her sweater and took both lace-covered breasts in his hands. Burying his head between the mounds, he kissed the skin over her breasts as he pulled the bra away. The stubble on his chin was rough, his lips and tongue wet and wild and wonderful as his hot breath whispered across her nipples and caused a fire to burn deep within.

He teased her. His tongue grazed a nipple, parrying and thrusting, wetting the tight bud until Melanie was wild with desire.

An ache stole through her, and she cradled his head to her breast. He suckled long and hard, and Melanie grasped his hair in her hands, her fingers tangling in his thick blond locks.

He began to move against her, and she felt his rhythm, still holding him close as he struggled out of his clothes and kicked his jeans away. Lord, she wanted him. She could barely think for the desire rippling deep within.

His eyes were gold and glowing with a passion matched only by her own as he discarded her clothes quickly. And then they were naked. Again in the barn, but this time the love between them was a savage, forceful desire that stripped them bare. "You make me crazy," he muttered, as if trying to get a grip on his exploding passion.

Was he going to stop? Now? Oh, God, no! "Gavin...please..." Writhing, she lifted her hips, and he ran his hand along her inner thigh, touching her moistness at the apex of her legs, and groaning in satisfaction at the evidence of her desire.

"Melanie..." he whispered, his breath fanning her skin, his tongue wetting a trail against her leg. "Oh, Melanie..." And she shivered in anticipation.

His hands once again found her buttocks, and she moved closer to him, trembling with desire as he found her, pleasuring her until she could stand the sensual teasing no longer.

"Gavin, oh, please..." She reached for him, drawing him up along her body, her hands forcing his head to hers, and she kissed him with all the desire flooding through her veins. Touching the flat nipples in his mat of golden hair, she sucked on his lower lip and he lost control.

"What do you want from me?" he rasped, his voice echoing off the old beams.

"Everything!"

Shifting, he opened her legs wide with his knees. He mounted her then, his legs fitting inside her own, before he plunged deep and she arched upward, meeting the fervor of his thrusts anxiously, closing around him again and again, their bodies fusing in savage fury.

Her fingers dug into the supple flesh of his arms as he entered and withdrew, pushing her to the edge of rapture, until at the sound of his primal cry, she shuddered, convulsing against him, a thousand sparks igniting and sizzling.

With a dry gasp, he collapsed atop her, crushing her breasts and pressing her hard against the rough denim coat. Perspiration fused their bodies, and his curling chest hair tickled her sensitive bare skin.

"Melanie, oh, Melanie," he whispered, his voice raw and hoarse. "Oh, God, what am I going to do with you?"

And what am I going to do with you? Wrapping her arms around him, she closed her eyes and tried to slow the still-rapid beating of her heart. She wasn't going to fall apart now, to weep for what might have been. But she held on to him tightly, as if afraid he might disappear.

When he slowly rolled to his side, she reluctantly released him.

"This is insane," he said. "Just plain crazy." He plucked a piece of straw from her hair and sighed loudly.

"So what're we going to do about it?"

"I wish I knew," he muttered. "I wish to Holy God I knew."

Chapter Thirteen

"I think it would be best if we went low profile," Gavin stated, finishing his second helping of slightly burned chicken pot pie. As if the passion that had exploded between them less than an hour before had been forgotten.

"Low profile?" Melanie repeated, unable to touch her food.

"If Michaels is really serious about making us the lead story in his next issue, we should diffuse it."

"By not being together?" Why did it hurt so much?

As if noticing her pain, he reached across the table and wrapped warm fingers around her palm. His thumb slowly rubbed the back side of her had. "I just don't want the focus of attention shifted from the lodge to us." He offered her a patient smile. "It's only for a little while, till the lodge gets on its feet. And believe me," he added with a devilish twinkle in his eyes, "it'll be as hard on me as it is on you."

"You think so?"

"I know it." With a sigh, he scraped his chair back and reached for his coat. "I've got to get back, but I'll see you at the resort, right. Rich says you've got some pictures on consignment in the ski shop?"

"That's right."

"And you'll be there for the grand opening?"

She nodded, though her throat was tight as she walked with him to the back door. "Of course."

"Bring your ski gear. Maybe we could take a few runs together."

"You'll be too busy."

"Then come up sometime before." He reached for the handle of the door.

"I thought we were going low profile," she teased, though she didn't feel much like joking.

"We will. I doubt if Michaels will catch us on Devil's Ridge or West Canyon." He smiled as he mentioned two of the toughest runs on the mountain.

"It's a date," she said as he drew her outside and swept her into his arms. His lips caressed hers in a kiss that was full of promise and pain.

When he lifted his head again, he groaned. "We've got to do something about this," he whispered, his voice rough as he rested his chin against her crown and held her close. Wrapped in the smell and feel of him, she hated to let go.

When at last he released her, she stood on the porch and watched as he ran across the yard and climbed into his truck. With a roar the engine caught, and as the pickup backed out of the drive, the beams of his headlights flashed against the old barn and the trunks of the trees in the backyard. As the light receded, she noticed the huge ponderosa with the gash in its bark, the ugly cut her father had made when he'd first learned she was pregnant all those years ago.

She closed her eyes for a second and wondered where she and Gavin would go from here. Would the future be bright and filled with happiness, or black with the loss of a love that was never meant to be?

"Don't even think about it," she told herself as she walked back into the house.

"I've got good news," Dr. Hodges said as he switched on the light and illuminated an X ray of Gavin's leg.

"I could use some." Gavin eyed the X ray but couldn't make head nor tail of it. He hadn't seen Melanie in days, and he was irritable. The lodge was opening the day after tomorrow, and he was up to his eyeballs in preparations. But he really didn't give a damn. He just wanted to be with her.

"The fracture's healed." Hodges studied the X ray again, narrowing his eyes, looking for some sign of the flaw that had sidelined Gavin.

Gavin felt a slow smile spread across his face as he thought about the season ahead. "I can race again."

"Well," Hodges said, his lips protruding thoughtfully, "there's no physical reason why you can't, at least not in your ankle. But if I were you, I'd give it a year before I raced competitively again."

"So you're releasing me?"

Hodges smiled a boyish grin. "For the time being. But if you have any pain—any at all—I want you back here, pronto."

"You got it." Gavin stood and shook Hodges's hand. He felt as if a ton of bricks had been lifted from his shoulders and he wanted to celebrate. With Melanie. This afternoon!

Melanie was miserable. The past few days without Gavin she'd been cranky and upset and her stomach had been queasy. "All because of one man," she chided herself as she snapped on the lights in the darkroom and walked into the kitchen.

"About time you finished in there."

Melanie nearly jumped out of her skin. Gavin was there, half-kneeling, scratching Sassafras behind his ears.

"How'd you get in?" she asked, drinking in the sight of him. Dressed in gray slacks and a pullover sweater, his skin tanned and his hair unruly, he was as handsome as ever. He glanced up at her and her heart turned over.

"Breach in security. The front door was unlocked. I heard you in the darkroom and I didn't want to bother you." He straightened and his eyes sparkled. "Come on, get your gear."

"My gear?" she repeated as his arms surrounded her.

"We're going skiing."

"Now? But I have work—"

"No time. We're celebrating." Wrapping strong arms around her waist, he spun her off the floor.

"Hey, wait. Stop! Your leg!" she cried, though it was her stomach that lurched.

"That's what we're celebrating," he said, dropping her back to her feet and planting a kiss against her forehead. "My health."

"Your health? Gavin, you're not making any sense."

He winked. "The doctor's released me. Given me the okay to race again!"

She felt her face drain of color. "This season?"

"As soon as I can pull it off. I'm rusty, of course, and older than most of the guys on the circuit. It'll take some intense training, but I can work out at the lodge. And once Ridge Lodge is up and running, Rich and the manager can handle the rest."

So he was leaving! Again! All her private hopes disintegrated. Her father was right. Gavin's first love was and would always be the thrill of downhill racing.

"Are you all right?" he asked, his eyes suddenly serious.

"I'm fine," she lied, forcing a smile that felt as fake as a three-dollar bill. "Just let me get my things." Wriggling out of his embrace, she ran out of the kitchen and upstairs. Her head was pounding, and when she looked in the mirror she noticed that her face had turned ashen. "Great, Melanie—you're a real trooper," she chided, changing into a black turtleneck and her new jumpsuit, a purple and sea-green one-piece that she'd found in a local shop before she'd quit working for the *Tribune*.

She found her skis, poles and boots and packed a small bag for her goggles, gloves, sunglasses and an extra set of clothes. Then, before she went back downstairs, she splashed water on her face and fought a sudden attack of nausea.

"Hang in there," she said angrily, furious with herself for overreacting to the news that he was leaving. A little blush and lipstick helped, and when she hurried downstairs, she'd pushed all thoughts of life without Gavin from her mind. They still had a little time together, and she was determined to make the best of it.

They drove to the lodge, and while Gavin changed, Melanie waited for him outside. The sky was blue and clear, and other skiers tackled the runs, gliding gracefully down the slopes or, in the case of the less experienced skiers, grappled with their balance as they snow-plowed on the gradual hills.

Melanie smiled as she heard the crunch of boots behind her. Turning, she expected to find Gavin but was disappointed. Jim Doel was walking toward her, and his face was firm and set.

"I'm surprised to see you here," he said.

Nervously, she replied, "Gavin and I decided to ski together before the crowd hits this weekend."

Jim frowned. "Look, I don't see any reason to beat around the bush."

Melanie braced herself.

"A lot of things have happened between your family and mine, and Lord knows if I could change things I would. I'm the reason you grew up without a mother and I've lived with that for eighteen years. I've also lived with the fact that I wasn't much of a father to Gavin, but he made it on his own. Became one of the best skiers in the whole damned country."

"You should be proud," Melanie said icily.

"Of some things. All I'm saying is that I'm sorry for the accident. If I could've traded places with your ma, I would've. But I couldn't."

"If you're expecting me to forgive you—"

"Nope. What I expect is for you to leave Gavin alone. You've messed with his mind enough." He raised faded eyes to hers. "He's got a second chance, you know. Most people don't get another one. And he loves racing."

"I know."

"So let him go."

She inched her chin up a fraction. "I'll never stand in the way of Gavin's career."

He didn't look as if he believed her, but she didn't care. She had something else she had to get off her chest. And, though a part of her longed to blame him for the tragedy, she knew it was unfair. He'd paid for it with every day of his life. "As for my mother's death, it was a long time ago," she said, offering a slight smile. "I hope you can put it in the past where it belongs. I have."

His jaw worked.

"And, though I doubt you and I will ever be close, regardless of how we both feel about Gavin, I'd like for us to try to be fair with each other."

His lips compressed. "All I want from you is a promise that you won't interfere in his life."

"How Gavin lives his life is Gavin's business."

"Glad you see things my way."

"But I do care about him very much."

"Then do what's best for him." With that, he strode toward the machine shed, and Melanie let out her breath slowly. She watched as Jim disappeared inside the shed, then she headed toward the lift. She wondered if she and Jim Doel could ever be comfortable around each other. Probably not.

Frowning, she adjusted her bindings and practiced skiing on the flat area behind the lodge.

"Hey! Let's go!" Gavin, already on skis, was making his way to the Daredevil lift. Wearing a royal blue jacket and black ski pants, he planted his poles and she followed. Her heart soared at the sight of him, and she shoved his father from her thoughts. Today she was going to enjoy being with the man she loved.

The lift carried them over snow-covered runs, thick stands of pine and a frozen creek. Gavin rested one arm over the back of the chair, and they laughed and talked as they were swept up the mountainside.

Cool air brushed her cheeks and caught in her hair. Gavin touched her cheek and she smiled, happy to be alone with him. At the top of the lift, they slid down the ramp.

"Follow me," Gavin urged, his voice excited, and Melanie only hoped that she could keep up with him.

Melanie's ski legs were better than she remembered, and she flew down the mountainside, snow spraying, hair whipping in the wind. Gavin, far ahead of her now, skied effortlessly. His movements were sure and strong, and as he glided from one plateau to the next, he waited for her.

At one plateau, she didn't stop to catch her breath but flew past him, her laughter trailing in her wake. Gavin gave chase and breezed past her along a narrow trail that sliced through the trees.

Exhilaration pushed her onward, and the wind rushed against her face, stinging her eyes and tangling her hair. She rounded a bend and found Gavin stopped dead in his tracks, flagging her down.

"Giving up?" she quipped as she dug in her skis and stopped near him. She was breathing hard, her chest rising and falling rapidly.

"No, I just thought you could use a rest." To her amazement, he pressed hard on his bindings, releasing his skis from his boots.

"Me?" she mocked, still gulping breaths of fresh air. "Oh, no, I could do this for hours! You're just wimping out on me."

"Ha!" He glanced up, and his smile slashed his tanned skin. "Well," he drawled, "I did have an ulterior motive."

"And what's that?"

"I wanted to get you alone up here."

For the first time she realized that they had skied away from the major runs and that the lifts were far in the distance. The area was secluded, trees surrounding the trail and the frozen creek that peeked from beneath drifts of snow.

Gavin reached down and unfastened her bindings, as well.

A thrill raced up Melanie's spine. "And what did you plan to do with me?"

"Just this," he said, taking her into his arms and pressing ice-cold lips to hers. They tumbled together in the snow and laughed as the icy powder tickled their noses and caught in their hair.

"Someone could come along at any minute," she protested.

"Let them." He kissed her again, and his lips warmed hers, heating her blood, easing the chill from her body.

Melanie's heart knocked loudly, her pulse leaped and she wished she could stay here forever, locked in his arms, the pristine stillness of the snow-covered forest surrounding them.

When he reluctantly drew back, his gold-colored eyes gleamed and he smiled at her as if they'd been lovers for years, as if all the pain and twisted truths of the past had never existed. "I love you, Melanie," he said, and tears tickled the corners of her eyes. She could hardly believe her ears. Gavin loved her? If only she could believe it was true.

"Well?" he asked.

"You know I love you, Gavin. I hate to admit it, but I probably always have."

He laughed. "What're we going to do about that?"

"I don't know," she replied honestly.

"Well, I do." He kissed her again and, pulling her against him, lay with her in the snow. Warmth invaded her body, and she closed her eyes, remembering how much she'd loved him. That love seemed to pale compared to the emotions that tore at her now.

Shouts and hoots interrupted the stillness, and Gavin, with a groan, struggled to his feet. He pulled her upright just as two teenagers swished past them, spraying snow and hollering loudly.

"Come on," Gavin said, eying the retreating figures. "Let's get in a couple more runs before I lose control completely."

"Or I do," Melanie thought aloud, stepping into her skis.

They spent the rest of the afternoon on the mountain, laughing and talking.

Finally, after dark, Gavin drove her home. He lingered on the doorstep, holding her close and pressing urgent lips to hers.

"You could stay," she offered, surprised at her sudden boldness.

"I have to be at the lodge."

"Tonight?"

"I should be."

She grinned up at him. "What would it take to change your mind?" she asked coyly, her fingers crawling up his chest.

He grabbed her hands. "You're dangerous."

"Am I?"

He kissed her again, harder this time, his lips sealing over hers, trapping the breath in her lungs. When he finally lifted his head, his eyes had darkened. "Oh, the hell with it! Since when was I responsible?"

Lifting her off her feet, he carried her inside, slammed and locked the door with one hand and hauled her upstairs, where he dropped her unceremoniously onto the bed.

A second later he was beside her, kissing her and removing their clothes, anxious to love her. And Melanie didn't stop him. Sighing, she wound her arms around his neck, tangled her fingers in his hair and pulled his head to hers.

Tonight, she thought. *I'll just think about tonight....*

She woke early the next morning. It was still dark outside, but Gavin was staring down at her, his hand moving slowly against the smooth texture of her shoulder. She could see his face in the half light from the moon sifting through the window.

"I've got to go," he whispered.

"Already?" She clung to him, his body warm as it molded to hers.

"No choice. The grand opening is tomorrow."

"At least let me make you breakfast."

He brushed a wayward strand of hair from her eyes. "You don't have to."

"I know I don't," she said crankily, unhappy that he was leaving her, "but I want to."

"Sure you do." He laughed as she climbed out of bed and, slipping into her bathrobe, struggled with the belt.

Downstairs, she started the coffee, opened the back door for Sassafras, then decided to get the paper. Donning a ski jacket over her robe, she hurried to the mailbox, grabbed the paper with near-frozen fingers and returned to the warmth of the kitchen.

She tossed the paper onto the table and returned the coat to the rack, then set about making waffles and sausage, suppressing a yawn and listening to the sound of water running as Gavin showered.

How right this all felt, she thought dreamily, wondering what it would be like to be married to him.

Within minutes Gavin hurried downstairs, his hair combed and wet, his expression positively devilish. "Well, aren't you the domestic one?" he joked, wrapping strong arms around her waist and standing behind her.

"Watch it." she warned, lifting her spatula. "I'm armed."

He laughed, his breath stirring her hair. "And I'm worried."

"Sit," she ordered good-naturedly, pointing with the spatula to the table. "You're the one who had to get up at this ridiculous hour."

He did as he was told, and as Melanie plucked the first waffle from the iron, Gavin snapped open the paper. Melanie placed the waffle and a couple of sizzling sausage links onto a plate, turned and set the plate on the table. As she did, Gavin's hand grabbed her wrist.

She giggled, thinking he was still playing, but when she caught his glance, she realized that something was horribly wrong. His eyes were hard, his nostrils flared and his mouth a grim, hard line.

"What—what's wrong?"

"Everything!"

"I don't understand."

Confused, she looked down at the table, then stood frozen, reading the headlines of the front page of the *Tribune*:

Gavin Doel Returns To Taylor's Crossing For Long Lost Love.

"Oh, God," she whispered.

"It just gets better and better," he said, his lips tight.

Swallowing hard, she read the article, written by Jan, which detailed their romance and the feud between the two families. There was a picture of her and Gavin at the lodge, obviously young and in love, and a picture of Jim Doel, the man who went to jail for negligently killing Melanie's mother.

"This is too much," she whispered, reading on and feeling sick to her stomach. There was nothing written about the baby, just Melanie's quick change of heart and short marriage to Neil Brooks.

"It could be worse," he muttered, "and it probably will be."

"What do you mean?"

"Just that Michaels isn't about to let up. Each week he's going to find something to dredge up. Again and again."

"The baby?" she whispered.

"Eventually."

"Oh, no." She sank into the nearest chair and told herself to be strong, that there was nothing more to worry about. She reached for Gavin's hand, but he stood slowly and impaled her with angry eyes.

"I think I'd better leave."

"Why?"

"Because I've got things to do." His face darkened with determination. "And I can't be sure that some reporter or hotshot photographer isn't camped outside your back door." There wasn't the least spark of friendliness—or love—in his eyes. His expression was murderous.

"You—you think I was a part of this?" she whispered, disbelieving.

His jaw clamped together. "I don't know, Melanie. Were you?"

"That's absurd! You know I wouldn't do anything . . ." But she could see it in his eyes—all the past lies and accusations surfacing again. Her world tilted, and her fantasy shattered. "You're right, you'd better leave," she said, standing on legs that shook and threatened to buckle.

He hesitated just a moment as a glimmer of love glinted in his eyes, but he grabbed his jacket and stormed out of the house, letting the door bang behind him.

"And good riddance!" she said, tossing his uneaten breakfast into the trash before she collapsed and slid down the cabinets to the floor. Tears flooded her eyes, and she tried to fight them back.

Pounding an impotent fist against the cabinets, she hiccupped and sobbed, and then her stomach, already on edge, rumbled nauseously. She scrambled to her feet, dashed to the bathroom and promptly threw up.

When she was finished, she sluiced cold water on her face and looked at her white-faced reflection in the mirror. *You've really got it bad,* she thought sadly. She hadn't wretched in years. The last time had been—

Time stopped. The world spun crazily.

With numbing disbelief Melanie realized that the last time she'd been so ill had been eight years ago, when she'd been pregnant with Gavin's child.

Chapter Fourteen

Melanie stared in disbelief at the blue stick from the home pregnancy test. But there it was—physical proof that her monthly calendar wasn't inaccurate. She was, in fact, pregnant. With Gavin's child. Again.

Ecstasy mingled with pain. What could she do? Sitting on a corner of the bed, she weighed her options and decided not to make the same mistake twice. She had to tell Gavin and she had to tell him soon.

Sighing, she shoved her hair from her eyes. She had to confide in him—there was no question of that. But she didn't have to marry him. In fact, she'd be more than willing to raise his child alone.

No longer a frightened girl of seventeen, she could handle the demands of a child and a career—if she ever got her career going again. Never again would she turn to another man. Marrying Neil had been a mistake she would never repeat. If and when she married, it would be for love.

And she couldn't imagine loving anyone but Gavin.

"You're hopeless, Melanie," she told herself, but couldn't ignore the elation that she was pregnant.

Suddenly she wondered how she'd be able to speak with Gavin alone tonight—opening night. She thought about avoiding the party but knew that both Gavin and Rich expected her to attend. As official photographer for the lodge, she could hardly beg out now.

She spent the day wondering how she would tell him. There was no easy way.

Finally, that evening, she took an hour getting ready for the formal party that would officially kick off the season and reopen Ridge Lodge. Tomorrow there would be races, sleigh rides, an outdoor barbecue and snowboarding and skiing demonstrations, but tonight the lodge would be ready for dancing and hobnobbing.

Not in a party mood, Melanie stepped into her one long dress, a royal blue silk sheath with high neckline and long sleeves, then added a slim silver necklace and matching bracelet. She brushed her hair and let it fall in curls that swept past her shoulders.

"Here goes nothing," she told Sassafras as she petted him on the head and slid her arms into the sleeves of her ankle-length coat.

She drove carefully to the lodge, joining a procession of cars up the steep grade and smiling to herself as snowflakes landed on the windshield. If Gavin's lodge failed, it wouldn't be for lack of snow.

The lodge was ablaze with lights. Torches were lit outside and every room cast golden rays from the windows and dormers. Melanie parked near a back entrance and, squaring her shoulders, walked through the main doors, where her pictures were now highlighted by concealed lamps.

Guests, employees, caterers and musicians already filled the lobby. In one corner a piano player and backup band were playing soft rock. In another a linen-covered table was arranged with silver platters of appetizers, and behind the bar two barkeeps were busy refilling glasses. Waiter and caterers hurried through a throng of bejeweled guests.

Smoke and laughter floated up the three stories to the ceiling, and Melanie wished she was just about anywhere else on earth. She spotted some local celebrities and a couple of famous skiers and their wives, as well as some of the more prominent townspeople.

She mingled with the crowd, searching for Gavin, wondering how she could break the news.

"Well, what do you think?" a male voice whispered in her ear. She turned to find a beaming Rich Johanson surveying the crowd.

"Looks like a success."

"I think so," he agreed anxiously. "And Gavin was worried!"

"That's what he does best."

"I—um, sorry about the article in the paper," Rich said. "I had no idea—"

"None of us did," she said. Then her heart thumped painfully. Behind Rich, through the crowd, stood Gavin, tall and lean, impeccably dressed in a black tuxedo. At his side, her arm threaded through his, was the most beautiful redhead Melanie had ever seen. With a sinking heart she realized the woman was Aimee LaRoux.

Rich, following her gaze, frowned. "Surprise guest," he said with a shrug.

"She wasn't invited?"

"Not by me."

But by Gavin. Melanie cast the unhappy thought aside. She trusted Gavin, and he had told Melanie he loved her, hadn't he?

"If you'll excuse me," she said, wending her way through the guests to Gavin. He hadn't seen her yet—his head was bent as he listened to Aimee—but when he raised his eyes and found her standing in front of him, he managed a tight smile.

Melanie returned with one of her own. "Congratulations, Gavin," she said. "The party looks like a big hit."

"Thanks."

"Oh, this resort is just fabulous!" Aimee said, bubbling. "But everything Gavin touches turns to gold."

"Not quite," Gavin said.

Melanie drew on her courage. "When you've got a minute—no, not now—I'd like to talk with you."

"Alone?"

She nodded. "That would be best."

Gavin glanced at his watch, whispered something to Aimee, then, taking Melanie's arm, propelled her quickly to the back hall. "Hey, wait, you've got guests," she protested.

"Doesn't matter." He strode quickly to his private suite and locked the door behind them.

"There's something you should know—"

"Mr. Doel?" A loud knock thudded against the door.

Gavin, swearing, opened it quickly. "What?"

The caterer, a tall man of thirty or so, stood fist in the air, poised to knock again. "I'm sorry to bother you, but the champagne is running low—"

"Open another case—there's more in the refrigerators near the back door," Gavin said, unable to keep the irritation from his voice. "And if you have any other questions, talk to Mr. Johanson."

"Yes, sir," the caterer replied.

Gavin closed and locked the door again. "Now—what's so all-fired important?" he demanded.

Her stomach, already knotted, twisted painfully. "You left the other morning in a hurry," she said, reaching for the back of a chair to brace herself. "And I didn't get a chance to say goodbye."

"Goodbye?" he repeated, frowning. He folded his arms over his chest and waited.

Her palms began to sweat. "Aren't you leaving soon...to rejoin the racing circuit?"

"I don't know. I haven't made definite plans. It all depends on what happens here." He crossed the room and stood only inches from her. "What's going on, Melanie?"

She cleared her throat. "I'm pregnant," she whispered, facing him and seeing the shock and disbelief cross his features.

"You're what?"

"Pregnant." When he paled, she added, "Of course, the baby's yours."

"But you said—I thought you couldn't have children."

"I couldn't—not with Neil."

"You're sure about this?" he said, still not making a move to touch her, his suspicious gaze drilling into hers.

"I took a home pregnancy test this morning, but no, I haven't seen a doctor. I'm late and I've been throwing up and I haven't felt this way since the last time." Her fingers were digging into the back of the chair, and she felt herself begin to shake.

"We'll get married," he said without a second thought.

"No."

His head snapped up, and he regarded her in disbelief. "What do you mean, 'no'?"

"I'm not going to trap you, Gavin. You have your life and it doesn't include me or a baby. You won't be happy unless you're racing headlong down a mountain as fast as you can."

"And so what do you plan to do? Marry another man?"

She sucked in a swift breath. "No. I'm going to raise this baby alone, the way I should have the first time. And I'm going to love it and—"

"You lost the first one."

The words crackled through the air, burning deep in her heart. "I won't lose this one," she vowed, "no matter what."

"You're right about that," he said, his disbelief giving way to a new emotion. His lips twisted, and his eyes turned thoughtful. "I won't let you," he said softly, kicking the chair from her hands and throwing his arms around her.

"Mr. Doel?" Pounding erupted on the door again.

"Let's get out of here," he whispered against her ear.

"But..." She cast a worried glance at the door.

"Come on!" Taking her hand, he opened the back door and hustled her down the steps of his private deck.

"Where are we going?" she asked, and his answer was a ripple of laughter.

When her high-heeled shoes sank into the deep drifts, Gavin lifted her easily into his arms and carried her toward the base of Rocky Ridge, where a gondola sat.

"You're not serious..." she whispered, but he was. He started the lift and ushered Melanie inside the gondola. The operator, recognizing Gavin, took instructions, and within seconds Melanie and Gavin were moving quickly uphill, the night dark around them.

"You're insane," she chided.

"Crazy. The word is crazy and I'm crazy about you." When the gondola was at the top of the lift, it stopped suddenly.

Melanie gasped. "What's going on?"

"Tony's giving us half an hour of privacy." Gavin drew her tightly into the circle of his arms. "And in those thirty minutes, I'm going to convince you to marry me."

"Gavin, you don't have to—"

His mouth closed over hers, and his tongue slipped intimately between her teeth.

Melanie's knees sagged, and he propped her up against the side of the car. "Marry me, Melanie."

"But I can't—"

He kissed her again, and this time she gave in, kissing him with all the fire that raced through her blood. She closed her eyes, unaware of the view of the lodge or the surrounding night-darkened hills.

Groaning, he lifted his head. "Well?"

"Yes!" she said, "Yes, yes, yes!"

His grin slanted white in the darkness, and he reached into the pocket of his tuxedo. Taking her hand, he placed a soft velvet box in her palm.

Breathless, she opened it to discover a large solitary diamond ring nestled in a tuft of black velvet. He slipped the ring on her finger, and it fit perfectly.

"You had this planned," she whispered.

"That's why the operator was standing by at the base of the lift," he admitted. "I was going to wait until the party had wound down a little, but I had already decided that I wanted to marry you and I wasn't going to take no for an answer. I planned to take you up here and propose."

"You did?" she asked incredulously. "But what about the *Tribune*? You accused me of—"

"I know. But we don't have to worry about the *Tribune* anymore."

"Why not?"

"I bought it yesterday."

"You did what?" She stared up at him, sure that he was teasing her, but his face was dead serious.

"Remember, I told you I had things to do. When I left your place I called the owners of the paper, made them a more than generous offer and bought them out. As for Brian Michaels—he's already packing, along with Jan."

Melanie could hardly believe it.

"Yesterday I decided that it was time to set a few things straight. So—if you want it, you can have your old job back, with a raise."

"And what about you?"

"I've decided that I don't need to race in Europe, unless my family needs a vacation."

"Will you be happy living here?" she asked.

"Only with you."

"But what about your father?"

"Oh, I straightened him out. And it seems that you two had a chat the other day. Dad's decided maybe he was wrong about you."

Melanie could hardly believe her ears. "So why did you put me through all this—this confession? Why didn't you propose *before* I told you about the baby?"

He took her into his arms again and pressed a kiss to her forehead. "Because I wanted to hear what you had to say—I had no idea you were pregnant. And then I wanted to make sure that you really wanted our child."

"Oh, Gavin, did you doubt that?"

"Not for a minute, love," he said, grinning ear to ear. "But I had to know that you were marrying me because you wanted to, not because you wanted the baby to have a father."

"That's convoluted thinking."

"No more than yours." He kissed her again, and she snuggled against him. "I can see it all now—the headlines in the next edition of the *Trib*: Doel Marries Girl of His Dreams."

Melanie laughed and glanced down at the diamond on her left hand. "It's my dream, you know. I've dreamed about this for so long."

"It's our dream," he replied, his voice tight with emotion. "And it's a dream that will last forever."

* * * * *

PASSPORT TO ROMANCE VACATION SWEEPSTAKES

OFFICIAL RULES

SWEEPSTAKES RULES AND REGULATIONS. NO PURCHASE NECESSARY.

HOW TO ENTER:

1. To enter, complete this official entry form and return with your invoice in the envelope provided, or print your name, address, telephone number and age on a plain piece of paper and mail to: Passport to Romance, P.O. Box #1397, Buffalo, N.Y. 14269-1397 No mechanically reproduced entries accepted.
2. All entries must be received by the Contest Closing Date, midnight, December 31, 1990 to be eligible.
3. Prizes: There will be ten (10) Grand Prizes awarded, each consisting of a choice of a trip for two people to: i) London, England (approximate retail value $5,050 U.S.); ii) England, Wales and Scotland (approximate retail value $6,400 U.S.); iii) Caribbean Cruise (approximate retail value $7,300 U.S.); iv) Hawaii (approximate retail value $ 9,550 U.S.); v) Greek Island Cruise in the Mediterranean (approximate retail value $12,250 U.S.); vi) France (approximate retail value $7,300 U.S.).
4. Any winner may choose to receive any trip or a cash alternative prize of $5,000.00 U.S. in lieu of the trip.
5. Odds of winning depend on number of entries received.
6. A random draw will be made by Nielsen Promotion Services, an independent judging organization on January 29, 1991, in Buffalo, N.Y., at 11:30 a.m. from all eligible entries received on or before the Contest Closing Date. Any Canadian entrants who are selected must correctly answer a time-limited, mathematical skill-testing question in order to win. Quebec residents may submit any litigation respecting the conduct and awarding of a prize in this contest to the Régie des loteries et courses du Quebec.
7. Full contest rules may be obtained by sending a stamped, self-addressed envelope to: "Passport to Romance Rules Request", P.O. Box 9998, Saint John, New Brunswick, E2L 4N4.
8. Payment of taxes other than air and hotel taxes is the sole responsibility of the winner.
9. Void where prohibited by law.

PASSPORT TO ROMANCE VACATION SWEEPSTAKES

OFFICIAL RULES

SWEEPSTAKES RULES AND REGULATIONS. NO PURCHASE NECESSARY.

HOW TO ENTER:

1. To enter, complete this official entry form and return with your invoice in the envelope provided, or print your name, address, telephone number and age on a plain piece of paper and mail to: Passport to Romance, P.O. Box #1397, Buffalo, N.Y. 14269-1397 No mechanically reproduced entries accepted.
2. All entries must be received by the Contest Closing Date, midnight, December 31, 1990 to be eligible.
3. Prizes: There will be ten (10) Grand Prizes awarded, each consisting of a choice of a trip for two people to: i) London, England (approximate retail value $5,050 U.S.); ii) England, Wales and Scotland (approximate retail value $6,400 U.S.); iii) Caribbean Cruise (approximate retail value $7,300 U.S.); iv) Hawaii (approximate retail value $ 9,550 U.S.); v) Greek Island Cruise in the Mediterranean (approximate retail value $12,250 U.S.); vi) France (approximate retail value $7,300 U.S.).
4. Any winner may choose to receive any trip or a cash alternative prize of $5,000.00 U.S. in lieu of the trip.
5. Odds of winning depend on number of entries received.
6. A random draw will be made by Nielsen Promotion Services, an independent judging organization on January 29, 1991, in Buffalo, N.Y., at 11:30 a.m. from all eligible entries received on or before the Contest Closing Date. Any Canadian entrants who are selected must correctly answer a time-limited, mathematical skill-testing question in order to win. Quebec residents may submit any litigation respecting the conduct and awarding of a prize in this contest to the Régie des loteries et courses du Quebec.
7. Full contest rules may be obtained by sending a stamped, self-addressed envelope to: "Passport to Romance Rules Request", P.O. Box 9998, Saint John, New Brunswick, E2L 4N4.
8. Payment of taxes other than air and hotel taxes is the sole responsibility of the winner
9. Void where prohibited by law.

 RLS-DIR

VACATION SWEEPSTAKES

MONTH 3 ENTRY

Official Entry Form

Yes, enter me in the drawing for one of ten Vacations-for-Two! If I'm a winner, I'll get my choice of any of the six different destinations being offered — and I won't have to decide until after I'm notified!

Return entries with invoice in envelope provided along with Daily Travel Allowance Voucher. Each book in your shipment has two entry forms — and the more you enter, the better your chance of winning!

Name ____________________

Address ____________________ Apt.

City ________ State/Prov. ________ Zip/Postal Code ________

Daytime phone number ____________________
Area Code

☐ I am enclosing a Daily Travel Allowance Voucher in the amount of $__________ Write in amount revealed beneath scratch-off

VACATION SWEEPSTAKES

MONTH 3 ENTRY

Official Entry Form

Yes, enter me in the drawing for one of ten Vacations-for-Two! If I'm a winner, I'll get my choice of any of the six different destinations being offered — and I won't have to decide until after I'm notified!

Return entries with invoice in envelope provided along with Daily Travel Allowance Voucher. Each book in your shipment has two entry forms — and the more you enter, the better your chance of winning!

Name ____________________

Address ____________________ Apt.

City ________ State/Prov. ________ Zip/Postal Code ________

Daytime phone number ____________________
Area Code

☐ I am enclosing a Daily Travel Allowance Voucher in the amount of $__________ Write in amount revealed beneath scratch-off

CPS-THREE